The Keepers

Smoke and Mirrors

JJ Hull

Paranormal Crossroads & Publishing

The Keepers, Smoke and Mirrors

Copyright © 2012 by JJ Hull

ISBN 978-0-9882412-3-7

www.paranormalcrossroads.com

This work is fiction. All of the characters, organizations, and events portrayed in this novel are either products of the author's imagination or are used fictitiously.

Image copyright Luxorphoto, 2011 used under license from Shutterstock.com.

Table of Contents

1. Chapter One 7
2. Chapter Two 10
3. Chapter Three 22
4. Chapter Four 28
5. Chapter Five 49
6. Chapter Six 69
7. Chapter Seven 97
8. Chapter Eight 118
9. Chapter Nine 125
10. Chapter Ten 137
11. Chapter Eleven 145
12. Chapter Twelve 157
13. Chapter Thirteen 159
14. Chapter Fourteen 167
15. Chapter Fifteen 172
16. Chapter Sixteen 186
17. Chapter Seventeen 192
18. Chapter Eighteen 205
19. Chapter Nineteen 219
20. Chapter Twenty 223
21. Chapter Twenty-One 239
22. Chapter Twenty-Two 256
23. Chapter Twenty-Three 268
24. Chapter Twenty-Four 277

The Keepers

Smoke and Mirrors

JJ Hull

CHAPTER ONE

Dustin

I found myself chained to a dirty dungeon wall. Apparently, I had been here for days. No amount of struggling freed me. I yelled, but no one came. Then suddenly, I was surprised when Geren entered the small, dark, damp room which held me captive.

"I must ask you," Geren started as he pulled a guards chair from its position by the door and sat down in front of me. "Why do you believe you have been allowed to come and go at will, to make your own plans?"

"Because it has been my duty to do what was necessary to find Bethany," I replied.

"Wrong," I heard his mind say.

"Then enlighten me?" I shot back.

"One day, you will take my place as head guard," Geren stated.

Who was he kidding? Only a son of his could take his place. I watched as a smirk crossed his face. He stared at me as the possible awareness of my parentage flashed suddenly across my face.

"Yes, I am your father," Geren stated. "Your mother is Mary Farris."

I felt sick. The idea that I used to be accepted by the Keepers inside the dome wasn't a rouse at all. Just the opposite, it was true. I had been fooled along with everyone else. Why didn't I see it before now?

My earliest memory was sitting alone in the hospital. Geren came for me explaining he was going to take me home. That is where my life in the world of the Dwellers began. I lived with Geren until I was old enough to start my training. Engraved in my memory was how proud Geren was as I was welcomed as an official member of Venema House upon the completion of my training. He wasn't proud because I was a lost kid he took in, I was his...

"My son, how long do you plan to rebel against Deward's demand?" Geren asked.

Deward had requested that I bring Elizabeth here at all cost. He intended to send her through the Black Arch for an eternity of reincarnations on the Earth Plane. The moment she would die on the Earth Plane, her soul would recycle right back into an Earth Plane baby. She would cease to be Elizabeth in the world of the Keepers or Bethany in the world of the Dwellers. The simple thought made me crazy. She was the light in my life.

"Tell me why you refuse to follow his order," Geren begged. "Let me help you."

"I am in love with her," I whispered.

"I see," Geren said as he stood and began to pace across the damp and muddy dirt floor. "Deward can be dealt with, when he understands the reasoning behind what we do. I once felt the same about Mary. I knew from the moment I looked at her. Did you know from the moment you saw Bethany?"

I nodded.

"I understand where you are coming from and I will speak with Deward today concerning a possible union," Geren stated as his eyes studied my face. "I need to know I can trust you."

I sighed and began, "I don't have anything to give or any way to prove to you..."

"Actually you do," Geren interrupted as he sat and tilted back on the two legs of the stool. "I will arrange her safety for as long as you want her. However, if you betray me, I will ensure she is granted instant travel through our Black Arch." His voice turned icy as he added, "I want your loyalty to me and me alone! Don't ever cross me. Do you understand?"

The line in the sand was drawn. His threat made the consequences quite clear for betraying his trust. "There is still another problem," I added under his steely stare. "She is in love with another."

"I am aware of the Keeper you talk about," Geren stated. "What do you propose to do about him?"

"I need to get rid of him!" I stated firmly grasping that this was the corner I was backed into. Elizabeth would never give me a chance, if Marvin was standing in my way.

"Yes! Now you're scheming like my son!" Geren replied with a chuckle. "Then, your problem is making her stay. You have your work cut out for you. She is already the scandalous talk of Venema House. She's cunning and might even give her sister, Tina, a run for her money."

CHAPTER TWO

Mark

I leaned against the wall while I waited for Anthony and his sister to exit the lift. They were due to arrive anytime and I was to escort them to Mr. Solliday's private office in Dogwood House. I had just finished escorting Trevor, Tilly, and Elizabeth there. Everyone was meeting with Mr. Solliday to be informed of the changes which were to shortly come. On the in between, I had gone to pack my belongings in order to ready myself for my new assignment. Saying goodbye to my bachelor pad, which I shared with my two childhood friends, hadn't been easy. It was a beginning, but also an end.

Both my childhood best friends had a reserved thrill over my new assignment. It was unusual for a new guard to be chosen for a special assignment. However, the look upon their face said what I felt. Assigned to watch a Humling child, could you get any lower?

Lenny, being a home agent, had been patently waiting for my first official assignment. I had no doubt that he had the perfect place picked out for me. Usually, special assignments signaled a guards right to get their own place. Since the three of us had a great bachelor pad, I probably wouldn't have moved anyway, or so I told myself. The look of horror on his face, when I informed him I would be living amongst the Humlings and wouldn't be requiring his services, matched what I felt.

His only verbal response, "This realtor doesn't deal in property outside the Keeper Dome!"

I overlooked the dig about my new accommodations being below him. The fact was, I would be living with my assigned family. Lenny had a great job which afforded him the bachelor pad we lived in. He had it so easy and couldn't possibly comprehend the pressures of my job. His was a cake walk. Moving people into new homes was a joy. Young people spreading their wings, newly weds building a life together, parents growing their family, retired couples, and snow birds were all excitedly cheerful.

Phillip had a different response questioning, "Is that safe?"

Of course, this would be a border agent's take. His time was spent protecting the outskirts of the dome. In his short time, he had seen an array of breaking and entering Humlings. If only he knew, Anthony my new landlord, was his worse nightmare. He had been sneaking into the dome down to a science.

My room mates big concern was hosting a big blow out to celebrate my new assignment. I didn't want the attention, but they saw my leaving quickly as another disappointment, adding distance between us. It was something I had done a lot of lately to my childhood friends. It wasn't unlike Trevor with his cousin Eddie. According to Trevor, they had done everything together until Trevor joined the Underground. Slowly becoming the keeper of many secrets was driving a wedge between them.

His story was similar to mine. I too was in training when I discovered the Underground. Having always loved to read, I was usually found with my nose buried in a book studying council cases. I began to discover a pattern of Dwellers who were being brought before the Council. The more I dug, I began to wonder where they were all coming from? This led to my questions and unknowingly drawing attention to myself. Eventually the Underground discovered me and I became a member.

I was taken under the wing of a wise spy named Ralph. In the beginning I hadn't seen him in that manner. Face it, he was handed a wimpy nerd to whip into shape. I couldn't lift any amount of decent weight and had no physical abilities. First and foremost for him was bringing me up to physical par.

His words still rang in my ear, "Better get some muscles kid or those Dwellers are gonna eat you for lunch!"

Those first few months I endured brutal workouts. I was exhausted with no desire to party with Lenny or putt around with Phillip. They didn't understand my new obsession with physical fitness. Then he put me on an intelligence regime. Every day he handed me a list of topics to study and quizzed me on yesterday's topics. I recently told Trevor I had read most of the books in the Underground archives. I hadn't mentioned most were read during this time period. Since

Trevor never asked me anything normal, I was now re-reading them to brush up on minor details. Looking back, I wouldn't trade any moments with Ralph. In a short time he taught me a lifetime of knowledge.

With all of my knowledge came the distance between myself and my friends. They didn't and still don't understand my leaving in the middle of the night to play basketball, my disappearing from functions, or the secrecy involving new acquaintances. In the end, I wasn't sure my relationship with my two childhood friends would ever be the same. This was the price a spy paid.

The lift dinged and I watched its door slide open. My fellow guard, Chester, stepped off the lift followed by Anthony. Then a young lady with sandy brown hair, pale freckled skin, and vibrant eyes came into view. She was beaming with excitement and I imagined it was due to visiting the dome. It was forbidden for Humlings to enter the dome unless summoned.

"Good morning," Chester greeted me. "They're all yours."

"Thanks," I said as Chester grinned at me.

"Hey," Anthony greeted me.

I nodded my head and turned my attention to the young lady. I extended my hand saying, "Hello. I am Mark."

She took my hand in hers returning, "I'm Emma."

"It is nice to meet you," I replied as I let go of her warm hand.

I turned to Anthony, whom I knew, even though he didn't know me. I extended my hand. "Mark."

He shook my hand returning, "Anthony. As if life were one big adventure he asked, "Where are we off to?"

"Mr. Solliday has requested to speak to you," I returned as I threw my heavy backpack over my shoulder. Then my attention turned to my suitcases and boxes which were piled on a rolling cart.

As I grabbed the handle, Anthony asked, "All of those are yours?"

"Yup," I replied.

"Are you going on a trip, or moving?" Emma softly asked.

"Sort of both," I replied to those incredible hazel eyes.

"Man you pack like a girl," Anthony returned.

"A girl?" I replied while digging in my pocket for my handkerchief.

I hadn't packed like a girl. Since I had no idea when I would be relieved of my new assignment, the pile contained everything I couldn't live without. I smiled to myself as I wiped my running nose. It hit me that he didn't realize that all this stuff and I would be moving to his home.

As I shoved the handkerchief back into my pocket, my hand rubbed the lift card. With it in my hand, I envisioned Mr. Solliday's office in my head. Suddenly, the door magically appeared in the wall directly ahead of us. Anthony's teasing demeanor faltered. He appeared as shocked to see the magical door as I was. When I was given the card, which resembled a regular destination card, I laughed to myself. A card that you only had to think the destination and a door that appeared to take you directly there was a fairy tale. I had given Trevor a hard time about his magical card. Before fielding questions from these two or appearing as if this were my first time using my card, I stepped up and swiped the card in the door lock. I held my breath as the door swung open revealing a huge office.

Anthony stepped out into the room with Emma at his heels. Obviously, he had not one ounce of fear in his body. Trevor's warning about his 'life's an adventure' attitude was proving to be on target. I also couldn't help but note how correct it was to place a guard in their household. Anthony gave no thought to Emma following him in to the unknown.

I wheeled the cart towards the door realizing this wasn't Mr. Solliday's office in the Administration Complex. I was about to step into Mr. Solliday's personal, plush office in his home at Dogwood House.

As my cart and I stopped just inside of the magical office door, we were greeted by a motley crew. Trevor, Elizabeth, and Marvin were seated on the couch in the sitting area which reminded me of someone's personal living room. Tilly was seated in one of the two stand alone chairs facing the couch.

Upon seeing us, Mr. Solliday stood, turned, and smiled a welcoming smile. He greeted, "Welcome. Mr. Spirs and our friends from Lakeland, please come in and pull up a chair." He held out his hand to chairs along the wall next to his massive desk.

"Thank you sir," Emma shyly replied as she appeared nervous in his presence.

I pushed the cart to the side of the office while watching Anthony claim the chair beside Tilly. I moved to carry a chair for myself. Emma bumped into me as she too was retrieving a chair. I grabbed the chair from her hands saying, "I'll get them."

Emma shyly smiled up at me as her finger wrapped her hair around her finger. She simply stood out in this crowd. Boy is she cute. However, I wasn't going to loose sight of my assignment. Messing with a Humling wasn't in the cards.

As I positioned the chair next to Tilly's, Emma said, "Thank you."

"You're welcome," I answered as I purposely placed mine next to hers.

"Great, now that we are all seated," Mr. Solliday began as he glanced at me and Emma.

"Why is that?" Tilly interrupted between chomping her gum.

Mr. Solliday offered Tilly a warm smile as he continued, "I have called you all here to discuss some changes that will immediately be put into affect. I believe they affect each of you."

"Changes?" Anthony repeated in an inquiring voice.

"Mr. Tabures," Mr. Solliday began. "Have you told Miss Bradford about your brother?"

"Neither of us," Anthony began appearing completely serious as he pointed between himself and Emma. "Spread that around."

"That is wise," Mr. Solliday stated. "However, now that Dwellers have entered the picture, can you imagine the problem we have?"

"Now, it makes since," Anthony murmured as if he knew a truth we didn't.

"His class trips have never ran over before," Emma concurred Anthony's unspoken thought.

Mr. Solliday held up his hand gesturing towards us saying, "Shall we fill all of them in."

"It's your show," Anthony retorted as he sat back in his chair.

"Daniel, their little brother," Mr. Solliday began. "Will go to the Earth Plane when his training is complete. He will become a great world leader who will be instrumental in the Earth Planes progression. There is a wise soul behind those child's eyes. His life at Home has been filled with extensive classes and he has been sheltered from undue influences."

Trevor loudly chuckled causing everyone to stare at him.

Anthony broke the silence questioning, "What is so funny about that?"

"Protected from all but you, his brother," Trevor taunted from under his breath.

"Hold on," Anthony demanded apparently offended. "We are extremely careful about outings, guests, and who Daniel has contact with."

"Get real," Trevor retorted. "Tilly and you are always sneaking off."

"What I do when Daniel isn't home doesn't affect him," Anthony challenged as he moved to the edge of his chair.

Mr. Solliday held up his hands to intervene the conversation. He turned to Anthony saying, "Your parents entrusted him to you and you have done a great job."

"Until I came along," Elizabeth interjected.

"You're no harm to Daniel," Marvin stated as he reached over to hold her hand in support. Marvin seemed a nice guy, but I wasn't sure involving himself with Elizabeth was smart. Like me and my sacrifices for the Underground, he had given up his life. However, his sacrifice was not for the Underground, but for her. He contended she was weak and needed protection. However, I knew she had strength. How else could she have tricked a slew of Dwellers to free herself and Tilly.

"No," Elizabeth agreed. "However, I brought the dark into his life didn't I?" Before Marvin could answer she continued, "Just as I have done to each and every one of you in this room."

"We can't focus on what has transpired in the past," Mr. Solliday consoled Elizabeth. "However, in the case of Daniel, I would be neglecting my duty to let any of the darkness influence his life. He must be protected from the Dwellers and must never know of their presence. We can't let anyone tarnish his pure way of thinking." Mr. Solliday stated and looked directly at me.

"That's where I come in," I announced to the room.

"I assume you introduced yourself on the way up?" Mr. Solliday questioned me as I once again stood to pull out my handkerchief.

"Of course," I replied.

Mr. Solliday returned his focus back to the room as he began, "Mr. Spirs is a council guard. I have asked him to protect Daniel while he is at Home."

"He is not in any danger when he's at home," Anthony adamantly disagreed. "With the exception of some childhood friends, no one comes around."

I blew my nose as everyone stopped to glance my way. Then Tilly grabbed Anthony's arm, leaned over, and began to rub Anthony's back to regain the room's attention.

"My job isn't to protect Daniel from your friends," I informed Anthony. "It's to keep an eye out for Dwellers."

"Dwellers?" Emma softly questioned while nervously twisting her hair around her fingers.

"Are you some kind of expert?" Anthony huffed.

"Mr. Spirs is indeed capable of spotting a Dweller," Mr. Solliday assured Anthony. "It's unlikely they would make an appearance in Lakeland, but adding a layer of protection is prudent."

Anthony's attention was focused on the cart with all my belongings piled on top of it as he asked, "Where will he be staying?"

"I will be staying with you," I stated as I sniffed in and dropped the gauntlet on him.

"I assume you have a guest room?" Mr. Solliday asked.

"We do," Anthony hesitated adamantly shaking his head negatively side to side. "However, having a complete stranger move in and live in my home… I'll pass."

"I don't think you have a choice," I retorted, wishing I could take that pass. I was as apprehensive about living amongst Humlings as he appeared to be having me in his home.

To that, Anthony stood and began to pace behind the chairs.

"You do have a choice," Mr. Solliday stated in a calming manner. "Since Mr. Spirs has been appointed by the Council, he will watch Daniel when he is not in class. Now, whether it is at your home or not is up to you."

"He doesn't get to come home unless he…," Anthony stopped as he pointed at me. "Accompanies him?"

"Got cotton in your ears?" Trevor mumbled with a smirk.

"Where would Daniel stay?" Emma quietly inquired.

"If you refuse to have Mr. Spirs as a house guest, I suppose Daniel will be forced to board at his school," Mr. Solliday conceded.

"Oh Anthony," Emma whined. "You have to let him stay. Daniel wouldn't understand not coming home."

"How would you propose we explain our sudden house guest to Daniel?" Anthony asked while still pacing.

"He is indeed a friend of Mr. Stillholm and Miss Bradford's. Correct?" Mr. Solliday questioned as he peered between Tilly and Trevor.

"Yeah," Trevor hummed.

"Any friend of his," Anthony pointed to Trevor. "Isn't a friend of mine."

"I'm a friend who needs a place to stay," I answered the lingering question.

"I don't like it," Anthony spewed at me. "Besides, what's up with your nose? Are you sick or something?"

"How in the world does their family drama affect us?" Trevor asked in a bored huff.

"I am asking the rest of you to avoid contact with Daniel," Mr. Solliday answered.

"No problem," Trevor agreed as a slight smile crossed his face.

Tilly stood, placing her hands on her hips. She appeared as if she might pace the floor with Anthony. With Trevor's deep feelings for Tilly and her unwise attraction to Anthony, Trevor was in a love triangle with no easy way out.

"If Anthony isn't allowed in the Keeper Dome and I can't go there, how will I see him?" Tilly screeched.

"Miss Bradford, as long as your studies are kept up, you may travel during daylight hours to Lakeland," Mr. Solliday stated shaking his head. Tilly opened her mouth, but before she could speak he clarified, "However, make sure your trips are when Daniel is in class."

The fortunes had turned. Tilly eyes flashed to Anthony as she gave him a flirtatious grin. Trevor, on the other hand, appeared as if his blood was beginning to boil.

"Why only during daylight?" Marvin asked.

"It's safer," I threw out, knowing Dwellers preferred to move around at night.

"Let me explain your new mode of transportation," Mr. Solliday continued.

"New mode?" Trevor threw out in a questioning voice.

"You should cease using the hospital to gain access to the Humling Subway," Mr. Solliday stated with raised eyebrows as he looked between Trevor, Tilly, and Elizabeth. None of them seemed to return his knowing stare. "A new lift will be place at the Lakeland Station. The town sees the lift as a way to boost their farmers market."

"Actually, it's to give me easy access to the dome if I should need it," I added.

"Their home is no where near the subway," Tilly spouted.

"It's directly across the lake," I answered.

"Not a escape route I want to take again," Tilly mumbled.

"I have a gift to give all of you," Mr. Solliday said as he stood and pulled a stack of lift cards from his pocket. He moved around the circle, handing them out. As he handed Tilly hers, he added, "The lift operators would appreciate it if you would discontinue using the fake cards. They cause a mess of reporting paperwork."

"Oh," Tilly hummed.

It surprised me they didn't realize lift operators were always council guards. I had only spent one day as a lift operator and I had been fascinated watching the Humlings beyond the doors. Now that I was faced with living in a Humling household, it didn't seem as fascinating.

"If you desire to venture out, apply for the proper paperwork," Mr. Solliday stated interrupting my thoughts. "As you now know, the rules have always been in place to protect you."

"These take us to Lakeland?" Marvin questioned.

"Yes," Mr. Solliday answered as he sat back in his chair. "Only Lakeland."

"Why are you giving us permission to wander outside the dome?" Marvin questioned.

"Mark needed the access and I feel it is safer to know where the girls are than to have them sneak away," Mr. Solliday honestly answered.

"Instead of telling them no," Trevor began. "You are taking the easier route."

"You can't stop a gnats fascination or them being drawn to fruit," Mr. Solliday stated. "You should understand this. Are you not the one maintaining the ladder for them?" It was apparent, to anyone watching the exchange, that Trevor was caught off guard by Mr. Solliday knowing something that he believed was a secret.

Mr. Solliday turned to Marvin. Suddenly, Trevor crossed the space between him and Tilly and plucked the card from her hand. He turned and held both his card and hers out to Mr. Solliday. "No thank you! We don't need these!"

"Speak for yourself," Tilly adamantly stated as Mr. Solliday took the cards and handed hers back.

Trevor once again made an attempt to grab Tilly's card as Anthony stopped pacing and warned, "You better back off!"

"Are you threatening me?" Trevor asked. "Wow! Why in the world would your parents leave a small child with such a hot head as you?"

"Hot head," Anthony repeated as he moved towards Trevor.

Tilly stood and stepped in front of Anthony in an obvious attempt to get between them. "Anthony," Tilly began.

"Tilly, step aside," Trevor interrupted.

As Marvin stood to grab hold of Trevor, Tilly swung around to face him. "Trevor Stillholm, you listen to me!" Tilly demanded looking directly into his eyes. "His parents will be Daniel's parents on the Earth Plane."

"So," Trevor countered.

"They had to go first," Tilly attempted to make sense of them leaving.

"Don't explain anything for me," Anthony disagreeably spouted from behind Tilly. "Especially to him."

I moved to be in position to hold Anthony back if needed.

"That's enough boys," Mr. Solliday stated appearing unhappy with the two of them as he handed Trevor back his card. "Both of you sit before I call for my guards."

"I still don't need the card," Trevor retorted turning the card over in his hands as he retook his seat.

"I simply thought you might on occasion have reason to want to visit Mr. Spirs," Mr. Solliday hinted to Trevor.

He was too emotionally wrapped up in his love triangle. Obviously, he had forgotten he was my partner.

"He's not welcome at my home," Anthony spouted as he glared at Trevor.

"Anthony, sit down," Emma said as she too was now standing.

"Like I would ever want to visit you," Trevor spouted back at him.

"Stop," Tilly said as she tugged on him.

"Hey man," I began as I sniffed. "Come on, sit down."

"Maybe we could all play basketball," Marvin added ignoring Anthony.

"That is all you guys think about lately," Tilly huffed.

"Do you even have a hoop?" I asked Anthony.

"If you like to play," Emma spoke up as Anthony didn't dignify my question with a response. "I'm sure we could find a place to put one."

"There's no need," Anthony quickly disagreed as he finally sat down and seethed. "The move isn't permanent and he…" Anthony pointed towards Trevor finishing, "better never plan on stepping a foot in Lakeland."

CHAPTER THREE

Elizabeth

Lost in thought, I stepped out into Elephant Room and was faced with Rhett's crew staring at me. It appeared their shift was over and they were awaiting the lift.

"Howdy gal!" Billy had warmly greeted me. "How ya doin'?"

I smiled at him, "Fine, thank you."

"Sure could use those ghost catchin' skills ya have," Billy continued. "Wanna join in a good ole ghost hunt?"

"She'll probably pass," Luke hummed. "Our last hunt ended so well."

To this Jason chuckled.

Marvin's Dad just peered at me, not speaking. Lately, all anyone could talk about was Marvin's overnight visit to my room. Mr. Lagedge probably heard the rumors and felt I had tarnished Marvin's reputation. Of course, Marvin seemed to take it all with a grain of salt, telling me, "Let them talk!"

"Now fellas," Billy said as he grinned at me. "That wasn't her doin'."

I looked past them and could see Tilly. What in the world was she doing here? They followed my gaze as I bid the group, "I better go."

As I approached Tilly, I realized her attention was on Andy who was standing tall next to Tiffany. Her dark curly hair made his blond hair appeared white. Tiffany was hanging on his arm, with one hand placed firmly on his chest. She gazed at him with a smile which made me queasy. Just as she had done to me by hanging on Marvin, she was now doing it to Tilly.

Suddenly, Tiffany gave Andy a tight hug as she peered directly at Tilly from over his shoulder. Whether Tilly wanted Andy or not, she cared enough for him not to want to see him with Tiffany.

As Tiffany released Andy and backed towards the double doors, Tilly's anger was written all over her face. With a flirtatious wave at Andy, Tiffany turned to exit the room.

Before I could catch up to Tilly to caution her to leave it alone, she rushed towards Andy.

"Andy, you can't date Tiffany," Tilly seriously said to him as she grabbed his arm.

"So, it gets under your skin that I am seeing her," Andy smugly replied.

"She's using you," Tilly hysterically cautioned.

"Right," Andy said under his breath as he turned to walk away.

Tilly once again grabbed his arm to stop him.

He spewed, "Your jealous!"

Tilly shook her head in disagreement, "I'm not jealous."

"Then tell me why you are here," Andy demanded.

"She was meeting me," I interjected.

"Just please trust me," Tilly stated in a begging voice.

"You have got to be kidding! Trusting you has gotten me nowhere in the past!" Andy spouted. The hurt flashed behind Andy's eyes for a moment. Then as if the emotion drained from his face he continued, "I'm a big boy, I can take care of myself." He then spun around and began to storm towards the double door.

Tilly on the other hand threw up her hands and stormed in the opposite direction towards the lift.

I yelled after her, "Tilly!"

"I'm okay," she half yelled turning and walking backwards. She then gave me a quaint wave and a forced smile.

A clear lie. Unfortunately, one I didn't have time to deal with at that moment. It was Wednesday and I had a Ghost Society meeting to attend.

Tilly and Rhett's crew were already on the lift. I stood hoping Tilly would spot Jason and get side tracked flirting with him. Her solution to any problem had always been a date or flirting with the opposite sex.

After the lift door slid closed, I hurriedly made my way to the ghost portal located in the coat closet within Rhett's quiet, dark office. The dark, wet, swooshing, cool air spilled out into the Ghost Society room as I exited the ghost portal shivering. The sensation of ice cold, numbing water from the invisible water shower had chilled me to the bone. Why did the portals have to be so cold?

"Welcome back," Spike hummed as he walked up on me carrying an arm full of bottled drinks.

"Let me help you," I said as I pulled two of the bottled drinks from his arm.

"Thanks!" Spike said. "Madeline was hoping you would come back."

"Why?" I replied as we began to walk towards the familiar long banquet table.

"I think she sees you as a new comrade to gang up on me with," Spike said with a cocky grin.

As I placed the drinks on the table, Madeline grabbed a bottle saying, "Hey!"

"Hi," I replied as I pulled the metal folding chair out to sit next to her.

She then turned to Spike and asked eyeing his hair, "Stuck your finger in a light socket again?"

"You're one to talk tonight," Spike retorted. "You turned your mop purple!"

As they bickered, I couldn't help but focus on the small round table which was still shoved into the back of the room. Rhett's Father, Royce, was seated at it. He was rumored to be one of the oldest ghosts and was indeed the oldest gentleman in the room.

Those around me gossiped that at one time Royce was my grandfather's best friend. Since they appeared to be about the same age, it seemed feasible to me. The tragic part of the Royce's story was why he chose to stay as a ghost. On the day of the event, when the dark Dwellers raided the world of the Keepers, his wife was kidnapped. His grief and desperation over not knowing what had happened to his wife had driven him to live another life on the Earth Plane. He eventually died on the Earth Plane and ended his path here as a ghost. My grandfather lost my grandmother on that day as well, but his path was different.

I could see Rhett in his father. Besides physically resembling each other with their tall, slender build, their mannerisms were very similar. He and Rhett were a huge mystery to me.

"What's the story with the old guy?" I interrupted the lively conversation at the table by asking.

"Old guy?" Madeline repeated as she followed my gaze. "Oh."

Spike turned around to look. "Royce," he answered in a hushed tone.

"Why are you talking so low?" I asked.

Their eyes shot to each others. It was Spike who answered, "Have you registered?"

"Registered?" I repeated feeling confused.

"Well yeah," Madeline answered. "Every ghost must register with the society."

"Why do you assume I haven't?" I asked in an attempt to bluff them.

"You aren't on the role," Spike stated with a serious but knowing look upon his face.

"Did you double check?" I returned feeling a little offended.

"No," Madeline quickly countered. "Lucy manages the role."

"That's why she befriended me," I thought out loud.

"She is nice to all new arrivals," Madeline agreed. "But she actually likes you."

"Right," I muttered to myself.

"She's not joshin' you," Spike added. "Look, until you've signed the role we normally don't talk about the inner workings of the Ghost Society."

"What's wrong with me asking about the old guy?" I answered.

"We didn't say that," Spike disagreed with a cocky male grin that Tilly would have loved.

"He's our leader," Madeline said in a hush of a voice.

"And why is that some big secret?" I asked rolling my eyes to look casual. "Arthur told me awhile back that he started the Ghost Society."

"It's more why he chose to be a ghost," Spike countered.

"He didn't want to go into the light because he claims his wife has disappeared," Madeline whispered like she was telling a big secret.

"He set up everything you see," Spike added in an equally hushed tone. "He battles those hunters."

"Except the one ghost hunter... His son," I threw out.

Spike smiled agreeing, "I'll give you that one."

"He claims there is no reason to go back," Madeline continued finishing Spike's thoughts.

"He tells new ghosts they have another choice," Spike whispered affirmatively.

They too knew Rhett's basic story. Only, I knew Royce did have a reason to go home. I couldn't help but wonder, what about Rhett? "The event," I mumbled.

"Yeah," Spike agreed peering at me strangely. "You know what Royce is talking about?"

I stuttered, "Just something…" Hmm… How to respond to that? I shuffled my feet nervously as I grasped for words.

"See," Spike stated. "Sign the role. He'll like you too!"

Arthur sat down. Quickly, the conversation turned to Humlings who went ghost hunting. Appearing to Humlings on the Earth Plane in ghost form was looked down upon. I assumed this was why they didn't like Charles' group from the hotel. They often appeared and played tricks on the hotel guests.

As I refocused on Royce, I could view him talking to a lady whose back was too me. I tried to be casual in my glances about, so as not to alarm anyone.

I was caught up in my own world watching the lady with shoulder length hair when Lucy interrupted my thoughts from over my shoulder, "Here we go."

"Huh?" I questioned caught off guard as she sat down beside me.

"The Ghost Council is up in arms this week about the ghost hunting societies on the Earth Plane," Lucy answered.

"Why shouldn't they be?" Arthur pointedly asked.

Their conversation then swung back to their boring conversation. When I looked back up, the small round table where Royce sat was empty.

CHAPTER FOUR

Elizabeth

I was torn, now that Dustin was gone. I was back to wondering why I hadn't really taken the time to get to know him better. Our relationship had always centered around me. The fact was, I knew very little about him.

So, here I was standing and facing the door to his room. Unbeknownst to me, he lived in the bottom of the Administration Complex in the Council Guard's Hall. I must have passed hundreds of guards on my way to Dustin's door. They were all housed here. I could see there was no better place to have Dustin constantly watched. It was a sensible place for my grandfather to stash my Dweller guard.

It was sad to stand before Dustin's door watching other guards shuffle past as if Dustin and the door never existed. Lately, I was the only one who seemed to remember he existed. Why had I never wondered or asked about where he lived?

With a sigh, I reached out and placed my hand on the cold door knob to his room. With one turn, the door cracked open revealing a pitch black room. I moved to run my hand along the wall to find the light switch. One flip gave me my first glance into Dustin's private life.

The room was eerily cold and dark. The walls were painted dark blue and black out curtains covered the small window. An unmade bed set against the far wall with a cluttered desk at its foot. I ran my hand down his clothes rack noticing all his stylish clothing, while I sadly waited for his return.

After exploring his room, I plopped down on his unmade bed and instantly the scent of him washed over my body. Calming peace filled every pore of me.

I laid back and wrapped myself in his black blanket, letting his scent overtake all my senses. It dulled my nerves. Lying in his mist, I could let go of the gossip, dirty looks, and daily struggles I had been subjected to.

Recalling the latest gossip that had been the topic of brunch conversation, I ran my hand over the empty spot beside me on the bed. Then I drifted back and replayed the moment.

"Please pass the two assignments which are due," Professor Zirak stated. Sighs broke the silence around the table.

"Go ahead, feed us some crap about the professor knowing why you can't complete your homework," Shannon venomously spit out as she rolled her eyes at me.

"There will be no additional assignments," Professor Zirak interrupted.

For the remainder of the brunch, the question on everyone's mind was why he hadn't assigned additional work. You could read the shock on my fellow trainees' faces. They wondered if I was getting off scot free or if my life plan and life theme were too juicy to share with the group. The stares said they probably thought the latter. However, their icy stares weren't for me alone. They eagle eyed Tilly, Trevor, and even Eddie. Poor Eddie had nothing to do with anything. It seemed, associating with me came at a cost. Those who chose to be my friend always paid for their choice in the end. There was an impending doom hanging over all of us. I inhaled another deep breath in an attempt to wash the thought away while lying on Dustin's bed.

Somewhere from the hall, muffled voices interrupted my thoughts.

As I opened my eyes, I spotted a shelf hanging above the desk near the ceiling. Four, neat, white boxes sat perched in a row up on it. Curious as a cat, I shoved the black, comforting blanket away and crawled off the end of the bed. Then I pulled the chair out from his desk and used it as a step stool to climb on top of Dustin's desk to stand.

With the first plain white box in my hand, I pulled the lid off and gently let it fall to my feet on the desk top. Old assignments from training were staring at me. I lowered myself to sit down on the desk. One by one, I removed the graded papers. On the final one, scribbled in Professor Zirak's messy handwriting, was a note telling Dustin how proud he was of him. As I stacked the papers back into the box, it dawned on me why Dustin had kept all of these. Each had either a personal note of encouragement or one of praise. Professor Zirak had probably been the only soul to ever praise him. Obviously, Dustin cherished them.

Rising and teetering on top the desk once more, I pulled the second box off the shelf. As soon as I removed the lid, I could smell the garlic. It wasn't like the stuff Marvin had retrieved from the city. This was pure Dweller garlic. According to Marvin, his garlic actually was making me stronger. I didn't have the heart to tell him the Keeper garlic didn't have the same effect. There was no comparison between the two. Since the dark Dweller garlic was more intense in smell and taste, it instantly made me feel strong. It seems, I inherited my father's Dweller garlic needing genes. Marvin's focus had been on making sure I ate enough of garlic to stay healthy, a sign of love on his part.

I set this box down extra carefully on the desk's edge. Since Dustin wasn't here and no longer needed it, I was taking the garlic. I knew as time went on, I would be needing it.

The third box held junk consisting of old real life movie ticket stubs, a napkin from a restaurant, etc. Nothing of value, but each item probably represented a fond memory of his. Otherwise, he wouldn't have kept them.

The last box baffled me. It contained a picture of a brown couch setting upon a dingy looking brown carpet in a darkened room. Book cases covered the walls behind the couch. I recognized the couch. It resided in Mr. Farris' home library. Instantly, I had to wonder if Dustin had left this for me and what it meant. Or, was this photo a trap? A picture planted to draw me out and away from safety.

Trevor

I felt as if I were the lookout for the sinking ship Elizabeth. She left me no option but to trail her, after I observed her disappear through the hospital door in the Keeper House lobby. I couldn't imagine where she was sneaking off to by herself.

Then, I followed her through the Humling door into the Humling Subway. I overheard her speak her destination, Stonehenge. I too stated the destination as I entered the subway train. After a blur of lights and short trip, the subway train halted and I shadowed Elizabeth, stepping off. Since Elizabeth and I were the only two exiting at this destination, the gig was up. We stood face to face with her staring me down.

"What are you doing here?" Elizabeth angrily asked. "Don't you have anything better to do than to follow me around?"

"Follow you?" I returned astonished at her over reaction. "You are my friend! Yeah, I trailed you. What on earth are you doing out here alone?"

"It's personal," Elizabeth said under her breath.

"What does that mean?" I questioned.

"That's none of your business," Elizabeth quickly retorted.

Before she expressed it, I already understood what was about to come out of her mouth.

"Please go back!" Elizabeth begged with a hint of desperation behind her voice.

I could see the internal struggle. Wherever she was going, she wanted to be on her way. She didn't want me to tag along. However, there was no way I would turn back. I knew she should have one of Solliday's guard following her. I wasn't going to take a chance that she dodged them. "I'm not leaving you out here!" I stated to Elizabeth's dismay.

"I wanted to be alone," Elizabeth mumbled with hands on her hips. Then she demanded, "Just go home Trevor!"

"No," I adamantly stated shaking my head.

"I don't want to put you in danger," Elizabeth mattered under her breath.

"If you're worried I might be in danger, then you shouldn't do whatever you're doing," I countered. I watched her as my words sunk in. "Where are we going?"

With a deep sigh, she answered, "Mr. Farris's home."

"Are you out of your mind?" I asked feeling deeply agitated. "Why would you even consider going there?"

"Dustin left something there for me," Elizabeth answered.

"This is about Dustin," I stated feeling heart broke. She once again was placing herself in danger and she didn't trust any of us to help her. What if she ran into Dwellers? After all the sacrifices we had all made for her. She repaid us by doing this.

"I hope you can understand," Elizabeth said as she hesitated to look me in the eyes. "I have to see this through!" As she looked up at me, she asked, "You're not going back, are you?"

I simply shook my head no as she turned to walk away from me. I followed the tight lipped Elizabeth as we exited the Stonehenge Station into the village of massive homes. We had reached an impasse and walked in silence.

The small shops we passed were filled with people. Each one seemed to be framed with magnificent flowers all placed in planters. Occasionally, as we passed someone, I found myself thinking they seemed to look right past us with no acknowledgement.

The shops eventually gave way to a residential neighborhood. All the homes would look alike, if it weren't for the different paint colors and landscaping. I could not help but notice odd things about the houses and people we were passing. In the yard of every house there was a person gardening and attending to the already immaculate yards that were filled with yard ornaments, flower beds, and shrubs. I believed the man at the last house was measuring the length of his grass with a ruler and cutting shreds of grass with the yard shears in his hands. I sure could think of better ways to spend a beautiful afternoon.

As I kept pace with Elizabeth, I couldn't fathom what she hoped to find. What in the world could Dustin have possibly left for her? I didn't like blindly following her.

Elizabeth's steps faltered as she stood before a white picket fence. As I peered at the two story brick home with brown shutters I asked, "Mr. Farris's home?"

"Yeah," she replied. She looked over at me as she continued, "I don't know what we will find."

I peered at the wooden flower boxes hanging under every window with an array of planted flowers, the vibrant green yard with flower beds in perfect symmetry. "You're worried it might not be as peaceful as it looks?"

"I don't know if this is a trap," Elizabeth countered.

"So the possibility has crossed your mind?" I countered.

"Of course," She replied. "I can't let go unless I know."

With that said, I held open the gate, resigned that what would come, would come. We had traveled too far to turn back. I followed on her heels as we climbed three steps onto the porch. The house appeared dark and abandoned. When she grabbed the door knob, I placed my hand on top of hers. "You aren't going to knock?"

"I hadn't planned on it," Elizabeth said giving me a devious grin reminiscent of Tilly. Clearly she had been hanging around Tilly too long.

"Then let me go first," I countered.

Elizabeth stepped back as I turned the door knob to the unlocked front door. It creaked open announcing to anyone inside our arrival. The dark house revealed the white glazed furniture of the living room and the strong smell of hospital disinfectant. In this drafty, cold, and stiff room I didn't detect anyone watching us. I peered down the hall and up the staircase finding no one.

I turned around to see Elizabeth waste no time quietly pushing open the frosted French doors leading to an adjacent room. It appeared she knew where she was going. I followed her through the door and scanned the room, finding it to be empty.

We were standing in a musty, smelly study. Massive book cases filled with a wide variety of books covered every wall. A wooden desk set under the window with a well used chair pushed under it. The floor was covered with a dirty looking brown carpet.

Elizabeth walked over and stood facing a brown couch. Then she methodically began to pull off the cushions and run her hands down the back of the couch.

"What are you looking for?" I asked.

She peered at me answering, "I don't know exactly."

"You're kidding," I retorted as the door of the study opened.

Mr. Farris limped in using a cane. Apparently, he was startled to find us in his study. Smiling at us he said to Elizabeth, "Good evening, Miss Cantrell."

Elizabeth gave him a small wave as she began to place the cushions back on the couch.

"I see you have once again found your way into my library," Mr. Farris stated as he limped further into the room.

The round, gray haired Mr. Farris didn't appear as if he were a danger to us.

"I suppose you are here for the book Dustin left you?" Mr. Farris inquired. "Or have you come to read... what book was that? Oh, more Art History?"

My moving between him and Elizabeth made both focus on me.

"A book?" Elizabeth repeated as she stepped out from behind me and began to scan the many shelves. "He left me a picture of your couch."

"You won't find it on any of the shelves," he replied. "It is a dark book, I wouldn't want anyone to know of its whereabouts." He walked over and knelt down looking under the leather sofa. His whole arm seemed to disappear and I heard the creaking of tape breaking and his arm emerged with the book in his hands. "This book you can not find in the Hall of Records. I only know of one other copy."

"I assume it was a gift from the wise man who gave you the rest of your library?" Elizabeth asked.

"Yes," he replied as they shared a friendly smile. "I worry you are heading down the same path as my dear..." He seemed unable to finish.

"Sir, I am very sorry about Mrs. Farris." Elizabeth seriously said.

"So am I," Mr. Farris returned.

"Dustin must have felt whatever was in the book would help me understand," Elizabeth threw out. "My life is such a mystery. I desire to know about myself, to fill in the blank spots."

"Dustin seemed solemn the day he brought this to me. He said I must keep the book and its contents between him and possibly one day you," Mr. Farris stated.

When I saw the handwriting scrawled across the front cover, I knew this book was of Dweller origin and not reading for the average Keeper. I moved closer to read Venema on its spine.

"I could also understand why Dustin thought I could successfully let it blend into my library…," Mr. Farris continued. "I was honored he would trust me enough."

"I'm sure he could see you were a lot like him, honest, hard working, and noble," Elizabeth replied.

As they shared another smile, Mr. Farris handed the book to Elizabeth. As the exchange took place, papers fell from the book. I moved to pick them up realizing it was a hand-written note from Dustin.

Elizabeth snatched it from my hand saying to both Mr. Farris and myself, "Thank you." She then shoved the note into her pants pockets.

Before anything else could be said, it was the sudden shock on Elizabeth's face which made me spin around. The Dweller named Collin was looming at the French doors. His eyes were as black as night and alarmingly focused eerily on Elizabeth. My head swung to peer at her. It looked as if she were holding her breath. I instantly knew his stare was rendering her unable to move.

Instantly, I moved to place myself in front of Elizabeth to break his gaze. With my hands out, I shuffled my feet backwards feeling Elizabeth doing the same behind me.

"No," Elizabeth said from behind me. Another long pause before she added, "I won't go with you."

It dawned on me that Elizabeth was hearing him in her head.

"You aren't going to take her," I stated to Collin's crooked grin.

"No," Elizabeth yelled answering an unspoken thought from behind me.

"Silly boy," Collin taunted me as he focused his black eyes on me. "Do you really think you can stop us?"

"I can," Elizabeth stated into my back.

Collin stepped forward as Mr. Farris stepped out in front of him. "I would appreciate your leaving," Mr. Farris sternly stated.

With a look of annoyance Collin stated, "I will only ask this once. Move aside old man."

Mr. Farris stood his ground. Collin's face turned menacing as he shoved Mr. Farris aside.

Elizabeth yelled, "No!"

I watched as Mr. Farris lost his footing, and then hit his head on the desk as he fell to the floor.

Suddenly, Elizabeth placed her hand around my waist, hugging my back. She mumbled, "Keeper House."

In the same instant, Collin grabbed my arm with his ice cold hand. We began to spin as Mr. Farris's home faded away into the swirling air around us. Collin's hand disappeared from my arm and excruciating pain filled its place. As Keeper House formed around us, we fell to the staircase in Keeper House with a hard thud.

Elizabeth instantly threw up her hands saying, "I dropped the book!"

"You're worried about the book?" I gasped in return as my burnt arm stung. "Honestly Elizabeth. We were almost captives of him!"

"Shh," Elizabeth said to hush me.

"I feel sick," I said off the top of my head as my stomach churned.

"Did you close your eyes?" Elizabeth answered. "Travel by..." Elizabeth touched the locket. "It can make you feel sick unless you close your eyes."

"There's not going to be a next time," I spouted. "No more Elizabeth!" In a low whisper I began to tell her the truth she needed to hear. "You wanted to go alone."

"I should have," Elizabeth grumbled.

"Then tell me this," I spouted back at her. "What did you plan to do if it was a trap? And since it was, what would you have done without me? You needed me to break his stare. You would have been captured!"

Elizabeth let out a heavy sigh. She understood that I was telling her the hard, cold truth.

I grabbed her hand forcing her to look me directly in the eyes, "No more! It is too dangerous."

Elizabeth

Since Trevor's burnt arm spilled the beans about our adventure, I had to work hard to ditch Tilly, Trevor, and Marvin who were all glued to my side. After all their lectures, I could appreciate Tilly's feelings of being trapped and not having freedom.

Since Marvin had plans tonight, he had been the easiest to shake. I was reminded of this during our conversation earlier.

"May I come over tonight?" I asked, erroneously hinting that I had no plans.

"On guys night?" Marvin returned.

"I'm sure Rhett wouldn't mind," I casually said to play the part.

"Guy's night isn't at Rhetts," Marvin answered.

I knew this. Wednesday was Ghost Society Night. I was curious as to Rhett's secretive comings and goings. He had a mysterious side to him, but he also liked routine. Rhett wouldn't be able to host guy's night and sneak away to the society meeting.

"Elizabeth," Marvin hesitated interrupting my thoughts about Rhett. "I can't take you home with me tonight."

"This again," I stated feeling his family didn't accept me or he feared they wouldn't accept me. This isn't how I wanted this conversation to go.

"You just don't understand," Marvin said as he looked at the ground. "My parents are…" As his arms crossed across his chest he cut me off, "Never mind. I really should get going."

With that he gave me a peck on my lips and he was gone. My instinct was to interrupt guy's night and force him to level with me. However, I couldn't do both. I had plans.

Rhett's light flipped off bringing my thoughts back to reality. I leaned against the wall of the Elephant room and pulled out the note which had fallen from the book at Mr. Farris's home. Trevor hadn't mentioned the note to the others and I had dodged all of his questions about it. How could I tell any of them that it was a personal note from Dustin.

Marvin would never understand. He was fooling himself to think Dustin was out of our lives forever and foolish to believe I could put his memory on a shelf. If there were once any doubt that I dated Dustin, it no longer existed for me.

Elizabeth,

If you are reading this simple letter, I know my fears have come true. We have been separated, not by memory loss but by the light and darkness.

From the day I first saw you, I knew my heart would forever belong to you. For all these months, I have replayed our memories in my head alone. I filled my time with a hopeless wish that you would remember us, the us that was happy and in love with each other. The us that completed each other. The us who lived to spend time together.

Your memory loss only showed me my dim future. It proved what we both knew in the back of both of our minds all those nights we spent wrapped tightly in each other's arms, our paths would one day divide us. You are light and embody all the goodness that the light brings. You are so beautiful, both inside and out.

I have an undeniable dark side which includes dark thoughts and deeds. A side you have never seen or acknowledged. This is why, you are better off without me, my love. Follow your heart always. Your happiness brings my greatest joy, even if your path no longer includes me.

As you read this book, be strong my love. Don't let your world make you crumble.

Dustin.

"Wow," I heard a catty voice call to me. "From white trash to circus clown?"

Instantly, I pulled up my long shirt and shoved the note back into my jeans pocket. She would be the wrong person to get hold of that note.

"Jeans under your, um… your costume," Tiffany hesitated while pretending to attempt to hold back laughs. "Cat got your tongue?" Before I could answer she belly laughed, "It that a mask?"

"We certainly are ready for Halloween!" Rodger added as he stood behind Tiffany. He then said under his breath, "Probably went mute kissing that traitor!"

"What?" Tiffany instantly spouted as she jerked away from Rodger's touch.

"What's wrong with you?" Rodger said. He was clueless as to how his comment had crawled under her skin.

Tiffany didn't bother to give Rodger a response. She turned on a dime and stormed off. Rodger followed her like a lost puppy dog who didn't know why he had just been scolded. He unknowingly had taken Tiffany's dark spewed venom for me and turned it upon himself.

It was time to pursue my plans for the evening. Rhett's light had turned off long ago. Only I knew the secret why he hadn't left his office. The time to go was now because I sure didn't want to explain my choice of clothing to anyone. I was confident I didn't need to knock as I approached Rhett's office door and entered it.

Wednesday couldn't come fast enough. Now, here it was! I daydreamed all week of getting to the next Ghost Society meeting and asking Lucy if she knew my mother. If I could find her tonight, I would approach her casually. Tonight's events would make it easy. The ghost society had a weekly theme. Tonight it was a masquerade ball.

I hurried to the closet and shivered as I descended the frigid ghost portal. I spilled out into the empty, octagon room rubbing my arms in response to the extreme chill. The damp portal left my body covered in goose bumps, like I was covered with crushed ice. The masquerade dress I was wearing left a little to be desired, as far as being warm.

The muffled sound of music was coming through the set of double doors to my right. As I followed the sound of instruments playing, I entered a cavernous room.

"Wow!" Spike said as he walked up beside me. "You look…" He paused as a dreamy, but goofy, grin crossed his face. "Incredible."

I peered at him, not sure how to respond.

"It's time for the round robin," Spike said as he pointed to the dance floor which was emptying.

"Round robin?" I questioned seeing men and women lining up in long lines down either side of the room.

"Yeah," Spike responded. "We all line up and it's the luck of the draw." Once again he pointed towards the other end of the room. "Whoever you meet at the other end when it's your turn, you dance with them for the next song."

"I see," I hummed.

"Elizabeth!" a masked girl with purple hair yelled as she moved out of line towards me. I might not have known it was Madeline if it weren't for her purple hair sticking out, all around her mask. She was dressed in a sparkle zebra print, spaghetti strapped, princess cut dress which flowed effortlessly into a floor-length skirt. She looked amazing.

"Where's your mask?" Madeline asked.

I pulled out the plain, black mask and held it out for her to see. It was plain, unlike the dress I pulled out of the costume props room at Grand Hall. The dress I was wearing had to be a relic.

"Put it on," Madeline stated with a giddy giggle as she focused on someone beyond me. Then she squealed in delight, "He's here!"

I peered over my shoulder to see a tall masked young man looking sleek in all black, with the exception of his red cape. "Who is he?" I questioned.

Madeline was staring at him and seemed to be so lost in admiration that she didn't hear me. "He is magnificent!"

"Who cares?" Spike spouted clearly irritated by the young man's presence.

"He is only the dreamiest guy around," another girl stated snickering as she walked up to Madeline. She too stopped to drool over the mysterious, masked stranger.

I followed their gaze back to his eyes. For a brief second I wondered if he had been staring at me?

"Come on," Madeline said as she pulled me towards the growing line of girls.

As she pulled me away, I heard Spike say under his breath, "Maybe I'll be the lucky one."

As I tried to eye the handsome masked man without looking at him, I noticed he was watching me too. What was with the guy's tonight? Had the portal iced my hair or something? Was it sticking straight up or something? Maybe my eyelashes had ice on them.

The buzz in line was all centered around the tall young man in the outfit with the long cape. To me he seemed like he belonged in, Keeper Warrior, the comic everyone enjoyed reading. He looked like a masked superhero. Every girl standing around me hoped to get to dance with him. They were raving about his dancing skills.

"Where's Lucy?" I asked interrupting Madeline's dreamy conversation and staring.

"She never comes to the dance," Madeline answered. With a sigh she continued glancing at me, "It makes her sad."

"Dancing makes her sad?" I asked feeling astonished. "Why?"

"She lost a love a long time ago," Madeline answered as she waved her hand like I was annoying her. "Lucy and her beau were accomplished, admired dancers. She doesn't want to remember the past and him."

As we neared the end of the line, everyone began to count the guys line and then the girls. Again and again they seemed to stop counting with their fingers pointing at me. Then the girls would proceed to give me a dirty look. As I peered over at the boys line, Spike was staring at me with a goofy grin. My gut told me dancing with him would be trouble.

I counted the girl's line in front of me; one, two, three, four, five. Then I peered over at the boy's line counting; one, two, three, four, five. I was perfectly paired with him, the masked superhero.

I nervously peered at Madeline who whispered to me, "Lucky!"

Glancing back across the room, it was Spike that caught my attention. Disappointment was all over his face.

"Tell me what it's like," Madeline continued. "They say dancing with him is like walking on air."

For a fleeting moment, I thought about offering to change places with her. However, tonight Spike was acting similar to Eddie. I clearly didn't need to fuel his fire.

"If only I was as lucky as you," the girl in front of me hummed before stepping out to the center to meet her dance partner.

I took a deep breath as I too made my way to the center. The masked young man stepped up and offered his left hand up. As I placed my right hand palm to his, his fingers closed around my hand. I hesitated a moment before placing my other hand on his shoulder.

"I don't know how to dance," I nervously blurted out.

As his hand wrapped around me and rested on my waist, a smile crept across his face. He confidently answered, "Follow my lead."

"I might step on your toes," I sputtered under my breath as my left arm rested on top of his.

"I have thick shoes on," he replied. With confidence in his voice he squeezed my hand as he asked, "Ready?"

I let out a nervous sigh, feeling Spike and Madeline stepping up close and waiting for us to move.

The Super Hero bent forward softly saying, "It's simple. I step forward with my left foot. One. You're going to step backwards with your right." As I stepped back he continued, "On the second beat. Two. You are going to step to the left with your left foot." I watched our feet as I stepped and he continued, " Three. Bring your right foot together with your left." As I let out a sigh he squeezed my hand again. "Okay. Four. Step forward with your left foot."

He stepped backwards as I stepped squarely on his foot with my wrong left foot. I tensed up as he brought his foot back up to mine.

"Wrong left foot," I stated in a nervous chatter.

After giving me a moment he calmly asked, "Ready?" To my shrug he again said, "Four. Step forward with your left foot." As I stepped he continued, "Good. Five. Step forward and to the right with your right foot."

Spike and Madeline whisked by us. I caught a glimpse of them floating across the dance floor.

"You should have danced with someone else," I stated as I peered up at him.

He ignored me as he stated, "Six. Slide your left foot to your right."

"Now what?" I asked.

"We do the steps over and over again," he stated. He went right into counting one through six, over and over again for me. When the song ended he smiled and whispered in my ear, "Now, you have the steps."

"Somewhat have the steps," I disagreed blushing.

"Dance a real dance with me," he stated not letting go of my hand and waist.

"Look around," I stated as I pointed to all the envious looks from the catty females in the room. "You could dance with anyone in the room. Why me?"

"Why you?" he repeated. "Because you owe me."

"I owe you?" I questioned.

As a smile crossed his face, he explained, "For teaching you the steps."

A new song began as I reluctantly agreed, "Okay."

I went back to watching my feet as he stated, "Relax your shoulders and don't watch your feet."

"I'll stomp your foot," I disagreed fearing my klutzy side.

To this he smiled as we began to slowly move while I counted in my head.

"So tell me," he started catching me off guard. "Do the simpler minded ghosts in this room know you are one of the hunters?"

I totally lost count of my steps and stomped his foot. To this he stopped and moved his and my hand over my head and spun me around. I felt like a giddy school girl, spinning to simply make my dress spin. When we came back together, I had temporarily forgotten about his odd question. As our hands came back together, palm to palm, I glanced up at him. The look of fascination across his face brought it quickly back to me.

"So do they?" he asked.

I responded, "No, they don't."

"Why do you choose to hang out here?" He threw out.

"Why do you?" I returned. "How long have you been a ghost?"

"A long time," He answered as he once again spun me around.

"Surely not longer than the old ghost," I said off the top of my head finding myself having an odd, fun moment.

To this he didn't reply.

"How long?" I asked.

"Hundreds of Earth Plane years," He answered as we spun around together in some type of strange couple move.

"Why hasn't your Keeper came for you?" I inquired hanging on to his arm as we stepped in synch.

"I thought maybe that was why you were here," he slyly stated.

As I raised the wrong foot and started to stomp his, I corrected myself. Feeling more confident I assured him, "That is not why I am here."

I took my hand from his shoulder and pushed up his mask. Surprised, it was Charles staring back at me.

As quickly as I de-masked him, he let go of me and moved to push the mask back into place saying, "Don't ruin this for me." He peered around to see who might have caught a glance of him. With a sigh, he again offered me his left hand.

As we stepped back up to each other to once again dance, I understood saying, "Sorry, I shouldn't…"

Instantly, his head shook no as he interrupted me, "You are only as curious as everyone else in the room."

If everyone knew it was Charles, no one would dance with him. Repeatedly, I was warned to stay clear of him.

"You can't be happy with the way others treat you," I stated. "Wouldn't it be easier to go Home?"

"Are you trying to talk me over?" Charles stated.

"Have you even seen you Keeper?" I inquired not understanding why his Keeper didn't attempt to help him.

Charles carefully watched me before saying, "I don't have a Keeper."

"Everyone has a Keeper," I intently disagreed.

"Not where I came from," Charles stated as he intently watched me. "The song seems to be ending." He stopped and held up my hand to his mouth, slightly kissing it. "Thank you for the waltz."

"You're welcome," I stated as he backed away.

I turned on a dime to walk back towards the door and outer perimeter of the room. Leaning against the wall, not ten feet in-front of me was the lady I had seen sitting with Royce during my last visit. Her shoulder length hair flowed around her face as she stared at me. I felt uneasy under her piercing eyes. Then, I smiled thinking somehow I knew her. At my hint of recognition, she disappeared.

"Wait!" I yelled making those around stare at me like I was strange and un-mannered.

Those lined up on the wall began to look about suspiciously before continuing to stare at me. I pointed to the place where she had been standing and contin-ued, "Did anyone see her?"

"A ghost seeing a ghost?" a bystander asked making everyone chuckle.

I blew off their laughter and stepped through the double door to leave the dance. I wasted no time moving through the familiar, empty octagon room and racing up the chilly portal. I pushed up the floor boards, crawled out into the closet, and pushed them back into place. I quietly shut the closet door when the office light flipped on.

I held my breath as I turned around finding Rhett staring at me with his arms crossed across his chest in disapproval. "What do you think you are doing?"

I began, "I was just... Um..."

"You don't belong down there!" Rhett interrupted my faint attempt to justify myself.

"And you do?" I threw out.

"Yes," Rhett angrily stated. "Of course I belong down there! I'm a ghost hunt-er."

"That's why you have your secret portal," I challenged. "That's why you go down there when no one knows?" I paused before adding, "What are you really doing down there?"

"Did it ever occur to you that I am still working?" Rhett retorted.

"By joining them?" I disagreed. "You are part of their group."

"How much do you know?" Rhett asked.

"Enough to know about their society," I threw out. "You do know that they, the ghosts, all know they are dead."

With a sigh, he walked around to his chair and plopped down. "I know, but you shouldn't."

"Everyone should know," I disagreed. "Knowledge is power."

An uneasy silence between us lingered. I pulled out a chair from his round table and sat, returning his stare.

"Does Marvin know where you are?" Rhett asked as he studied my face.

"No," I answered.

"I saw you dancing," Rhett threw out with a knowing look.

I growled, "That wasn't…"

"How do you think Marvin would feel?" Rhett threw out.

"About the round robin?" I growled back. "I didn't pick him to dance with!"

"Sure," Rhett stated. "The first dance."

"I didn't do anything wrong," I adamantly stated mad that he would insinuate I was a cheater.

"Sneaking down my portal, attending a ghost meeting, and dancing with some strange guy isn't wrong?" Rhett asked not grinning. "All I am saying is that I don't think it would go over well with Marvin."

"So that's how this is going to go?" I questioned. "You're blackmailing me to keep my mouth shut!"

Rhett threw up his hands and leaned back.

"Marvin trusts you," I stated. "I thought I could too! You intend to hold this over me!"

"You can trust me!" Rhett retorted. "But can I trust you?"

"If you wanted my trust," I stated. "Then why not just ask me not to say anything about your presence there?"

"Because this is bigger than the two of us," Rhett answered.

"It's less about Marvin and more that you don't want me to expose you, them, or the truth about ghosts," I threw out.

Rhett simply shook his head in agreement. We had reached a silent understanding between the two of us. However, this wasn't over. This mystery was mine to solve. I still had unresolved questions.

CHAPTER FIVE

Elizabeth

"Where are we going?" I asked Marvin as we strolled in the warm sun light towards Table Rock Lake.

"We have been invited to dinner!" Marvin said as he nervously shoved his hands in his pockets.

"That bad of an invitation…" I assumed out loud as I pulled his nervous hand out of his pocket.

"No, not bad," Marvin stated with a reassuring grin. "I want you to meet my parents. Well, my mom actually."

"We are going to your home for dinner?" I questioned in horror. I should have dressed more appropriately! He had already been reluctant to take me home.

"I thought you would be happy," Marvin threw out to my apparent panic.

"You really should have told me," I scolded Marvin. "I would have worn something other than this." I never would have worn sweats and T-shirt to meet his mom. I ran my hand up to my hair pulled back into my usual pony tail. I could feel pieces of hair escaping. "Look at my hair!"

"Elizabeth, you are beautiful just the way you are," Marvin countered with a loving look. "You've already met my dad. It's just mom." He shrugged and once again shoved a hand in his pocket.

"Then why are you so nervous?" I asked while bracing myself for lightening to strike.

Marvin once again began to walk as he explained, "Mom has strong opinions about certain things."

"About the girls you date," I assumed.

Marvin chuckled a little before answering, " Yes, about girls. However, mostly about other stuff."

"Like?" I prodded.

"She's obsessed with cleaning," Marvin split out as we approached the row of massive brick homes all setting in a row along the lake side street.

"Cleaning?" I repeated. "You haven't taken me home because your mom likes to clean?"

The front porch was welcoming as we turned to walk up the side walk. Marvin peered at me saying, "Just follow my lead when we go in."

"Okay," I replied to his strange demeanor.

The door opened with Marvin's dad stepping out onto the porch to welcome us. He was as clean cut as ever with crisp, starched shirt, slacks, and dress shoes. However, he appeared nervous like Marvin. Together, their jitters were giving me the jitters.

"Elizabeth," Marvin's dad greeted me. "Welcome."

"Thank you," I replied as Marvin's mom appeared behind his dad peeking out.

"Mom," Marvin greeted as he moved to the door, kissing her on the cheek. "I want you to meet Elizabeth." He then glanced at me, "Elizabeth, this is my mom, Susie."

"It's nice to met you," I said as I held out my hand.

I could see Marvin and his Dad's eyes dart to each other. His mom appeared to be taking me in as she looked me over from head to toe. After an awkward silence while holding my hand out, she sighed as if shaking my hand might catch hers on fire. She extended her hand and then hesitated, pulling it back slightly. Marvin made a slight noise which caught her attention. She then appeared resigned that there wasn't an option about shaking my hand. Once again, she extended her hand and grabbed mine for a split second. It was more of a slight touch that a real, genuine hand shake. However, Marvin and his Dad collectively let out the breath they had been holding.

I looked over at Marvin who gave me a reassuring grin as he extended his hand for me to follow Marvin's mom who had already disappeared from sight. His hand found its way to my back. The simple touch of his hand was comforting.

I stepped into the entry way and paused. There was a bench hugging the wall beside the door. On the opposite side I could see a line of neat shoes placed together as pairs with the heels against the wall.

Marvin pushed his way towards me as he whispered, "Do what I do."

He sat down on the bench and I found it cozy to sit next to him. The door shut with Marvin's dad just standing there waiting for something.

"She better take her shoes off!" Marvin's mom called from somewhere beyond the entry hall. "I don't want dirt on my floor!"

Before anyone could answer I yelled back, "Of course, Mrs. Lagedge." Marvin's dad nervously smiled down at me.

"Here," Marvin said as he pointed to the bleach smelling carpet square his dad was holding for me. I watched as he pulled another one off a shelf above our heads and handed it to Marvin. "Place your shoes on this carpet square, your socks into your shoes, and the square into the row along the wall."

Upon closer look at the line of neat shoes, all pairs were setting on individual carpet squares. I smiled beginning to feel as if I had stepped into the twilight zone. Tilly had once visited here. I couldn't believe she hadn't told me about this odd ritual. I did as I was told following Marvin's lead.

I was flabbergasted as Marvin then pulled a washing tub from under the bench. He stepped into it and let his feet soak for a moment in the water. He plopped down on the edge of the bench and pulled one foot out of the mixture and began to dry it with one of the fresh towels hanging from the bar behind the bench. Then the other.

As he peered up at me he said, "It's simply water with a little bleach in it."

Marvin's dad leaned forward and whispered, "Susie takes foot hygiene very seriously."

"Disinfecting your feet is a quirk with her," Marvin said sheepishly and looked away.

It was no wonder he hadn't wanted to bring me home. This was weird. Marvin grabbed my hand as I stepped into the mixture. It was cold and made my feet curl. I then sat down and pulled my chilled feet out quickly. As I dried them, Marvin's mom reappeared. She looked very unhappy that I had honored her foot rule. It was obvious she had hoped I wouldn't. Now, she would have to let me in her house. A feeling of being totally unwelcome spread over me. What did his mother have against me? I didn't know her!

I forced a grin as Marvin discarded the towels into a hamper. He grabbed my hand and our fingers interlaced causing Marvin's mom to visibly shiver. As if the sight sickened her, she turned to walk away.

"What are we having tonight?" Marvin called after her.

No answer came and Marvin's dad answered, "Her favorite."

"Dad," Marvin whined. "How could you let her make that?" He shrugged as Marvin explained, "Beans and corn bread."

"What's wrong with that?" I questioned.

Again, their eyes shot to each others. I held up my hand to stop them. Whatever it was, I would soon find out. Marvin's mom appeared with a box in her hands. She then pulled out something from the front of the box. I was shocked to see her reveal a pair of latex gloves. A moment of panic overtook me.

"For you," she said as she reached out to hand them to me.

Marvin grabbed them before I could and sternly said, "No mom."

"You are holding her hand," his mom replied. "How do I know where her hands have been. How do you know. You should probably wear them too!"

"Umm…" I hummed realizing she must be germ phobic. I held out my hand to his mom for a pair. "It's okay. I'll wear them."

"No Elizabeth, that's okay," Marvin's dad assured me from behind putting a hand on my shoulder. "Susie, we are not going to make our guest wear those," he stated firmly staring at his wife.

"No really," I again stated as I peered at Marvin. "Give me the gloves."

Marvin placed the gloves back in my hand and appeared to be angry by the glares he was giving his mother.

For the first time, she smiled adding, "Marvin you know where to get yours." She turned and hummed walking down the hall, "Then you can hold hands all you want. Germ free!"

Marvin followed his mom red faced. I was left with Marvin's dad. He led me in silence to the dining room. Along the way, I noticed that the furniture we passed was covered in plastic. The dining room table had a clear, plastic table cloth across it. The chairs themselves were covered in plastic as well.

"Which one should I sit in?" I questioned.

"Either side," he answered. "I will be sitting here." He patted a chair at one end of the table next to him. "Susie will be sitting there." He pointed to the opposite end of the table hinting to me.

I took his hint and seated myself directly next to Marvin's dad. Hopefully Marvin would sit between myself and his mom. I could use all the help I could get not to be in her direct line of sight. I was feeling really antsy.

"Pour yourself some tea," Marvin's dad stated. "I'll see what's keeping them."

Silence fell as I looked around the table. The setting was simple, but pretty. The plates were a pale pink with delicate flowers circling the outside edge. That's when I over heard Marvin's mom saying, "I just can't place my finger on it. I know her from somewhere." Then, she came through the swinging door carrying a pot. I assumed it was filled with beans. Following in tow were Marvin, carrying corn bread, and Conrad trailing with a relish tray of chopped onions and pickles.

They placed their items on the table and took their seats. Marvin's mom was still intently watching me.

"Shall we eat," Marvin's dad asked hoping to hurry the dinner along.

"Hold on," Marvin's mom said holding up her hand. "I can't shake the feeling that I should know you."

Marvin's hand found it's way to my leg. "Mom, quit."

"Do you work?" she asked.

"No," I said. "I'm in training."

"Which house?" she asked.

"Keeper House," I replied.

"Who are your parents?" she asked.

"What is this?" Marvin asked. "Fifty questions?"

"Yes," Conrad agreed. "Let's just have a nice dinner."

With that he handed me the plate of corn bread.

"Marvin brought her home in hopes I would get to know her," Susie persisted. "Tell me about your family."

"Why are you so concerned about her family?" Marvin stated trying to deflect his mom.

"I'm just trying to place where I know her from," Susie stated.

Marvin peered at his dad for help.

"Now I see," Susie stated. "The two of you are hiding something from the crazy lady? You hid your last relationship as well."

"I'm not trying to hide her," Marvin stated. "I want you to get to know her. Elizabeth is the woman I'm in love with."

"In love with?" she gasped. "If you are so in love with her, then what are you hiding from me?"

"My mother's name was Christy," I stated.

"Christy...?" she repeated slowly and suddenly appeared deep in thought. As I watched her thinking to herself, I could not miss her visibly shiver. "That name," she mindlessly stated. "I've only known one Christy."

"Do you need butter for your corn bread?" Marvin's dad quickly asked. I turned to look at him. It became obvious that he knew something concerning my parentage and was trying to redirect the conversation.

"Thank you," I said as I took the crystal butter dish.

"You know the Christy I'm referring too," Marvin's mom pointedly stated turning to Marvin's dad. Marvin's dad shook his head in agreement. She continued, "She once was a friend. However, she didn't have the character I thought she did." She was deep in thought as her head shook. I wondered what was up. Then, as if shaking off a horrendous memory she continued, "She turned to the dark side!"

"Susie," Marvin's dad called. "Please pass the salt."

"She ruined her life," Marvin's mom said under her breath as she reached and passed the salt. "Then she added, "With Satan's spawn."

To this, Marvin almost choked on his water.

"What's wrong with you?" Marvin's mom questioned while intently staring at him. "You know all about the league with darkness."

"That's not fair of you to say," I blurted out feeling irritated with her opinion.

"What's not fair?" Marvin's mom repeated turning to me. You could have heard a pin drop as she zeroed in on me like a bird after a worm.

Marvin's hand found its way to my leg. Just as he often did when dealing with Tiffany, he was trying to convey he had this one. With a deep breath he began, "Mom..."

"No," I interrupted him. I didn't need him to speak for me. She would either accept me, or not. "Your saying Christy ruined her life is unfair."

A look of fear spread across Marvin's mother's face. Then shaking, she peered down the table at Conrad asking, "Are we talking about Rhett's Christy?"

"Yes mom," Marvin stated in a firm don't mess with me voice.

"I assume we are discussing Christy Solliday," I stated. Then to clear up any misunderstanding, "She is my mother."

Mrs. Lagedge's hand flung itself to her chest as she began to hyperventilate. "I told her not to have anything to do with that… That Dweller the last time I saw her," she gasped out in between breaths. Her eyes were fixed on me as she bolted up, clutched her chest, and leaned over. "Oh… Your father is…!"

Marvin's dad threw his napkin on his plate and buried his head in his hands.

She asked, "Conrad, you knew about this and yet let her enter our home?"

I unintentionally shook my head affirmatively causing her to hysterically scream at us, "They've found us!" She looked at Marvin's dad with desperation in her eyes and voice, "They're using her to… Oh, my God! Marvin…" The shock caused her to drop to her knees. "They've got to Marvin!"

The loud thud of her falling to her knees caused Marvin to jump to his feet and rush to her side.

"No!" She sobbed over and over again. "They can't have you Marvin. No, no, no!" I could see her grab both sides of his face demanding, "Don't let them use you. She's a demon!"

Marvin grabbed both of her hands and pulled her to her feet. As her eyes flickered to mine she screamed, "Don't you see the darkness? She has his eyes! Don't peer into those eyes." She closed hers as Marvin pulled her under his strong arm, apparently holding her up. "Her soul will steal yours!"

"Stop!" Conrad stated as he motioned for Marvin to take her down the hall.

"You too," she screamed. "You sat too close to her. She has cast a spell of darkness on you!"

Marvin began to drag her away. "Don't breathe! Don't breathe!" Marvin's mom hysterically yelled as she tried to hold her own breath. "Her germs are in floating in the air. She's got to your dad!"

"Mom," Marvin muttered disgusted.

"Marvin, please don't breath." Then her attention focused on Mr. Lagedge who was still standing at the end of the table. She reached over Marvin's strong arms for him yelling, "Conrad, don't inhale!" As they disappeared she screamed, "There's no way to decontaminate! We'll have to move!"

"Great!" Marvin's dad said under his breath as his legs seemed to give out with him plopping back down into his chair. "She'll have bulldozers here tomorrow to tear the house down!"

I didn't know whether to sit or run at this point. I could still hear hints of Marvin's mom's voice begging him not to have anything to do with me. She was never going to accept me.

"Guess you could say I know how to clear a room," I said under my breath.

When I glanced over at Marvin's dad, he was sitting with a blank embarrassed stare. When he looked at me, I could see the regret behind his eyes.

"I see why you haven't told her," I said with deep sorrow.

"You just don't understand her reaction," Marvin's dad assured me. With a sigh, he shoved his chair back, stood, and began to clean off the table.

"I'm sorry," I stated feeling empathy for Marvin's dad.

He attempted to force a smile. When he failed, he sadly stated, "It's I who am sorry that she can't accept you. Marvin is deeply in love with you or he wouldn't have brought you home knowing her extreme quirks."

His mother was right, he should have run from me a long time ago. Who knows, after this fiasco, he might run from me now. Would he choose his mother or me? He shouldn't have to make that choice at all.

Marvin yelled for his dad from somewhere down the hall.

"I'll go ahead and leave," I informed him ending the horror of the night for all involved.

"Marvin will be out shortly, if you want to wait," Mr. Lagedge stated.

I held up my hand to stop him, "No. I don't think Mrs. Lagedge considers me a welcome guest. I will exit graciously."

The look across his face spoke volumes. He agreed. "Marvin can catch up with you later."

Mark

Although I couldn't hear the exchange between Trevor and Anthony as I peered out the window, I understood Trevor had come to take Tilly back to the dome. Her presence here had been minimal. She was reduced to sneaking away from Trevor to see Anthony. Trevor was right to worry about this budding relationship. Dating a Humling was bound to bring trouble.

It wasn't that I objected to Anthony. In the scheme of things, Anthony and I probably would have been great friends if he were a fellow guard. He was cool.

However, I couldn't help but feel bad about the love triangle Trevor found himself in. He had deep feelings for Tilly, but she seemed torn between him and Anthony. Since I was a council guard, I knew the price Trevor and Tilly would pay for their trip to the Earth Plane. Tilly was to be Trevor's wife. It was council mandated, making the whole situation between Anthony and Tilly ridiculous.

Anthony held open the door of his buggy for Tilly. Tilly glanced between Trevor and Anthony before focusing her attention on Trevor. Her hand ran down his chest as she gave him a flirtatious look. Tilly exchanged words with Trevor before she smiled at Anthony and crawled into the buggy. It was obvious Trevor was angered.

Anthony shrugged innocently as he shut the door and began to round the back of his buggy. Only I saw the moment he smirked when Trevor wasn't looking. He was playing Trevor, making Trevor come across as an overprotective, overbearing friend. Obviously, it wasn't working for him. He stood frowning and seething as Anthony hopped in the driver's seat.

Trevor, defeated, began to walk towards the road. Leaving my place at the window, I could hear the roar of the dune buggy as Anthony revved it and sped out. I was left with no choice but to inform Trevor of what I saw. Anthony's smirk, fully aware of Trevor's feelings, was the same as a punch in the face.

The door slammed behind me as Emma hummed from the swing, "I gather you saw it too?"

I nodded affirmatively as I hurried off the porch, down the cracked sidewalk, and out the gate to catch up with Trevor. Adrenaline filled Trevor was moving.

I yelled, "Trevor!"

He didn't stop or respond to my calling. Beginning to jog, I caught up to him. His skin was flushed with anger and it oozed out of his demeanor.

"What do you want?" Trevor growled at me.

"You need to change your game plan," I answered.

"Get lost," Trevor retorted with clenched fists.

"He's playing you off as the fall guy," I threw out. "Don't you see that?"

"What?" Trevor spouted back.

"You keep charging in and demanding that Tilly come home with you," I began trying to explain.

"Anthony isn't good for her," Trevor growled.

"Look man, Tilly's a rebel," I stated. "She is never going to respond to your demands. She lives to rebel at authority. You trying to control her makes him look good. He knows this and he is using it against you."

"So, you're suggesting that I do nothing?" Trevor replied appearing angrier than before.

"In the end she's yours," I threw out. "The two of you will marry. It is council mandated. He is a flash in the pan."

"So the council guards know," Trevor spit out. "What did you do, research the wayward ways of me, your new apprentice. Did you enjoy reading about Tilly's and my antics?"

"Trevor, back off," I retorted. "Everyone knows about the stunt the two of you pulled. Use it to your advantage!"

"Don't judge me as a user like Anthony," Trevor retorted as he stormed off. "I don't take advantage of anyone!"

Judging him? My attempt to talk sense into him had backfired.

All of this was a reminder to me to take a hands off approach with Emma.

I now found myself living in a cheesy movie where the spy character falls in love with the nerd who is actually really cool and beautiful. Emma was something to behold, but I couldn't get involved with her. I had already gone too far the other night. I knew better. I was a Keeper and she was a Humling.

I settled down under the massive tree in the yard and pulled out my pocket knife. Whittling always cleared my mind. I looked up when I heard the front screen open and then slam shut. Then I heard the thud of shopping bags being set down. The sun was almost down as I closed my knife and pocketed the small whistle which I had carved over the last few hours. Anthony and Tilly had already returned. Now I knew Emma was home. I recognized all of their voices in a muffled, unpleasant exchange as I approached the screen door. Apparently Emma was reading Anthony the slight riot act. He deserved it.

I cringed knowing Daniel would show Emma my gift. I was having second thoughts about it. Emma might take it wrong.

"Emma!" Daniel exclaimed right on queue. "Look what Mark got for you. It came from the city!"

"He took you to the city?" Anthony inquired.

"Yeah," Daniel excitedly answered. "It was fun! We went to three stores."

"A rolling tote," I heard Emma say from beyond the door.

"He rattled on about you carrying groceries," Daniel added.

"Where is he?" Anthony asked.

"Outside whittling," Daniel answered. "He said he needed to clear his head before bed."

"Where should you be?" Emma questioned turning the focus on Daniel.

"Bed," Daniel huffed.

I could hear Daniel's feet running around in a circle possibly around the rolling tote. He asked, "Do you like it?"

I heard the wheels as they clanked across the tile floor. "I love it," Emma replied.

"Of Course," Anthony huffed.

I entered the back door and crept to my bed that night envisioning her perfect, freckled face smiling. Emma worked hard with little appreciation from her brothers. I justified the rolling tote in my mind as the least I could do for her since it would make her grocery trips much easier. She cooked for all of us, cleaned, and even did my laundry while Daniel and I were out. The real truth was, I had never been so excited to buy a gift. I felt an undeniable urge to make her happy. I told myself it was a brother's feeling I was experiencing. I was bonding with her and not so different than Trevor trying to keep Tilly safe.

Elizabeth

Marvin arrived to get me, wearing a backpack. He seemed very nervous and intent that we needed to hurry as if we were on a schedule. After the parent episode, I hadn't seen him. It had been a couple days and I was beginning to feel shaken in his love for me.

"Where are we going?" I asked relieved to see him smiling at me.

"We're going to take a hike," Marvin replied seeming to get a sudden nervous jitter.

"Lets do something else," I begged as I put my hands around him and snuggled my head into his chest. "I don't want to hike."

"Come on!" Marvin said and then led me down to the foyer. He seemed a little put out that I didn't want to agree to his plans for the evening. I didn't want to sour whatever he had planned, especially after his family's reaction to me, so I gave in. His family didn't accept me and we both knew it. It was the elephant in our relationship which we were ignoring.

We walked up to the lift where he produced two official looking lift passes.

"We have passes?" I asked.

"Yes we do," he replied with a grin.

"Who issued them to you?" I questioned.

"All in who you know," he replied.

Why was he being so mysterious?

"Why don't we use the cards Mr. Sol..., my grandfather gave me?" I asked.

"I've had these longer than we've had our new cards from him," Marvin answered.

"Princess," Leo exclaimed as the lift door opened.

"Princess?" Marvin repeated in a questioning tone.

I slightly shook my head no at Leo before returning, "Good morning Leo."

"I have fresh cookies for you," Leo replied as his small hands held up the familiar brown paper bag containing gingerbread treats.

"Thank you," I said taking the bag.

As Leo's stare moved from me to Marvin, Leo spouted, "What are you staring at?"

Marvin returned a dirty look while producing the cards for Leo stating, "Tanyard Creek."

"Princess, do you really want to take a hike?" Leo pointedly asked. "It zaps your energy!"

My mind screamed, "Not really."

Leo must have read my face as he continued, "Don't let the big oaf push you around. He is capable of hiking!"

"Watch it?" Marvin stated tapping the little man on the shoulder and staring him down.

"Leo," I said in a disapproving tone.

"Just saying," Leo hummed. "I have your best interest at heart. You are my friend!"

Marvin grabbed my hand as he pulled me back into the lift. He mouthed to me, "Princess?"

"Something he nicknamed me," I whispered back.

As I peered up at Marvin, he appeared increasingly nervous. He shoved his hands into his pocket. I could read him like a book. I wondered if he could read me.

"Are you okay?" I asked.

A week smile crossed his face, "Never been better."

Leo interrupted my conversation with Marvin as he stated, "Tanyard Creek."

I mouthed thanks to Leo as I brushed past him. As we stepped out of the lift, I viewed an incredible green park nestled below a damn. It was a sunny, beautiful day with a breeze gently blowing. A narrow, paved path descended down the small hill into the park. Marvin grabbed my hand, interlocking our fingers. We walked in silence as the path turned into a dirt one. There were several trails jetting off the main path as we meandered along.

As we crossed a low water bridge, Marvin stated, "There is a marvelous water fall near the top."

"Is that where we are going?" I inquired.

He gave me a goofy, nervous grin as an answer. We continued to ramble down the dirt path. The path turned several times before it steeply ascended. Marvin allowed me to take the narrow path first with him following closely behind me. Several hikers passed us walking and half way sliding down.

Once we reached the top, a noisy water fall was raging with water hitting rock ledges on the way down. It was an awesome, natural beauty. I leaned up against a protective wooden railing, watching it.

I was caught off guard as he wrapped his arms around my waist and pulled me against him. His head leaned against mine and nuzzled itself there. I could feel his face in my hair and his breath on the top of my ear. I was aware of my heart accelerating as his breath sent shivers down my spine. He was always so careful and reserved. His breath was as ragged as mine. This was not like him.

I turned to look him in the eye. "What is all of this about?" He leaned in and gently kissed my lips. Feeling sensations run through my entire body, I pulled away from his kiss. I had not felt this type of passion since Dustin. It was so wrong to be comparing how the two of them made me feel. I stepped back and looked at him.

Wow, did he look nervous. My thoughts were confirmed as he began to jingle the change in his pocket while looking at his feet. "You're killing me," I said as I read his demeanor. "Spit it out! What is wrong?"

He took a step forward to diminish the space between us. His eyes flickered to mine and held their glare. He knelt on the ground before me. He grabbed my hand.

"Elizabeth Marie Cantrell, will you marry me?" He asked and then dug into his pocket and pulled out a mind blowing ring. "I love you. There will never be anyone else for me. Will you spend an eternity with me as my wife?"

"Marvin, I don't know what to say," I said in shock.

As I looked at Marvin, I knew he was simply perfect in every way. He was handsome, muscular, and athletic. I was always put first when he was around. He made me feel safe and secure. Most important though, I knew he was my soul mate. He was right, we were meant to complete each other and be together. I loved him!

"Say yes," he responded as I could read in his face that I might say no.

After all we had been through, my heart and body wanted to collapse into his arms and simply say yes. However, my mind knew that even after all we had been through, I couldn't make him choose between his family and myself. We needed to talk about that elephant. "What about your Mom?"

With a sigh, he pulled himself up to sit on a bench beneath the railing with the ring still resting on the end of his fingers. He didn't answer.

"I can't and won't," I began. "Make you choose between me and your family."

"There is no choice to be made," Marvin adamantly disagreed. "You are my soul mate." He paused for a moment before asking, "Can you deny that we are soul mates?"

"No," I answered as I moved to share the bench with him. "I know we are soul mates, but I can't change how your Mom feels about me."

"You don't understand," Marvin hummed.

"Then make me," I begged. "Explain to me that your family doesn't matter. I know better! By choosing me, you will be disowned by them. I don't understand your mother's aversion to me and my parents."

"It's a long story," Marvin muttered under his breath.

We watched the waterfall and listened to its roar.

"I didn't expect Mom to have the type of reaction she did," Marvin stated breaking the silence. "I never dreamed it would be so extreme."

"She flipped out!" I stated. "She called me a demon!"

"It had less to do with you, than your heritage," Marvin mumbled. "Your father."

"My Dweller roots," I mumbled in return.

"Mother is petrified of Dwellers," Marvin stated as he stared out over the waterfall.

"You have a healthy fear of them, but you don't go into hysterics," I retorted.

Marvin's head turned to look at me directly as he stated, "My grandparents, my mother's parents, were taken the day of the event."

"I'm sorry," I quietly stated. "I didn't take them!"

"The Dwellers weren't looking for my grandparents, they were looking for Rhett's father," Marvin began. "Rhett was home with his mom on that morning. When she noticed the Dwellers, she sent Rhett to my grandparents house. My mother and him were hidden by my grandparents in a cabinet. The Dwellers took them as well, but they couldn't find Mom or Rhett. They couldn't find the children."

"I'm so sorry," I replied. "What does that have to do with me. I am a Keeper!"

"You have nothing to be sorry about," Marvin corrected me.

"How old was your mother and Rhett?" I asked.

"Mom was six and Rhett was four," Marvin answered. "Mom can't move past it. She can't get the horror of the day out of her mind and she's convinced the Dwellers will one day come back for her."

"I was her nightmare suddenly calling!" I sputtered.

"Yes and no," Marvin said. "Your father represents the darkness she fears." He huffed a little saying, "That is why she obsessively cleans. She has always thought cleaning stops Dwellers from being able to enter her house."

"Your dad's comment," I recalled.

"Comment?" Marvin questioned.

"He said under his breath that your mom would bulldoze the house," I replied.

"No, they are moving," Marvin stated. "Mom already has moved in with extended family."

"What!" I returned. "They are moving after one visit from me?"

"Not because of you," Marvin disagreed. "Because of my mom's unrealistic fears." He grabbed my hand, "You are not a Dweller." He let out a sigh, "It's for the best. They are moving as far away from me and you as they can get."

"She's scared of a second event, isn't she?" I questioned. When he didn't respond I inquired, "This is why you moved out? You knew you couldn't see me and remain at home!"

"Yes," Marvin answered. "Not because of you though. When we were attacked in Lakeland, I knew I was marked. I moved out to protect my mother. Dad can take care of himself."

"Marked?" I inquired.

"When you cross or get the best of Dwellers, they are relentless about revenge," Marvin stated. "They refer to those they are seeking as marked. I couldn't chance bringing night mare Dwellers to my parents door."

"When did your dad figure it out?" I asked.

"Not long after I moved out," Marvin admitted.

"I assume he didn't want you involved with me," I threw out.

"Probably not," Marvin stated. "He didn't say anything because he trusts Rhett. The two of them trained together. They are best friends. Rhett introduced my parents. Dad trusts Rhett and knows I'm too old to make demands of. Dad respects me as a man."

"Don't you see why we can't do this?" I stated folding his hand on the ring.

"It's already done," Marvin answered. "I have announced you as my soul mate publicly."

"You shouldn't have," I stated shaking my head in disagreement.

"I asked your grandfather for your hand in marriage," Marvin stated. "I told Dad after my Mom fell asleep after the dinner. He knows and supports me. All Dad wants is for me to be happy."

"Happy without them though, correct?" I asked. He didn't have anything to say. "We can't."

"You're saying no?" Marvin asked with eyes tearing up.

"Not until your family accepts me," I stated. "I know we are soul mates and I want nothing more than to marry you... All I am asking is that we give your family some time."

"What if time doesn't change anything?" Marvin questioned in return.

I moved to snuggle up to Marvin as he leaned back against the railing in a defiant pose. "We'll cross that path at some point in the future."

"I will put it here," Marvin said as he pointed to the inside pocket of his coat. "This pocket is over my heart. My heart and the ring is what I will give to you for eternity. Forever and a day." He then moved towards me and he wrapped me in his arms. I didn't deserve him. He was holding me lovingly even though I had turned him his marriage proposal.

CHAPTER SIX

Trevor

Tilly and I trudged along towards our seats in class in silence, after she asked me if I ratted to her father about Anthony. The truth of the matter was… I had. Anthony was more than a thorn in my side. I wanted, no… I needed him gone! However, I knew better than to let Tilly get wind of my devious act. "You actually think I had something to do with your father finding out about Anthony?"

Continuing to give me the silent treatment, she simply glared at me from her seat on the un-trainable side of class.

"I often find myself welcome at your house," I returned as I offered up a stick of her favorite bubble gum. "Seriously, your parents barely tolerate me. We aren't exactly friends!"

Tilly exhaled loudly as she grabbed my offer of peace. "The way you've been acting lately," she huffed. "I wouldn't put it past you."

"Well, if that's really what you believe…!" I threw back at her.

"I wouldn't put it past you!" Tilly said as she stared me down looking for any hint of deception. "However, I have come to the conclusion it was Tiffany."

"Tiffany," I repeated not sure if I really heard her say that.

"Don't look so shocked," Tilly stated as she grabbed my arm. "Look, it just smells like something she would do."

I stood confused. How did that add up in her head. "What did your father do?" I asked.

"Threatened to rat me out to Mother if I continued to see him," Tilly huffed. "The nerve!"

"Your mother will flip," I said under my breath.

"Just slightly," Tilly agreed as she rolled her eyes.

"Am I to assume it's over with you and Anthony," I questioned and then held my breath.

"Trevor Stillholm," Tilly spouted as her arms flew to her hips. "Have I ever let my parents dictate my life?"

"Well no," I said with a chuckle.

"Exactly!" Tilly replied with a satisfied look on her face. "I should invite Anthony to dinner to spite my father. Can you imagine a Humling sitting at their dinner table? In their eyes it would be like inviting the garbage man."

"Tilly," I called in desperation. "You wouldn't?"

"Don't get excited," Tilly countered. "I should, but I won't because I won't subject Anthony to their scrutiny."

"But you're not going to stop seeing him?" I retorted in a questioning voice.

"Watch and see!" Tilly hummed as Elizabeth plopped down in the chair beside her.

Anyone could see her raw determination to see Anthony. At this point, I simply had made things worse. He was now more desirable to her, especially since her father had threatened her.

As Professor Presnell began to drone on and on, my mind drifted to Mr. Bradford and the conversation we had yesterday about Tilly's rebellion. She left me no choice but to pretend I supported her. Anthony wasn't likely to be around for long. I would play it cool. Then I began to think about my conversation with her father.

"Mr. Bradford," I called to get his attention. He had been content to let whatever was bothering me to fester as I sat across from him in his Underground office.

He peered up with a cocky grin, "Ready to spit out whatever is bothering you?"

"When Humling parents go to the Earth Plane and leave their children to follow them, do they leave a plan?" I blurted out.

"A plan?" Mr. Bradford questioned as his grin slid away. He dropped his pen and leaned back in his chair peering at me.

"Yeah," I repeated. "Like who goes first and when."

"I'm too smart for you to beat around the bushes," Mr. Bradford threw out.

"I'm curious about the family that Mark is living with," I stated hoping to end this sticky situation I was getting myself into.

"Missing your partner or is Mr. Lagedge no help?" Mr. Bradford asked once again with a smirk on his face. When I didn't crack at his humor, he turned serious as if he could read my mind. "That wasn't exactly what you meant. There's something more?"

"Tilly has been seeing the oldest boy, Anthony," I stated.

He openly chuckled before adding, "Just another attention getting stunt."

"You knew?" I questioned feeling incredibly dumb. Why had I chosen to bare my soul to someone I couldn't trust.

"Yes and no," Mr. Bradford said with a sigh. "Yes I knew she was dating someone she didn't want us to know about. No I didn't' know he…," Mr. Bradford visibly shivered as if the thought detested him. Then he stated, "He's a Humling."

He had no idea how serious it was. "What if she is serious about him?" I said in dismay.

"Trevor, give it a week… Month tops!" Mr. Bradford stated as he picked back up his pen. "You, as well as anybody knows, Tilly isn't serious about any particular boy."

"This one is different," I disagreed. "They have been on multiple dates each week. I know Tilly well enough to know she never dates anyone more than once or twice."

He stopped with wide eyes as he pointed his pen at me. " You're jealous!" He threw out. "I knew it."

"I'm certainly not jealous," I disagreed. "Just tell me. Is there a plan?"

"In their case, there must be since the youngest is to be a great leader on the Earth Plane," Mr. Bradford answered. "You want Anthony gone, don't you?"

"Anthony taking a trip to the Earth Plane wouldn't hurt my feelings," I spit out.

"Hmm..." Mr. Bradford hummed. "I'll check." As I looked back at him he seriously told me, "Your path is set. Don't let the Humling crawl under your skin. In the end she will be with you. Remember the two of you are council mandated."

I shook my head to pacify him as he seemed to genuinely attempt to console me.

"Don't worry," Mr. Bradford said as he peered at me with a cocky grin. "I'll take care of it."

It left me wondering if we just had our first father son moment. Mr. Bradford went back to work and silence fell over us once more. In my mind, I knew I should feel guilty about what I had just done. However, my heart had no regret. Mark was right about Anthony. I had been left with no choice. There was something shady about Anthony that I couldn't put my finger on. I disliked him and he felt the same about me.

A knock interrupted my thoughts and Professor Presnell's lecture. Annoyed, she stormed to the door flinging it open. From my place on the un-trainable side of class, I couldn't see who was standing just outside the door. Aware of the visibly foul mood of the professor, I felt sorry for whoever it was. They had, unknowingly, stepped into her crossfire.

Professor Presnell stepped out into the hall. However, all of us could hear, "I don't accept this. You can't waltz in here and expect to get your girlfriend out of class, much less think I would allow Miss Bradford or Mr. Stillholm to go along as well."

In response I heard Marvin, "But…"

"Don't ever interrupt my class again," Professor Presnell spouted as she stepped back into the room. With that, she slammed the door in his face. Since she had been fuming all morning over something, her extremely red complexion didn't seem to get any more flushed by the unwelcome interruption.

The population, of those deemed un-trainable and sectioned off to one side of the room, had grown. The majority of the trainees participating in the burn video came from Administration House. Since Professor Presnell was their leader, she had taken the disappointing behavior very personally. All those in the video had joined our un-trainable side of class the morning after the video aired. However, something unexplainable transpired last night in Administration House. Ruthanne had been paraded before the class in disgrace and asked to move to our side upon entering for the morning. I couldn't explain why Presnell seated her next to me.

I tore a sheet of paper from my notebook and scrawled across it, What happened last night? While folding the paper multiple times, I could feel Tilly hold out her hand over my shoulder. Obviously, she expected my note was for her. I reached out and placed the note on Ruthanne's desk, not Tilly's. With wide eyes, Ruthanne placed her hands over the minutely folded note looking up to see if the professor had noticed the exchange. Tilly loudly popped her gum, sending me a message, as Ruthanne began to methodically unwrap the note.

Guilt had gripped my soul when I glanced at Ruthanne when she entered. She, for obvious reasons, appeared extremely unhappy. She deserved someone better than me. Someone who would let her and be her whole world. I had no way of knowing how much she knew about where I had been and what I had been doing over the last few days.

She would never understand my need to protect Tilly. Plus, I seemed to be the only one who was concerned about Tilly's welfare. I decided I would never forgive the others, after looking at Tilly's bruised face. Her being captured and beaten still sickened me to my core. Tilly's fascination with Anthony had gone beyond ridiculous and it seemed there was nothing I could do to open her eyes to his lack of concern for her.

Ruthanne slid the note back to my desk. I glanced over at her and realized I had once again became preoccupied with Tilly. I sat back in my chair and quietly unfolded her return note.

Ruthanne answered in writing, "Janelle was found with Mike in her dorm room last night. Tiffany claimed she felt unsafe since Mike could easily sneak in. Janelle was told to apologize to Tiffany for not considering her safety or feelings about their jointly shared dorm room. Janelle refused. Her punishment is not walking with this trainee class as we graduate. Janelle's parents are extremely upset. Since Janelle and I are in the same boat, She's not alone."

I glanced at Ruthanne who seemed to be doodling on her notebook. What did that mean? I scrolled, "What did you do?"

I folded the paper again and stretched back out my hand with the paper slightly nudging her arm to get her attention again. She took the note and looked up at the professor before beginning to unfold it.

Ruthanne had gotten lost over the last couple days in the shuffle. I hadn't even considered my abandonment of her. The thought made me physically ill.

My spying led to more scrutiny being placed on Tilly and Elizabeth. I'm sure my fellow trainees wondered why I was trailing them. Not to mention, there were obvious questions about Mr. Solliday's visit to their dorm room and how Rhett and Marvin were involved. Tilly reveled in her new found fame for being devious and played it up every chance she got, much to my dismay. Destiny told Eddie that everyone wondered what we all had done. Some even speculated we would be sent to the Black Arch, if we kept up our obvious antics.

The scribbling of Ruthanne's pencil ceased. Once again, the small folded note appeared in Ruthanne's outstretched hand. I quickly took it. Slowly, I unwrapped the many folds revealing Ruthanne's answer, "Professor Presnell blamed the whole thing on me. I knew Janelle was waiting for Mike to come over while everyone went to Harmony practice. I covered for her. My punishment is that I won't be walking at graduation either."

Aghast, I looked over at Ruthanne and my blood began to boil. Her fellow trainees had been ruthless in making her do all kinds of work while they played. Why in the world did she cover for Janelle? Ruthanne wiped the corner of her eyes and I reached my hand over to hold hers. This simply wasn't fair. I glanced back at the remaining note, "Janelle is now my room mate. We are indeed in the same boat!"

I gasped.

Before I knew it, Professor Presnell was storming in my direction and peering at my desk. Instantly, I tore the note and shoved a portion of it in my mouth. Tilly leaned over from behind me and got her hands on a portion of the note, ripping it from my hand.

Professor Presnell with an outstretched hand demanded, "Spit it out, I'll take that note!"

I swallowed the part of the note, that was in my mouth, whole. Professor Presnell forcefully grabbed the bottom of the note which my hand was tightly clutching as I gagged, coughed, and willed myself not to puke. She stared at it with the disappointment of it being blank. Disgust spread across her face. Then she moved to Tilly, "Miss Bradford, take whatever is in your mouth and put it in my hand!"

"Really?" Tilly innocently questioned.

"Now!" Professor Presnell demanded as the vein in her neck pulsated with anger.

I watched in horror as Tilly stood and spit a huge ball of pink bubble gum into the professor's hand.

"Well!" Professor Presnell huffed with an aghast look on her face.

"What?" Tilly innocently replied. "You told me too!"

"The note," Professor Presnell spewed as she held her bubble gum filled hand out away from her body. "I want the note!"

"What note?" Tilly seriously asked with a fake, puzzled look on her face. Tilly began to peer around. "Did any of you see a note?"

A loud thud, thud, thud on the classroom door interrupted the enraged professor before she could pounce on Tilly who stood fearless. After all these years, Tilly still amazed me. Professor Presnell was slowly turning a deeper shade of red over the interruption. She stomped to the door and dumped Tilly's chewed bubble gum into the trash can as she wiped her hand across her blood red skirt. Then she took a deep breath to regain some type of control before pulling the door open. She glared at the person on the other side snapping, "Yes?"

"Mr. Solliday has sent me with this note for you," Mark said as he held up a small envelope and peeked through the door at the class.

In a huff, Professor Presnell snatched the note and ripped it open. After a quiet moment she spewed, "No way! Mr. Lagedge already attempted to get them out of class."

"Huh," Mark hummed in response.

"Who are you?" Professor Presnell demanded with her hands on her hips.

"Mark Spirs," Mark replied.

"Shouldn't you be at work?" Professor Presnell returned over the rim of her red glasses.

"I am ma'am. I'm a council guard," Mark defended himself. "Do you really think the note isn't from Mr. Solliday?"

"You are a council guard?" Professor Presnell questioned in disbelief. You could see the angry wheels turning in her head.

"Yes ma'am," Mark returned.

"What does the Council want with them?" Professor Presnell asked in a sudden overly sweet voice.

Mark shrugged replying, "I'm just the messenger."

Elizabeth

I had never visited the Ghost society on the weekend. Now was the perfect opportunity, because everyone had plans but me. Marvin was helping his parents move. Ruthanne had demanded Trevor's attention for a date. Tilly had happily sneaked away to see Anthony. Destiny was paling around with Janelle. I was alone and free as I stepped out into the octagon shaped room of the Ghost Complex.

I was surprised to see people sitting at the long tables and even more surprised to see that they all seemed to be up to their ears in paperwork. Some of the ghosts were using calculators to add data, while others appeared to be reading files. Lucy was seated at our usual table with many boxes of file papers surrounding her.

"Silver hula hoop!" An older man announced walking through the double doors.

Everyone turned as another gentleman replied, "What will kids think of next?"

The two men seated themselves.

"Really," the lady sitting across from them answered in clear disgust.

I began to walk towards Lucy. She noticed me and gave me a warm smile. As I pulled out a chair, she asked, "I thought you'd be out on a Saturday night."

"I am a wall flower," I responded to avoid the question.

"Well, at least you weren't involved in the U. F. O. madness," Lucy stated under her breath.

"U. F. O.?" I questioned.

"Our streaking across the sky in competition to see which of us can make ourselves known to the Humlings as an U. F. O.," Lucy explained. "There is a lot of paperwork involved." She took a deep breath as she once again gave me a warm smile. "Are you here to register?"

I hesitated trying to think of what to say.

She continued, "Not ready yet?"

"Not ready," I replied squirming.

"The light is still calling you then?" Lucy questioned.

My best answer was to not answer.

"Okay," she replied to my unspoken thought as she watched me. "I'm here when you are ready." With another grin she returned to checking boxes and filing papers.

"What are you working on?" I asked as I pointed towards all of Lucy's file boxes, interrupting her diligent work.

"The Ghost Society membership paperwork," Lucy responded. "I think you would find it boring." Again a warm smile flashed across her face. "I have no idea where Madeline or Spike are tonight."

"That's okay," I replied. "I'll see them at the next society meeting."

Instantly, she frowned.

I stared as her mood soured causing me to ask, "Did I say something wrong?"

"No sweetie, it's not you! I registered a new ghost earlier this week who was a famous Earth Plane dancer," Lucy huffed. "She has turned our next week upside down. She wants to teach everyone hip hop."

"Isn't it great!" The middle aged lady from the next table piped up.

"Speak for yourself," Lucy huffed back at her. "We had bingo planned!"

"Lucy, sometimes you are a Debbie downer," the lady answered in a matching huff. "Bingo versus hip hop dancing? Is there really any comparison?"

"We have a schedule for a reason! It is to keep things in order," Lucy adamantly returned.

The other lady stood, "You've complained all week!"

Lucy watched saying nothing as she moved several tables away. Then she looked back at me and whispered, "I just don't like dancing!" Then she seemed to mutter under her breath, "I sort of deserved that."

I peered around making sure no one was in ear shot. "Tell me why you don't like to dance."

"You don't want to hear an old ladies sob story," Lucy answered.

"You're really not that old," I countered.

She just looked at me.

"What?" I questioned. "You are only as old as you feel!"

"Usually it is someone my age who spouts that," Lucy conceded. "I was once your age. Do you have someone who you once loved?"

"I do," I adamantly stated.

"You remember him," Lucy assumed. "I can see why you don't want to register."

"Obviously you remember your love and registered anyway," I returned.

With a deep, heavy sigh Lucy agreed, "You are right. I met my heart throb when I was about your age. I knew right here that he was the one," Lucy pointed to her chest. "We were soul mates."

"What happened?" I asked.

"He never took the time for me," Lucy muttered and looked away. "He was always busy with books."

"That's awful," I emphasized as my mind spun.

As she glanced back to me she continued, "I don't know if he ever realized we were soul mates." Again she took another long painful sigh. "After each life on the Earth Plane he spent all his time reading books and analyzing the life he just led. He desired nothing more than his quest to learn as much as possible. When he began to live one Earth Plane life after another, I knew it was over before it ever began. He had no time to discover me."

Her words reminded me of Mr. Farris. I had no real words to console her.

Lucy she shrugged and continued, "Rather than be ignored, I choose to live as a ghost."

"What if he secretly misses you and does know you are his soul mate and you are oblivious to it?" I asked.

"By now, he probably has a whole library full of his precious books and I am shelved right along with them!" Lucy huffed as she began to shove what was left of her papers into the filing boxes. Her mood had soured and it appeared she wanted to run away and possibly cry. "I'm going to check out early tonight."

"Okay," I stated as suddenly the doors flung open and Charles and his crew stepped through. "Let me take over your job."

"On second thought, maybe I should stay," Lucy said as she peered at them.

"No," I answered her. "I will be fine."

I glanced at Charles as he sauntered by the table. I expected a hint of recognition from him. When I caught him glancing my way, I gave him a small wave. He didn't acknowledge me. How could he ignore me after our dance last week?

As Lucy left me sitting by myself, I knew it was time to get back to the dorm at Keeper House and simply call it a night. This evening had been a wash.

Collin

Hunting Keepers always gave me a sense of thrill and accomplishment. They were a feeble people who were always concerned with others. They had next to no self preservation skills and had a tendency to walk around care free with their guard down. Watching their fear as I turned my eyes upon them was addictive. Their pure panic gave me a high. I was the junkie who could never get enough. I was their worst unexpected nightmare!

Tonight, I had pledged to Tina to be on good behavior. That is how I found myself sitting on this bench watching the unassuming Keeper crowd walk back and forth. I was a shark sitting and smelling the blood of other fish. Yet, I was forcing myself to ignore my instincts to devour the smaller, weaker Keeper fish. My only companion was the hard, cold bench I sat on.

Tina had attached herself to that disgusting boy, Harry, for the evening. He didn't ooze goodness and light like most Keepers. As a matter of fact, Harry had a stalking problem and didn't handle rejection well. When Tina discovered that he had darkness within him, she felt he was the perfect alliance for her plan. I refused to allow her to travel to the Keeper world by herself. I was her guard and responsible for her. Harry was still the enemy. So, I was dumped on this bench to wait for her return. Since Bethany could hear if we used telecommunication, Tina would speak to me with her mind only if she were in danger.

Tina's plan was formed out of jealousy. Piper, her grandmother and our leader, adored Tina. The thought of Bethany coming into the picture and disrupting their bond was more than Tina could bare. Tina did not wish to share Piper. She wanted her sister to disappear in the same manner as their father, Walter. The plan was simple. We would capture Bethany and ensure she was sent through the Dweller Black Arch to live recurring lives upon the Earth Plane.

The only problem with our hatched plan was Dustin. He was such a thorn in my side. Maybe we could ensure he too would trip and fall into the Black Arch. He had an entirely different take as to what should happen to Bethany. Geren and Dustin talked Deward, Piper's husband, into the crazy idea of Bethany and Dustin being a couple. Dustin felt he could teach Bethany the dark side. No way would I let Dustin come out on top. If he actually married Bethany, he would be royalty. I wouldn't bow down to Dustin.

One thing was certain, I would be punished for concocting this plan with Tina. It was a price that I would gladly pay. However, Tina was a princess and had favor with a bigger fish than Deward. Piper would never allow Tina to be punished. If I had any fear of Tina being punished, I wouldn't be able to allow Tina to carry out her plan. In the end, Deward, Geren, and Dustin would be forced to forgive her for pushing her sister through the Black Arch. Our plan was formed out of shared hate for Bethany and everything she would bring into our lives. We had to strike first.

Elizabeth

Those seated around the table in the ghost society were a little gloomy due to none of us having learned hip hop moves. Lucy had gotten her way with the schedule. I thought playing Bingo wasn't a bad way to spend the night. However, the others didn't see it that way.

The chatter at my table had been about a teenager whom everyone called Streaker and he had a problem. He liked to run naked in front of huge Earth plane crowds and then disappear. The venue this week was his biggest ever. A national baseball game was his target. He ran across the field and then disappeared into thin air when security guards were closing in. To his delight, he left many Humlings asking, "Where did he go?"

Just as the bingo caller called, "Blackout this time," the double door to the room flung open.

Charles was standing with his group of misfits peering into the room with mischief written all over them.

"Get a life," Madeline said under her breath rolling her eyes.

"I 16," the bingo caller yelled.

"Just pay them no attention," Spike countered without looking to see who she was looking at.

I couldn't help but glance at the group and their intrusion.

"Who's he looking at?" Madeline questioned.

"I 29," the caller yelled.

I felt as if Charles's eyes were burning holes right through me.

"Just ignore him," Lucy warned as she peered up at him.

Uncomfortably, I tried to look anywhere but at him.

"B 6," the caller yelled.

"Mark your board," Spike stated as he leaned over placing a marker on B 6 for me.

"Thanks," I replied.

"Why do we need to play black out?" Arthur questioned.

"No patience old man," Spike countered in a playful tone.

"N 33," the caller announced loudly growing weary with the repetitive drill.

"Black out does take awhile," I conceded. I watched as color seemed to drain from Arthur's face and shock spread across Spike's. I didn't think what I said was that shocking. "What?"

Arthur pointed behind me. I looked over my shoulder and at a cold staring Charles looking over my shoulder.

"O 68," the caller continued.

"Um," I hesitated. "Hi."

"Hello," Charles replied to me with a slight grin. He pointed to the empty chair beside me asking, "May I?"

"No," Spike answered for me from across the table as he stood up causing his chair to screech across the wooden floor below him.

I, as well as most sitting around me, glanced at Spike.

"N 42," the called continued yawning.

"It's not taken," I replied giving Spike a strong look.

"Great!" Charles answered as he pulled the chair out to sit down.

"The rest of us…" Spike growled. "You are not welcome at our table!"

"B 2," the caller yelled.

"That's right," Madeline agreed.

"We can't ask him to leave," I stated. I saw no reason to be rude to him.

"You might not wish him to leave," Arthur adamantly stated. "But we do."

"N 43," the caller continued.

"However, I am a gentleman," Arthur stated as he stood to stare down Charles.

"Oh…" I replied not knowing how to respond.

"You are new at the table," Arthur informed me. "You should have respected our wishes."

I couldn't believe Arthur was so short with me. "I never meant…"

"Don't apologize," Lucy interrupted me while peering around at everyone.

"B 8," the caller yelled.

Meanwhile, Arthur started dumping his markers back into their container. Clearly, he was moving to a different table.

As I watched Madeline and Spike beginning to do the same, Spike pointedly asked me, "Are you staying or is your allegiance to us shaky?"

I peered over at Lucy who appeared to be very unhappy.

"O 73," the caller continued.

When I didn't return an answer, Spike replied, "Whatever."

Following suit everyone else at our table got up and moved, except Lucy.

"G 50," the caller yelled.

"You can go whenever you want," Charles stated to Lucy. "You wouldn't want to ruin your social status being seen sitting with me."

Lucy looked at me with sad eyes before scooting her own chair back and standing.

"B 9," the caller added.

"That was really rude," I reprimanded Charles.

He just shrugged as if to say, "Oh well."

"You aren't worried about my social status?" I questioned.

"I 23," the caller continued.

"You have that number," Charles responded as he picked up a marker and added it to my board. "Why should I worry about your social status?"

"Why should you?" I repeated. "Those are my friends!"

"You aren't really one of us," Charles countered giving me a knowing look. "Besides, I didn't really think you cared what any of us think."

"B 5," the caller yelled.

"What would make you assume that?" I questioned.

"You didn't run when you discovered who you were dancing with," Charles answered. "If you had cared for your friends, you would have run." He chuckled a little, "Not only would you have ran, but you would have ratted me out."

"I still could," I hummed. "I should have last week after you ignored me."

"I 19," the caller continued.

"I really shouldn't be paying you any attention," Charles said under his breath. "You could bring me trouble."

"I could bring you trouble," I repeated offended.

"In a heartbeat," Charles replied defending himself. "All of my friend's agree."

"Just who brought who trouble?" I questioned. "My standing up for you has brought me trouble with my friends." I huffed under my breath, "Now, I am gossip bait for your little…" I closed my eyes and took a deep calming breath, "For your group."

"You don't get what I'm alluding too," Charles answered.

"Then why don't you explain it," I growled at him.

"You don't see it, do you?" Charles questioned.

I leaned back in my chair questioning myself, What had I missed? "Enlighten me!" I replied.

"Why do you think everyone treats me and my friends like we have the plague?" Charles began. "Your friends scatter like flies when we enter the room." He pointed to Spike and Madeline who were seated a couple tables over, "I'm sure they have told you to stay away from me and my group."

"They did," I admitted. "They believe you are trouble."

"I know who you are," Charles stated.

"Go on…" I replied fishing to see what he knew.

"Not only are you a ghost hunter!" He leaned very close finishing, "You have darkness in you. I can see it."

Again, I glanced over at Spike and Madeline who were intently watching us. Suddenly, I wanted to be seated far away from Charles. He could blow my cover big time.

"Do you want to know how I know?" Charles asked catching my attention. With my slight nod he continued, "Everyone says I'm crazy for telling you this, but here it goes! I was once a Keeper."

"Once?" I repeated.

Charles leaned over close to whisper, "I have darkness in me also."

"How did you end up here?" I asked.

"When I was a Keeper, I made the worst mistake of my life," Charles said hanging his head in regret. "I was brought before the Council and they sentenced me to be sent through the Black Arch." He unbuttoned the button on his shirt sleeve and began to roll up his sleeve revealing huge scars. "Do you know what these are?"

I peered at his visibly scared arm. "Burns," I said under my breath.

"Yes," Charles stated as he rolled down his sleeves. "Keepers who are sent through the Black Arch spend their first ten to twenty years as a slave. You do not have any idea what that is like." He rubbed his arm and shivered, "The scars are just an outward appearance of Dweller torture."

"I'm sorry," I seriously whispered. Everyone kept eyeing us.

"N 40," the caller seemed to bellow interrupting our conversation and making me jump.

"You have another one," Charles stated as he put another one of my markers on my bingo card.

I pushed all the markers off my card demanding, "Stop."

"I did what I had to in order to escape slavery," Charles continued. "In the Dweller world, you must win your spot to go to the Earth Plane."

"Win it?" I questioned.

"Come on," Charles stated. "Don't play dumb!" He sat back in his chair and stared at me. "I intended to stay as long as possible on the Earth plane to escape return to the Dweller world. In my Earth Plane family, I had a sister who died when I was a child. She waited for me as an Earth Plane bound ghost and showed me I could become a ghost and not have to return to the Dwellers."

"How many ghosts are Dwellers?" I asked as I looked around.

"None," Charles quickly corrected me. "Dwellers can never be ghosts. They can't enter this world. If we were truly Dwellers, we couldn't come here. We are Keepers or Humlings who are living amongst the Dwellers, doing our best to exist in the Dweller darkness."

"Your group?" I questioned.

"None of them have Keepers," Charles answered. "And the Dwellers won't be looking for them here." He chuckled, "Well, Brian is the exception. That is why I let my group play dirty tricks on the hunters."

"O 62," the caller once again yelled catching my attention.

"I have found peace," Charles stated. "So, it really doesn't matter that they all suspect, that the rest of the Ghost Society dislikes me. I don't care that I'm an outcast." He sighed. "It's better than going back to be tortured, live as a slave, or be a second class citizen."

"How do you know about me?" I pointedly asked.

"The garlic," Charles stated. "You reek of it! There was something about it the first day I saw you. But when you showed up here, I put out my feelers." He chuckled, "Little ears go by unnoticed."

"What did she overhear?" I asked.

"The ghost hunter talking to Royce and the lady with shoulder length hair," Charles stated. "Your mother."

"My mother?" I repeated.

"Yeah," Charles replied. "I thought you might not know she is hiding here like

I am. She is enemy number one in the world of the Dwellers. Every Dweller knows of her. There is a hefty reward for anyone that can bring her to Venema House. After my sister overhearing your secret, I couldn't shake the feeling that I should level with you."

"All of your group knows?" I asked.

"They have known you were a ghost hunter from the first night you visited," Charles stated. "But we are outcasts, why should we warn the unassuming ghosts." He peered deeply at me, "Brian is the only one who doesn't realize your family history."

"Might as well tell him too," I huffed.

"No," Charles said with a relieved smile. "He's a little sporadic, which makes him fit well into our group. However, he can't keep a secret. Telling him would be telling everyone." He peered out saying, "Appears your friend can't contain his jealousy."

I followed his stare to see Spike leaving with Madeline following on his heels. As she was pointing towards me, they appeared to be having words. I left destruction in my wake everywhere I went.

With my friends leaving, I knew my visit to the Ghost Society was finished. Tonight was guy's night and one hadn't been held in a long time. I knew as I made my way there, my presence would be pushing the envelope. I wasn't sure Marvin would be happy to see me. He acted as if tonight was extremely important. I suspected it was because this would be the last to be held in the empty shell of his childhood home.

Standing on the porch of Marvin's lonely townhouse, I sensed the life had been sucked out of it. A sadness had engulfed it! As my knuckles were about to rap the door, the door slowly creaked open. I was certain Marvin's mother was already gone. She had guarded the door on my last visit. I pushed the door open remembering how unwelcome I was by Marvin's mother on my previous visit. I stepped inside the entry way and paused. Missing were the carpet squares for shoes and the foot washing bench. I was glad. It was unbelievable that anyone could put up with that ritual for a lifetime. Marvin's father, Mr. Lagedge was a saint.

A single light was shining from the dining room. I stepped past a few remaining cardboard boxes which lined the entry way. They appeared to be Marvin's childhood possessions. If there was a single ounce of Marvin's innocence left,

I was about to shatter it. The one person he fully trusted was Rhett and I had stumbled upon Rhett's secret world which Marvin knew nothing about. Earlier, I had discovered the scope of his deception. Marvin deserved to know.

A sign stating, "Wear gloves!" Was placed on the dining room floor next to a single box of rubber gloves. All of a sudden, I could hear a laughter echo from somewhere beyond the kitchen. I followed the sound and it became clear the sound was traveling up a staircase off the kitchen.

Taking a deep breath I took the first step to descend the staircase as I announced myself, "Hello!"

A dead silence followed below as I descended a couple more steps. Marvin appeared at the bottom of the staircase. He peered up at me expressionless before greeting, "Elizabeth?"

"Geez!" I stated off the top of my mind to his warm reaction. "Don't be so enthusiastic about seeing me!"

"Sorry," Marvin disagreed. "It's just…"

From the last step, I could see Billy who interrupted Marvin, "Howdy gal! I wasn't expectin' to see you this evenin."

I waved to all the familiar faces around the guy's game table as Marvin intently asked, "Is something wrong?"

I forced a weak smile at him as he returned a worried look. He reached out and grabbed my hand as he informed the group of guys, "I'll be back."

He started to climb the stairs as I placed my free hand on his arm stopping him. I turned to the group asking Rhett, "May I talk with you too?"

Rhett's eyes flashed to Marvin. Then he looked around the table before pushing his chair back. He then arose and peered at me agreeing, "Sure."

Marvin pointed up the stairs. I began to climb with him and Rhett behind me. Once we stepped off the top of the stairs I began, "I'm sorry to interrupt your guy's night."

"What is it?" Marvin asked with concern in his voice. Then as his thoughts shifted to the obvious, with a hint of true annoyance, he asked, "Why are you wandering around at night?"

As Rhett stepped out into the kitchen, he pointed towards the room off the dining room saying, "To talk, let's go in there. It's more private." Marvin shook his head in agreement as Rhett closed the door to the basement.

"Well?" Rhett questioned.

"I found my Mother!" I blurted out talking way to fast due to being nervous.

"Whoa," Marvin said peering at me. "Back up and slow down." Marvin waved his hands, "You found your mother?"

"She's going to be very unhappy," Rhett stated under his breath.

"What?" Marvin huffed as he glanced between us. He then focused on Rhett asking, "You know where Elizabeth's mother is?"

"You don't want to know," Rhett quickly retorted to Marvin. "The more you know, or the more it is perceived you know, the bigger target you will become."

"At this point, I'm already marked," Marvin returned.

"My mother is a ghost," I spit out again speaking too fast.

"She's in hiding," Rhett added. "Let it go for Marvin's sake!"

"Why did you not tell me?" I asked Rhett. "You know how alone I have felt!"

"Elizabeth, you have spent too much time in Ghost Relations," Rhett retorted. "You don't know the disappointment of talking to someone who doesn't know who you are."

"You think my mother doesn't remember me?" I asked. Rhett didn't answer. I was appalled. "You don't think my mother will remember me, her daughter, but she remembers you?" Again, no answer, "I don't believe that!"

"You should," Rhett retorted. "Not everyone who is a ghost remembers."

"The man you sit with doesn't remember you, does he?" I questioned wanting answers.

"We have a strong friendship," Rhett answered. "One that took a long time to build. I started visiting him as a child."

"Who are you referring too?" Marvin questioned lost in the conversation.

Rhett turned his back to both of us and peered out the window.

I answered Marvin, "His father, Royce."

Marvin stepped backwards and leaned against the wall as he mumbled, "Does Dad know?"

Rhett turned answering, "He highly suspects why I can't catch Royce, the famous ghost."

"Does Dad know you only pretend to look for him?" Marvin asked.

"It always appears as if I'm looking for him," Rhett nodded answering. "Without your Dad's ignoring the obvious, I couldn't cover my tracks so well."

"Dad always said you were too smart for ghost hunting," Marvin countered.

"Marvin," Rhett hesitated. "I made tough decisions back then. Being near my father took priority."

"Over you happiness?" I questioned leading the conversation.

"We aren't so different from the ghosts I hunt," Rhett countered. "We tend to make decisions based on our emotional ties."

"Does your father know Mr. Solliday is my grandfather?" I asked.

"Stop digging," Rhett coldly retorted. "I'm going to tell you the same thing I just told him. The more you know, or appear to know, the bigger target you are!" Rhett tossed his hands up as he continued, "If my father or your mother were to come back, they would be targets. Don't you see that they are safer where they are?"

"Is everything all right?" Mr. Lagedge asked as he entered the room. "I heard loud voices."

Rhett's eyes flashed to him. With a forced grin Rhett stated, "Just some good old teenage drama."

Mr. Lagedge didn't appear to buy it as he glanced at Marvin who had his hands shoved in his pockets, a thing he did when he was nervous.

"Dad, I better walk Elizabeth home," Marvin stated clearly trying to end the conversation before it started.

"That's a great idea," Rhett hummed. "I'm ready to get back to the game."

"I can walk myself," I stated not wanting to pull Marvin away from his guy's night.

"I hear it's not safe to wander around alone," Mr. Lagedge stated to my dismay.

"Thanks Dad," Marvin stated for the support. "Don't worry, I'll come straight back."

"Okay son," Mr. Lagedge answered as he turned to get back to the guys in the basement.

"Don't lead them to her," Rhett stated in a low demanding voice as he passed us.

Trevor

I stuck my head into Mr. Bradford's door saying, "You wanted to see me?"

"Yes," Mr. Bradford responded as he looked up waving me in. "Have a seat."

I pulled out the chair across from him and reluctantly sat down. My last talk with him didn't get me anywhere. It only served to make Tilly view Anthony as a way to rebel against her parents wishes.

"I'm ready to hear what you have to say to me," Mr. Bradford said clearly happy with himself.

"I don't know what you think I know," I stated feeling a little confused.

"Have you seen Mathilda this evening?" Mr. Bradford inquired.

"Tilly," I corrected. "No, I haven't seen her."

Since being summoned out of class by Mr. Solliday, I assumed Tilly was in her room at Keeper House. The girls were asked not to go out at night due to intelligence about increased Dweller movement at night. If she were out, I didn't have anything to do with it.

"I can't think of anything I've done that I should apologize to you for," I said off the top of my head.

"It isn't what you've done," Mr. Bradford said with a cocky grin. "It's what I have done!"

With that, he fiddled with the button on his desk while happily humming. The wall behind his desk slid away revealing the shelves and shelves of radio receivers. "I made a very special recording!" He stated as he rounded his desk and began to fidget with one receiver. He continued, "I wasn't sure I would get to hear the end result!"

"The end result of what?" I questioned.

"I did what you asked," Mr. Bradford returned. "The Tabures boy is gone!" He held up his hand to stop me from commenting. "You'll hear."

With that, the receiver came to life and I heard Tilly speaking.

"What's wrong with you today?" Tilly asked with a hint of annoyance in her voice.

I could hear a heavy sigh. "I have bad news," I heard Anthony's voice respond. "I don't know how to tell you this." A long quiet pause, "I don't want to tell you this."

"Whatever it is, it can't be that bad," Tilly reasoned. After another long pause her voice stated, "You're scaring me. Are you breaking up with me?"

"Never," Anthony instantly returned.

"Then spit it out," Tilly responded after a loud pop which I recognized as nervous bubble gum popping.

"I will be going to the Earth Plane," Anthony's voice replied.

"Well sure," Tilly stated. "I've known that all along. Daniel's training is moving along and you are going to escort him down." Another pause. Tilly's voice seemed a little panicked, "Why are you shaking your head no?" Another pause, "Daniel is finished with training?"

"No," Anthony answered. "I have been notified that I am to start planning my life on the Earth Plane having nothing to do with Daniel."

"No," Tilly replied with shock in her voice. "You can't go."

He seemed to say under his breath, "I just don't understand it."

"What about Emma and Daniel?" Tilly pointedly asked. "Are they going too?"

"That is what I don't understand," Anthony returned. "Daniel and Emma need me! My parents planned for me to go last. Dad was specific. He never would have left Emma alone to care for and guard Daniel."

"You have to reason with whomever told you to start planning," Tilly begged. "Use the care of Emma and Daniel as an excuse to why you can't go!"

"Turn it off," I stated to Mr. Bradford. "I've heard enough."

"Isn't it great," Mr. Bradford happily grinned as he stopped the recording.

"You did this?" I asked to cement in my mind how devious he could be. I made a mental note, you couldn't or shouldn't trust Mr. Bradford.

"Hey man, you asked me too," Mr. Bradford reminded me in a veiled threat.

"Point made?" I replied.

Tilly would never forgive me if she thought I was behind this. It was a gamble I wasn't willing to take and Mr. Bradford knew it.

I stated, "You have me." The black mailer had become the black mailed.

"You didn't miss much from where we stopped," Mr. Bradford stated as he rounded his desk to sit across from me. "Mathilda..."

"Tilly," I interrupted.

He gave me a frown before continuing, "She has been plotting ways for the Tabures boy to stay. It is so reminiscent of your plotting with her in the middle of the night."

"You listened in on us way back then?" I asked in shock at his deception.

He turned serious before continuing, "I understand why you want Anthony gone. He is becoming too big of a threat." He once again fidgeted with the button and the wall slid back into place, shutting its secrets inside. "Look, I cashed in a few favors. Surprisingly, a few of the other dad's in the underground understood my situation," Mr. Bradford stated as he leaned back in his chair.

"Anthony was to go last in his family," I spit out knowing how important Daniel's safety and care was.

"Not now," Mr. Bradford hummed.

"I thought the kid, Daniel, was special and required all kinds of special attention?" I threw out in a question.

"Luckily for us," Mr. Bradford flashed a slimy grin reminding me of Mr. Brassbuckle. "Your partner, Mr. Spirs, is an acceptable stand in for Mr. Tabures." He plopped down in his chair. "Actually he is better."

It was different to spy on someone you didn't know. I detested Anthony, but somehow I felt slimy for listening to Tilly's private moments. "Do you not think it was an invasion of Tilly's privacy?" I asked.

"Recording her?" Mr. Bradford returned. "She's my daughter."

"That is questionable," I said under my breath and shook my head slightly.

"I raised her," Mr. Bradford seriously stated. "As her father, I have the right to pry. Isn't that what any protective parent would do?" When I didn't respond he continued, "It was tricky recording that conversation!"

Since Tilly would never invite Anthony to her house, the listening devices and spy recordings had a far reach.

"How did you do it?" I asked. "… Record her at such a distance."

"Wouldn't you like to know?" Mr. Bradford hummed in delight. "By the way, you haven't thanked me!"

Since Tilly was sure to go crazy, thanking him was the last thing I wanted to do.

CHAPTER SEVEN

Elizabeth

Marvin wouldn't have wanted me to venture outside the dome without my locket, but I couldn't find it for some reason. Not wanting his lecture, I purposely left Marvin a note about going to Lakeland. It was the right choice. Now that I was back safe, he would have nothing to be upset about. Besides, my adventure out today should be blamed on Tilly. She was missing. Having had no luck tracking Tilly down inside the dome, I figured she had sneaked out to see Anthony in Lakeland.

I had just knocked on the screen door of Emma's house when I heard Anthony yell from inside, "Come in!"

The screen door squeaked as I opened it and entered. Anthony appeared from the darkened hall inside with an unusual sad frown on his face. When he approached me he greeted, "Hey."

"Hey," I repeated back at him. That is when I noticed Daniel curled up in a chair. "How are you Daniel?"

"Bored to tears," Daniel returned.

"Where's Emma?" I asked.

"Outback," Daniel impatiently returned. "When are we going?"

"When Mark is ready," Anthony answered.

"Where is Mark?" I asked.

"Outback," Daniel whined and stomped off.

"What's that about?" I inquired.

"Emma's garden," Anthony stated as if that totally answered my question as to her whereabouts. He shook his head, "It all started when Emma and I came home from the city and found that Mark had taken a day off and picked vegetables for Emma."

"That was nice," I replied not seeing it as a problem.

"You don't understand!" Anthony sarcastically replied. "Emma told him he didn't have to do that. Then he responded that he did it because she cooks for him every night." Again he shook his head. "You know, Mark is the brother Emma has always wanted."

"Are you worried Mark is taking your place?" Daniel hummed. "He is nicer to her than you!"

Anthony tossed a pillow at him, "No."

"Then why do you always peep at the two of them?" Daniel questioned.

"Why don't you let me worry about the two of them," Anthony stated. With a sigh he turned to me, "If you want Emma, you'll have to pull her out of the garden."

"Actually, I'm not here to see Emma," I retorted. "I was hoping to catch Tilly."

"Tilly?" Daniel questioned. "When was she here?"

Anthony motioned for us to go out onto the front porch. Once there he said, "Sorry. I didn't want little ears to hear."

"I'm not little," Daniel huffed from the other side of the window. "I'm an old soul, remember?"

Anthony scowled at the window. We moved further into the yard. Stopping under a huge oak tree, Anthony again tried to explain, "I wouldn't want Mark to get word that Tilly was visiting here when Daniel was home. That would be all I need."

"I understand," I said. "So Tilly was here?"

"Early this morning," Anthony replied. "She had job interviews all day and was in a hurry." He kicked his feet a few times acting like he knew something I didn't. He definitely had a secret.

"I haven't seen her today," I stated. "I'm worried about her."

"I know why," Anthony said. "Your locket is missing. She had so much to do today, she planned on using it to travel."

"My locket?" I repeated as my hand flung to my chest in a panic missing my invaluable piece of jewelry that I had tried to put out of my mind. It was my safety net.

"I take it you didn't tell her she could borrow it," Anthony replied rolling his eyes.

"Not exactly," I huffed back thinking about my tossing our room upside down earlier looking for it.

"Well, she did mention ending her day by dropping in on her parent's home," Anthony stated. "She said something about not wanting to run into the Queen."

"Ice castle don't you mean?" I hummed in response.

"She calls it that too," Anthony stated grinning. "It can't be that bad."

"Obviously, you have never been there," I stated.

After speaking with Anthony, I left and made my way to Tilly's home. As my hands rested on the wrought iron fence surrounding the stately colonial home, the Bradford's Ice Castle, I knew that anyone who had ever visited here would have that frigid opinion. There were no trees, bushes, flowers, or life. Only cold and impersonal rocks graced the yard leading up to the six white pillars of the porch.

The one thing that didn't make sense was why Tilly would blow off going on job interviews today, especially since she had my locket to travel by. Standing and peering at Tilly's childhood home, my gut screamed she wouldn't want to move back into this lifeless estate after Keeper House. Tilly might procrastinate, but she would want a job to enable her to graduate. She had tasted freedom and would now never be able to live under her mother's thumb.

As I pulled open the heavy, tall wrought iron gate which blocked the entrance, I stepped through and then heard, "May I help you?"

Instantly, I spotted a gray haired woman. She stood, blending into the tree shadows of a tree in the Bradford's neighbor's yard. As she walked over to her side of the fence, I gave her a smile and began to explain, "Hi. I'm here to see the Bradford's."

"Dear, they aren't home," she returned.

"I guess they are at work," I assumed out loud.

"Vacation," she retorted with what seemed to be a calculated grin. "They won't be back for weeks."

Instantly, I felt relieved. Now, it all made sense. Tilly was inside enjoying the quiet of her childhood home feeling free to do whatever she wanted. "I'm here to see their daughter," I replied to her stare.

"I don't know if the girl is home," she replied.

The girl. Hmm... Considering how snobbish the Bradford's were, they probably didn't socialize with either neighbor next to them. The gray haired lady didn't seem like Mrs. Bradford's high society crowd. That had to be why she didn't seem to know Tilly's name. Pointing towards the house, I said, "I'll see."

She nodded and stared as I sauntered up the walkway to the massive wooden front door which waited. Once standing under the stiff and starchy archway, I pounded on the massive wooden door. Knowing that Tilly's room was upstairs and at the back of the house, it would take a lot for her to hear me.

When the door instantly opened, I was shocked to see a middle aged lady standing before me in a maid uniform. It wasn't the same young maid I had seen on my prior visit.

She coldly and intently asked, "May I help you?"

"I'm sorry, I thought the Bradford's were gone," I replied off the top of my head.

"Then why are you here?" She huffed as if my standing before her was an annoyance.

She was their maid alright. Her cold and impersonal attitude was a true reflection of this property. "I might ask the same thing," I said under my breath.

"Whether they are gone or not," she growled. "I maintain the upkeep and integrity of the home."

"Is Tilly home?" I asked, cutting to the chase.

"You may come in if you wish to look in her room," she replied as she stepped aside and held her hand out to invite me in.

"So she's home?" I again questioned.

She didn't reply or move her outstretched hand. Reluctantly, I stepped inside the door feeling that her behavior was odd. Would she not know if Tilly were home? I heard the door shut behind me as I stepped into the foyer. Then, I walked straight down the center of the massive, stark white, formal living room. The house had an extremely eerie feel. I turned around and the maid seemed to have disappeared. As I heard footsteps over my head, I had to wonder how she climbed the stairs so quickly.

As I hurried around the classic, long table in the dining room I heard in my head, "One."

Instantly, I stopped dead in my tracks in a panic.

"Two," Collin's voice echoed.

If Tilly was home, she was in danger. I cautiously moved through the arch on the other end of the dining room.

"Three," Collin's voice echoed in my head.

My hands started to sweat as I tried to walk without making a sound. I spun around and glanced all around me in fear.

"Four," Collin stated.

I held my breath and tip toed down the hallway past a home office.

"Five," rattled into my head.

I peeked around the door of a bathroom that was ajar.

Seeing no one I began to step past as I heard, *"Six."*

The commercial kitchen was visible ahead, just past a few more doors.

"Seven," Collin called.

Then, Dustin appeared in one of the doorways. He put his finger to his mouth to say be quiet. His hand reached out for mine as he asked, "Are you okay?"

I shook my head and whispered in return, "Boy am I glad to see you."

"We must get out of here," Dustin stated softly.

"I think Tilly is here," I whispered. "She's in danger."

Dustin shook his head no. In the same instant, a bat hit the back of his head knocking him cold. He fell into me pulling us both to the ground.

"Eight, nine, ten," Collin said in rapid secession as he towered over us. *"Ready or not, here I come!"*

Frightened at the unexpected assault, my hand flew to my chest. Instantly, I felt my bare skin reminding me I had no locket. As I struggled to push Dustin's weight off me, another set of legs stood over me. They belonged to the maid. Why had I not read the signs? My gut had told me there was something wrong with her.

Panic set in as I pushed and pushed to get Dustin off of me. The maid leaned over and with one hand rolled Dustin away.

Collin's strong hands gripped my arms pulling me to my feet. With a crooked, evil grin he said, "Hello." With a chuckle he added, "I'm so glad you have came to play our game today."

"You're hurting me," I whined as I struggled to get out of his grip. I was sure he was going to leave bruises.

"Then don't struggle and remain calm," Collin replied in my head.

I watched in horror as the gruff older guard, Geren, appeared from the kitchen. He stepped over Dustin shaking his head in apparent disgust.

I felt Collin tense up as he eyed the fierce looking older man and said in my head, "What are you doing here?"

The maid gave Collin the same calculated smile she had given me. I could see in her eyes an evil demeanor.

"Traitor," Collin yelled from behind me to the maid.

"Can it," the gruff older man replied without saying a word.

"I caught this one," Collin stated with a proud voice. "I intend to send her through the Black Arch."

"No," the maid disagreed looking me over from head to toe.

"We will take her back to Deward," Geren stated in my head.

Collin was now so tense, I was sure his skin would crack like windshield glass that had been shattered. "Tina wants her sent through the arch."

"Tina may be a princess," Geren stated. "But so is this one." *With a quick look which stated his word was final, he stated in my head, "She goes back to Deward. Her fate is up to him. That is final." Then he pointed towards Dustin, "However, I can decide his fate."* I watched in horror as he reached over and jerked Dustin's locket from around his neck. "He won't need this."

Off the top of my head I stated, "How will he travel..."

"He won't," Geren coldly interrupted me. "I can not trust the two of you together. Without his locket he won't be able to access our world or help you."

"This is my lucky day!" Collin stated in my head.

With an evil grin Geren continued, "Dustin has no sense when it comes to you. You are simply too much for him to handle. Together, you spell trouble."

"Cut the head off the snake," the maid stated in agreement. "A Dweller without a locket is a blind, headless, slithering reptile. He is useless!"

A smiling Geren took pleasure in shoving Dustin's locket into his pants pocket. "He is now in the same boat as you," Geren chuckled. "Both of your lockets are lost."

"How did you know?" I questioned.

Geren answered me with a vicious grin spewing, "I know everything!"

Collin leaned his head next to mine. I could feel his hot, stinking breath on my ear. "Your friend took it. And that is where we found it, with her."

I gasped and clutched my chest as it felt like my heart was going to stop.

Collin stated, "Tilly is now mine. She is my reward for capturing you."

Marvin

I arrived home earlier with expectations of spending a quite evening with Elizabeth. As I walked up the freshly mowed path to the house, I could see a note thumb tacked to the door.

Marvin,

Tilly has been missing in action all day. I plan to go retrieve her from Anthony. Don't worry! I will have Mark or Tilly escort me back.

Love, Elizabeth.

I pushed open the door, entered the house, and plopped my bag down on the table. It was eerily dark as I moved into the living room and flipped on the light. I was caught off guard and alarmed to find Dustin sitting in a chair in the corner.

"What are you doing here?" I questioned as I stood dumbstruck.

"I need your help," Dustin quietly answered.

"And why would I help you?" I questioned in disgust.

"Because we both now have the same goal," Dustin solemnly answered.

"Has something happened to Elizabeth?" I asked as I felt my heart rapidly beating. My muscles nervously flexed. I would skin him alive if he harmed her. Relief washed over my body as I heard the door open. I knew Rhett would be there to back me up. I had reinforcements! Dustin did not seem to react and sat perfectly still. I repeated, "Has something happened to Elizabeth?"

"Ask him about Tilly as well," Anthony stated in a demeaning voice from behind me. I turned and couldn't believe he was standing behind me with Gary trailing behind him. It took me a couple moments to regain my train of thought. I was in shock seeing them!

"Tilly isn't with you?" I asked.

"No, not since early morning," Anthony stated. "The more I thought about Elizabeth coming to our place and asking about Tilly, the more I knew something was wrong. I gather Elizabeth hasn't made it back here?"

I turned to Dustin in disgust. Now that I thought about it, he was always the source of the problem. I lunged towards him. Anthony tried to hold me back but I was adrenaline filled! He could not stop me and I intended to beat Dustin to a pulp. We wrestled on the floor after crushing the coffee table. I could feel my overpowering him when I was pulled away by three sets of arms. When their hands began to relax from around my arms, I lunged at the non-moving Dustin again. Again, I felt arms pull me back.

Then my voice of reason, Uncle Rhett spoke. "Whatever the reason for his visit, we need him alive to tell us."

I tried to calm myself by taking deep breaths. Dustin was beginning to move. Uncle Rhett let my arm go stating, "Marvin, control yourself!" Then he turned to Dustin. "Why are you here? I'm sure you must have good reason!"

Dustin pulled himself up and leaned against the couch, "I came back today to warn Elizabeth not to go to the Dwellers to try to save Tilly."

I heard Anthony exhale and then watched him stagger, grab the edge of a chair to steady himself, and then lean over as if he had been punched in the stomach.

Dustin noticed Anthony's demeanor and stated, "I'm sorry. I would have brought Tilly back with me, if it were within my power."

"Who is this clown?" Gary asked as he let go of me.

"How did the Dwellers get Tilly?" Uncle Rhett asked not giving me enough time to answer. He also seemed shook.

"She used Elizabeth's locket today," Dustin stated.

"I told her to give it back to Elizabeth and not use it," Anthony stated in a panic.

"Using another's locket is viewed as stealing…" Dustin started.

"And the punishment is being sent directly to the Dwellers," finished Uncle Rhett shaking his head and biting his lip.

"I knew it," Anthony said as he punched the wall. "I just knew there was something wrong with her having that locket."

As Anthony took another swing at the un-offending wall, Gary stepped in with his hands up to stop him from hurting himself.

"So, how did Elizabeth find out Tilly was missing?" I questioned not wanting to believe my ears.

"She didn't know the Dwellers had Tilly," Dustin answered. "I found her today at the one place the Dwellers were watching, the Bradford's house." He placed his head into his hands. "The Dweller guard's have her. Once Tilly was taken to Venema house, Collin's interrogation discovered the Bradford's house was empty."

"They are on vacation," Uncle Rhett hummed.

"They knew it would be a quite place to wait for and capture Elizabeth," Dustin stated.

"They knew Elizabeth would sooner or later look for Tilly there," I stated.

"The Dwellers are no fools!" Dustin said. "I hoped to find Elizabeth before she made her way there."

"How did they take her if she didn't have a locket?" Uncle Rhett questioned.

"They placed a Dweller locket around her neck," Dustin answered as Uncle Rhett look disgusted and worried.

"Why haven't you gone back to the Dweller world to help them?" I questioned feeling like my heart was in my shoes. He was supposed to protect her.

Dustin unbuttoned the first couple buttons of his shirt and it was visible for us to see.

"They took your locket," I retorted.

Dustin nodded, "She won't be able to free Tilly or herself."

"Why did you bother to come here when you could have stayed and helped them there?" Anthony questioned.

Dustin looked away from the three of us, "They were torturing Tilly! I couldn't help her. I could not bare to hear the screaming, so I came here. I couldn't bare the thought of Elizabeth witnessing the atrocity."

This seemed to be more than Anthony could bear as he lunged for Dustin, "We'll send you back where you belong, Dweller!" Gary and I moved to pull him back and stood holding his arms securely. We could see the panic and hear sobs coming from him.

Dustin got up and paced a few times, stopping in-front of Anthony, "I wish you could send me back! I have no way of getting there!"

"They don't expect you back, do they?" Uncle Rhett asked. "They don't want you back!"

"No, I betrayed them when I tried to warn Elizabeth," Dustin answered as he began to pace again.

I could see Anthony's body shake. I understood and began to sweat as I wondered if Elizabeth was facing the same treatment. The thought was making me feel crazed. "Will Elizabeth face the same fate?"

"Not likely, she is royalty," Dustin answered. "They might punish her but nothing like…" He stopped and I knew how he would have finished that sentence. "I must find a way to get back."

"That's fine with me," Anthony spewed. "They can have you!"

"Think whatever you want!" Dustin yelled at Anthony.

"Anthony, Marvin." Uncle Rhett stated firmly trying to control his own outrage. He looked at Gary, who he didn't know. "We need Dustin! He is the only one who really knows the world of the Dwellers. He is our road map to rescuing them!"

"I came here tonight, because I desperately need your help," Dustin stated. "Venema house is well guarded and I can't go for them by myself."

I let go of Anthony and sat down in a chair. How could I trust him? He was a Dweller. Then again, it seemed I had no choice.

"I think we should go approach Mr. Solliday for assistance," Dustin suggested.

"I agree," stated Uncle Rhett. "We need his help and lockets to travel by."

"We need a well thought out plan to save them," Dustin stated. "If they are left there in darkness, they will fade away."

"I don't think you know either of them very well," spewed Anthony. "Especially my Tilly, even if you could box her up, you couldn't crush her spirit."

"If we don't succeed, I hope you are right." Dustin answered gloomily.

Elizabeth

I had not mastered travel by locket and normally found myself flung upon whatever surface graced the floor, when I landed. However, the transition from the world of the Keepers into the darkness with Collin had been seamless. He was gripping my arm and held me in place when we landed with a thud on our feet. As he inhaled a huge, deep breath, he filled himself with darkness. I blinked as I waited for my eyes to adjust to the hot, pitch black darkness.

"Can't see," Collin stated in my head as he chuckled from beside me.

The sound of his voice rattled my thinking. Two fiery red lights shined from the front of a massive building. As I attempted to focus on them, multi colored flashing, bright lights leapt and danced across my vision. I blinked trying to get the sensation to go away.

Suddenly, Collin flung me into the air like a rag doll. As I flailed about in the air, I could see a dried, dead tree rapidly approaching beneath me. I fell into the tree limbs and foliage. All air was forcibly exhaled from my lungs. I fell to the dirt below gasping for air, any air. I couldn't breath.

"Get up," Collin demanded. I tried to inhale, but the breath had been knocked out of me, Collin once again growled, "Get up!"

I tried to peer up at him, but I still couldn't breath. The kaleidoscope of colors were still flashing before my eyes. I was unable to see him. I struggled to kneel before Collin.

Collin's hand effortlessly pulled me to a standing position by the hair. I whimpered at having to move my tingling arms. I hurt all over from the fall.

"One thing you will know," Collin growled. "In my world, you don't cross me."

"Let me go," I yelled back while rapidly blinking my eyes and hitting at him with my hands which was to no avail.

"What do you need to say?" Collin asked. When I didn't respond he lifted me further into the air by my hair. Now on my tiptoes he again taunted me, "What do you need to say?"

In tears, as my hair began to pull and break from my head, I responded, "Please!"

"Wrong," Collin coldly smirked. His stare turned menacing as he flung me once again to the ground. Just as frightening, he was on top of me. His weight held my body down and his arms pinned mine to the ground. "Again, what do you need to say?"

"Get off of me," I begged as the colors swirled before my eyes making me feel sicker.

"Maybe I need to teach you a lesson about my power," Collin taunted as he moved closer to whisper in my ear. His ragged, hot breath on my ear and neck sent chills through me. "Maybe, the same lesson I intend to teach your dear friend when she awakes."

"You better not touch Tilly?" I growled back feeling instantly panicked. I wanted so badly to strike him. I pushed with all my might against his rock hard hands. I couldn't budge them.

"I taught her how to address me," Collin stated. He moved to stare at me, eye to eye. His eyes turned black. "Master."

"You are not my master," I disagreed feeling totally unable to move under his stare.

"All you need to know is that Dustin can no longer protect you from me," Collin growled as he sat straight up letting go of my arms. The black, lifeless eyes remained staring at me. I now realized he understood they left me immobilized. "Don't ever cross me."

"I know you want me gone," I quietly stated to his threat.

Collin looked away. I breathed deeply in an attempt to regain power in my arms and legs. I could answer my own question. He might be able to toss me around, but he wouldn't cross Geren.

Collin jumped to his feet in one motion and once more demanded, "Get up!"

"I don't think I can," I honestly returned.

Collin bent over and jerked my arm up, pulling me to my feet. "You are so weak!"

As I began to swagger, he held me in place. Acknowledging his super human strength in the darkness, I agreed in my head. I was no match for him. I still couldn't see much through the rainbow of colors which swirled in my vision. I also didn't think my legs were ready to work on their own. My arms were still tingling. Surprised, Collin simply stood beside me, my anchor, holding me up.

A row of old fashioned kerosene lanterns hung on tall poles. While blinking the swirls back, I could see they circled Venema House and signaled the edge of the grounds. If it wouldn't cause Collin serious trouble, I knew he would push me beyond the grounds to get rid of me. After breathing deeply, my rubber legs finally regained their strength.

Collin began to drag me up the stone steps leading to the double wooden door leading into Venema House. I attempted to take it all in. However, my blurry eyes were still making me nauseous. I closed my eyes and decided to let Collin lead me through the narrow, dark halls.

The throbbing pain in my temples led me to believe I was going to throw up. When we abruptly stopped, I opened my eyes to find I had a blind spot in the center of both eyes leaving me to shake my head and rapidly blink my eyes. Collin once again tugged me to get me moving, I stumbled and fell down realizing we were descending a staircase.

I reached my hand out attempting to steady myself by placing my hand on the rock wall as Collin tightened his grip to keep me from tumbling down the stairs. He growled, "What are you doing?"

"There is something wrong with my eyes," I said as the terror of not being able to see was sinking in.

"Don't play games with me," Collin warned.

"I'm not," I protested shaking my head.

With that, Collin removed his grip from my arm and nudged me to move on coldly saying, "I don't know what you are up too. You say you can't see… Prove it!"

I kept my hand firmly on the rough wall. I scooted my foot out until I knew it was no longer on the step and stepped down. I missed the next step and before I knew it, my knees hit the cold, slab rock steps hard. I had no time to concentrate on them when my elbows hit next, then my cheek bone. Knowing half the bones in my body were already broke, I could feel my feet pulling me over as they went over my head.

Elizabeth

I stood before a cracked mirror in my dark dungeon room, peering at my bruised face. The staircase had left its print across my cheekbone. My prison room had only the three comforts of a working sink, a mirror, and silence for my pounding headache. The semi dark seemed to help it. I had been hearing my heartbeat in my temple for days. Looking at my reflection in the mirror, I realized I looked dreadful. Sick, dirty, and disheveled described my appearance. It was a joke that I was a princess in Venema House.

Although my eye sight had returned to normal, my headache hadn't totally subsided. I was waiting for it to explode again at any moment. The dungeon had one tiny light which hung in the center of the room and flickered sporadically. I had longed for days to turn it off. The ceiling was round and met the center block walls at shoulder height. Bright orange floor tiles served as my bed. After the fall down the staircase had knocked me out, I had laid on them for days unable to move. The only bright side of my hell was my numb arms had returned to normal.

Peering over at sleeping Tilly, my bruises and stiffness were nothing compared to her wounds. The few times I had caught her right eye open, her intense pain seemed to shut her down. She would pass back out. Due to a swollen shut eye and battered cheek, I couldn't recognize the left side of her face. The rest of her body looked like she had wrestled with a ferocious wild animal. I knew all her torn clothing and injuries were due to Collin. The scrapes and gashes all over her body was huge and crusted over with dried blood. After seeing the scars on Charles' arms, there was no need to hold out hope. I knew the majority of those cuts would leave scars. Today, it didn't matter how nauseated I felt or how much my head pounded, I would need to somehow get her on her feet.

Hearing the lock turn on our door, I winced and spun around. The door flung open and Collin, with his ratty hair and crooked grin, stepped through. He peered at me spouting, "I heard you were up." Then he peered over at Tilly and moved towards her.

"Leave her alone," I loudly stated.

He peered at me, "I see she isn't awake yet." His mind thought, "But once she awakes, I can play with my new toy."

"She's not sleeping!" I yelled back at him. "She's unconscious! Look what you did to her."

"I have one final lesson which I will enjoy teaching her when she awakes." His thoughts pounded like a drum in my head, "She didn't fear me. Until now, I dare

say she has never feared any man. That was her downfall. I taught her the most important lesson a slave needs to know, to fear her master." With a cold voice Collin added out loud, "That is something you must learn, if you're going to survive in the darkness."

"Turning away from Collin, I heard him in my head. "Everyone should follow my lead. Who cares that Bethany was Dustin's girl!"

Me? Dustin's girl? I thought to myself.

The thought instantly caused Collin's demeanor to change to anger. "You will never cross me!"

Collin held his hand out towards the door, "Let's go."

"Where are we going?" I cautiously asked with my feet planted firmly.

"Now!" Collin demanded reaching out and jerking my hair.

With a sigh and a wish for Collin to let go of my hair, I reluctantly moved towards the door.

As we passed under the door frame, Collin warned, "Don't get any ideas. I wouldn't want anything to happen to you."

As I let him lead me up the dungeon staircase, I knew his warning was valid. He had let me fall down the stairs. Compassion or empathy were not words in his vocabulary.

I was caught off guard when Collin's mind seemed to be ranting as I listened in my head, "If Piper and Tina didn't care about Bethany falling down the staircase, Geren shouldn't either. His anger was uncalled for. Others should follow my lead! I should be in charge, not them. I am darkness."

There was a long pause in his thinking. I knew he had obviously gotten into trouble for his rough treatment of me and he was stewing about it.

"Geren is wrong if he thinks I can't handle what he can dish out. Power is fear. I instill it. Others should follow my lead! Bethany is falling into line!" I heard him think. "Weak!"

A silent chuckle came to my mind. Feeling he might beat me over my chuckling at his ranting, I tried to push it out of my mind.

"Guess I did make my point with her," Collin's mind stated.

The staircase gave way to a series of long, dark halls. As we passed a pale young lady, I saw fear in her eyes. She stood as flat as possible against the wall while she gaped at me. Collin raised his hand, acting as if he were going to hit her, causing her to flinch and cower to the floor.

"I love it when they flinch," I heard him think. *"I should have stopped and made her lick my shoes clean."*

He really seemed to revel in the reaction to his bullying demeanor and demands.

"Why would you do that?" I questioned.

"Don't! Questions are not yours to ask," Collin coldly returned.

"I manipulated Tina's plan," I heard Collin thinking again. *"If all had went the way we planned, I wouldn't be baby-sitter to the Venema black sheep."* He shook his head in disgust, *"If only that red-headed freak, Harry, had done his part."*

Harry? What part had he played in all of this?

As we entered the last hall, I knew it would give way to a massive room where the Venema's liked to congregate. It would have two thrones looming as the focal point of the room. That is where my grandparents would be sitting. Around the outskirts of the walls set a series of chairs which were just as ornate but smaller in size for the rest of the family. The closer your chair was to the thrones, the more important you were. My chair was as close to the door as it could get. As a matter of fact, I had never actually sat in mine. It was upholstered in an atrocious…

I stopped dead in my tracks causing Collin to whisper with a menacing growl in my ear, "Are you afraid?"

Afraid? I was terrified! Why did I suddenly remember my entire dark life so well? The nauseous feeling returned. It was all I could do not to puke all over his dirty boots and ragged old pants.

His strong hand suddenly gripped my arm roughly as he jerked me from my place and into the massive, dimly lit room. It was all just as I remembered. Although there was no sun to shine through it, the ceiling was glass. The sky above the glass ceiling was pitch black with no stars shining. Around the edges of the glass was intricate paintings of lightening and dancing flames. I remembered one of the slaves painting the mural the last time I was here. The paintings gave way to stone walls.

"What's wrong with her?" I heard a voice say in my head.

For the first time, I zoned in on all those seated who were watching me. I guess I did appear to be staring off into space. With their eyes locked on me, I peered around surprised at all of the familiar faces.

"She's a space cadet," someone answered.

As Collin dragged me into the center of the room, I watched my grandparents look me over from head to toe. Once my eyes caught those of my grandmother Piper's guard, it was her who held my attention. I remembered the family I couldn't remember back in the dome. My dark grandmother was the mother figure in Dustin's life as a child. He had told me… I suddenly remembered everything about Dustin. The journals sprang to life. They were my memories and his.

"Bethany," my grandfather interrupted my mind's chattering. "It would be polite for me to welcome you home. Kneel and kiss the dark ring on my finger!"

"There's no need," my grandmother adamantly stated in a huff. "She doesn't know what allegiance is."

Grandmother Piper held the real power. I remember her banishing me to the dungeon on my last visit. It wasn't an event I read about in Dustin's journal. I remembered the horror of it! The last time I saw Piper, it was clear that she never intended for me to stand in her presence again.

"The only one in this court that would welcome you…" Collin happily hummed in my head, "Is gone. Dustin is history!"

"Oh, spare me," my sister replied to Collin in my head. She jumped up and growled out loud, "Why must we talk about him?"

Dustin's presence in my life would be a great loss this time. As I peered around, it was clear no one in the room cared for me. If it weren't for Dustin, they would have succeeded in depriving me of ginger during my last dungeon visit and let me become a withered, weak, snake like person.

My sister stopped her strutting across the room to give me a pure evil grin. "Collin, why don't we talk about your new slave. I'm sure my sister will enjoy hearing your plans for her."

"Enough," my grandfather stated in a final tone. "I awarded him a slave for the capture and return of Bethany. He has redeemed himself." He grinned at Collin before he shivered as his thoughts shifted. *No more talk about that disgusting girl. Only Collin would want her. She's rat bait!*

My anger rose at their thoughts and treatment of Tilly. She wasn't a toy for Collin to play with or rat's bait. She was a real person! If there was anything I could do for Tilly, it was to leverage any power I had to protect her. "I demand to understand how Tilly came here! She's my enemy and I want her for a slave," I screamed and tried to move towards Deward as Collin's hands held me back.

"My, my… Maybe there is some darkness there after all," Deward stated with a calculating grin. "She is your enemy, is she?"

"How did you capture her?" I once again demanded. "She was mine to capture and bring back!"

That's our little secret," Piper stated while picking at her nails. "Why should we share the details or her with you?"

"I'll tell you," said Tina as she stepped forward. "It will serve you right to know you caused your friend's downfall. She is not your enemy!"

Calculated chuckles came from those in the room. They saw through my lies about Tilly.

If a Keeper uses the locket of another Keeper, it is like stealing," Tina continued. "You are damned to come straight to us." She smiled as her finger ran across my chest area in a taunting manner. "Of course, your dear Tilly wouldn't know because they don't teach travel by locket anymore. Lockets are now forbidden to be used in the Keeper world. She took your locket and now she is ours to do with as we please."

"She's mine," Collin contradicted Tina is my head.

"Let me be truthful," Piper stated as she stood. "It is only by Deward's grace and Collin's wishing her for a toy that your friend will survive here. He has no taste in women!" She paused shaking her head in disgust. "To each his own, I guess."

I could hear Collin literally growling in my head like a rabid dog as he twisted my arm painfully behind me.

Piper walked over to Deward and flashed him a calculating grin, "Deward won't stop me from getting rid of her, if you give us one ounce of trouble."

Collin's whole body seemed to tense up. He was the cat and I knew he wasn't going to let me take away his prey which he intended to play with. He was awkwardly bending my arm so hard, I thought it might pull out of its socket. Not only was Tilly his target, I was too. I was left with no choice. I had to keep Tilly safe. I would be on a short leash.

"Leave the boy's reward alone," Deward sighed. "A man needs his toys. Keeper ones are hard to come by."

"We are bestowing upon you a gift today," Piper hummed glaring at Deward over the toy remark.

I asked to Piper's cold stare, "My gift?"

"Your new guard of course," replied a young man who stepped up beside me, hastily jerking my arms from Collin's fierce, painful grasp. His demeanor was equally as frightening. "I am Samuel."

CHAPTER EIGHT

Tilly

Iawoke and laid perfectly still to avoid pain. I was lying on the floor on cold, hard tiles. My mind was trying to trick me into thinking I was lying in a warm, fluffy bed. My dream last night was so pleasant. However, the moment I opened my eyes, I would be faced with my harsh reality. Fortunately for me, my body hurt too much to move or show any sign of life. I looked as though I was asleep or passed out.

I longed to return and feel as I did in my dream last night. Anthony was there tenderly cradling me in his arms. I remember peering up into his worried eyes. I understood his fear in my dream. There, in his dream arms, I felt warm for the first time in days. My nightmare seemed unending.

In my dream, as I lay in his arms in a haze, I overheard Elizabeth say to someone, "At first, I didn't dream that tremendous uproar was caused by you."

"You had to know we would all come," Marvin returned.

Drifting in and out of reality, I began to smell ginger. I became aware that both Trevor and Rhett were rubbing ginger smelling gel all over my cuts.

"I am fine," Elizabeth stated somewhere in my fog. "Don't waste the cream on me."

I could hear someone huff, Marvin I assumed.

"I may look bad," Elizabeth's voice countered. "But, she is the one who needs our full attention. Give the rest of it to Rhett."

As I felt Trevor's hand rub the sap under my right ear, Anthony holding me winced before I could. In my haze, I knew my condition was serious. I slowly raised my hand to discover a rough stinging cut under my ear. As I pulled my hand back, I opened one swollen eye and looked at my fingers. It was red with my own blood. I might have felt alarmed if Anthony hadn't rubbed my hand on the inside of his shirt, gently removing the blood from my weak limp hand. I felt safe in Anthony's arms and closed my eyes being too weak to keep them open.

I assume Anthony thought I was asleep when he asked someone, "There are so many cuts. How did she get them all?"

I heard Dustin's voice say to someone in the room, "They often extensively torture the body. Her falling into a deep slumber protected her from further abuse."

"They tortured her until she no longer had consciousness?" Trevor asked in a broken voice.

I instantly knew how upset Trevor was by the sound of his broken voice. In my dream like state, I was too tired to say a calming word to him. I wanted desperately too. In my dream haze, I could not force myself to speak.

"Only pure evil would do that to her," Marvin replied to him.

"She will recover," Rhett stated. I could still feel him rubbing gel on me. Why was he in my dream? We weren't particularly friends.

Then as dreams do, it flickered. I was in a new scenario. I slightly remembered resting on Anthony's lap. He was leaned against the wall and breathing heavily, fast asleep. Elizabeth and Dustin sat on the floor with their backs to me like they were look outs. Beyond them, I could see a row of sleeping bodies. Marvin, Rhett, and Trevor.

"At what point did you forget about me?" I heard Dustin whisper.

"I never forgot you," Elizabeth's voice disagreed. I cracked one eye open. It was much too intimate when she laid her head over on his shoulder.

"You remember us?" Dustin asked as he leaned his head on top of Elizabeth's.

"Yes," Elizabeth whispered.

"Does Marvin know?" Dustin questioned.

"Why does it matter to you?" Elizabeth returned.

"Why does it matter?" Dustin repeated as his head lifted, shaking from side to side in disbelief as he stared off into space.

"I'm glad he doesn't know," Elizabeth said as she lifted her head from him. "It doesn't matter. You and I are the past. It was another life. Don't you see that Marvin is now and my future."

"You are choosing him because he's comfortable," Dustin disagreed still peering off.

"Marvin is who I love," Elizabeth countered.

"You really think he can make you happy?" Dustin questioned. Elizabeth and Dustin peered into each other's eyes. It wasn't the look of friends, but the look of lovers.

Through my slightly cracked open eye, I couldn't believe what I was seeing and hearing. This had to be a dream and a nightmare mixed.

"Why did you accept my dating Marvin for so long?" Elizabeth asked.

"Your happiness," Dustin paused taking her hand and holding it to the side of his face. "That's what I care about."

My dream then flickered to the door of the dungeon opening and someone waking me. Instantly, from his throwing me about like I was a rag doll, I recognized the dirty shoes as Collin's. I had seen those filthy shoes every time my body hit the floor from his throwing me. Several other Dwellers stood in sets of dirty shoes. Instantly, I felt panicked. Then a pair of skater shoes stood protectively in front of me. I closed my eyes to play comatose as I held onto the edge of Trevor's pant leg. Was he real?

With eyes closed I listened to the voices in my dream that had turned into a nightmare.

"Move," Collin demanded.

"Make me," Trevor growled back.

"Make us," Anthony interjected. I felt Anthony step over me. I knew it was him because I recognized his smell.

Suddenly, Trevor's pant leg jerk from my hand. Pure panic overtook me as I heard myself gasp. I buried my head under my arms in fear, blowing my cover.

Next, I felt cold hands grip both of my arms, pulling me to stand. As I cracked open my eyes, Collin's intense stare terrified me. I began to tremble as he stated, "Hello! Are you ready to play?"

What happened to the pleasant dream of me in Anthony's lap?

Then, Elizabeth pushed through the blur of men who were busy scuffling with each other. She grabbed Collin's arm and begged, "Leave her alone!"

"Take your hands off of me," Collin demanded as he peered at her. "Have you forgotten your place?"

I could see a moment of fear flash across Elizabeth's face. Collin saw it to and chose to ignore her.

"She needs more time to heal," Elizabeth stated as she pulled on Collin's arm to no avail.

"Your point?" Collin once again asked peering at Elizabeth.

I watched as both of them seemed to look off into the air. Collin sighed and let me drop like dead weight to the floor. I screamed in pain and then saw a hint of a smile on Elizabeth's face.

"I'll be back," I thought I heard Collin warn Elizabeth before my head began to spin round and round.

Next in my dream, I heard everyone in the room arguing from my sprawled place on the floor. I could barely keep my swollen eyes cracked enough to watch the dream happening.

"Elizabeth, I won't leave you," Marvin angrily said. "No!"

"They won't hurt her," interjected Dustin. "She's one of them. Royalty!"

"I'm the only one who can stay," Elizabeth argued. "They will continuously torture like that," Elizabeth stated pointing to me. "Any one of you."

"Why don't you stay," Marvin questioned angrily as he looked at Dustin.

Elizabeth placed her hand on his cheek, "Because I owe him."

Marvin fell very quiet and seemed resigned that Elizabeth's mind was made up. He turned to Dustin saying, "I have a hard time trusting you with my life."

"Your life?" Dustin repeated. "I thought we were talking about Elizabeth's."

"We are one and the same," Marvin said turning to look at Elizabeth. "You are my whole life and my life doesn't exist without you." He turned to Dustin, "Entrusting her to you, is trusting you with my life."

"Yes," Elizabeth quietly said shaking her head.

Marvin glanced back at her before starting to move away.

Elizabeth reached out and clung to him as she said, "Marvin, I have made up my mind. In this moment, I know what is right. You complete me. We are soul mates."

Had my nightmare jumped scenes again? Now it was a love story?

The hazy figures in the room stopped to peer at the two of them. Although I didn't understand their shock, it's reality spread across their faces. You couldn't deny Marvin & Elizabeth loved each other.

"I am saying yes," Elizabeth continued as she patted Marvin's chest.

Marvin lovingly peered at her for a moment before he grabbed her, picked her up, and spun around with her in his arms. He was giddy when he set her down. You could have heard a pin drop as he pulled out a small, red box from his inside coat pocket.

I heard gasps all around as he once again knelt on his knee, "Elizabeth Cantrell, will you marry me?"

"Yes, my heart desires no other," Elizabeth agreed.

"Forever and a day," Marvin responded.

My dream had turned into a pleasant one. I like pleasant dreams.

"Forever and a day," Elizabeth repeated as she held her hand up staring at the ring. I watched as her facial expression changed. She looked distraught as she peered up at Marvin and asked, "I want to return to the Keeper world with no memories of this place."

Dustin stepped over me as he began to pace the floor.

"That includes our now moment," Elizabeth continued unaffected by Dustin. "Tilly lies on the floor broken. I do not wish to remember that along with our forever and a day. I want to return a blank state. You and I will find our way to each other again."

Marvin was shaking his head no as he took Elizabeth's hands inside his.

"Promise me to never remind me or tell me anything about this moment in time," Elizabeth finished as she continued to peer up at Marvin.

"Elizabeth, you will always know something is missing," Dustin interrupted as he once again stepped over me.

Elizabeth's eyes never left Marvin's, "Promise me."

"Anything for you my love," Marvin hesitated. "I promise."

Peace spread over me. It was a wonderful love dream moment. If they had found a way to love each other, things would work out. My dream was shifting. I wanted to sleep. Then as if seeing pictures flash before my eyes, I had foggy flashes of lights, of being jarred, and of an urgency of those around me. I recalled bits and pieces of the two men in my life bickering with each other. Why were they blaming each other? Trevor was blaming Anthony and Anthony blaming Trevor for what had happened to me. In my dreams, they were fighting each other. Then as all dream do, my dream ended. All went black.

In the blackness, I lay still. I was afraid to open my eyes to more of Collin's torture. For the first time, I realized I had gotten myself into more trouble than I could handle. I remembered clearly taking the locket. As I lay perfectly still, I felt like I was dreaming about the day I took Elizabeth's locket.

Elizabeth's alarm went off. I jumped up from my makeup table and onto Elizabeth's bed stepping over her legs which were exposed. She was wearing foreign sweat pants. I leaned as far as I could to flip the button to stop the annoying beeping. I walked the length of her bed never causing her to stir. She was earthquake proof! As I stepped off the end, I moved to turn the lamp light on between our beds. The light reflected off the magical locket. In an instant, my mind was made up. I would use Elizabeth's locket to assist me in my travel. I was oblivious to the danger of using the locket.

Back to reality. That dream faded. Not even my drifting in and out of dreams could keep me from my reality. Collin, the ratty haired Dweller, had captured me as I used that locket. The beating, or my lesson as Collin called it, was something I wished I could forget. My mangled body and bruises were the outward evidence of what he did. I had been tortured. I wasn't sure any of my beauty had survived.

I inhaled a deep breath from my place of silent terror on the cold tiles in the dungeon. That is when I felt a hand rub my hair. I opened my eyes to find Trevor lying beside me on the edge of my bed. His hand was robotically rubbing my hair. I peered around through my one swollen eye that would open, realizing I was in Rhett's living room on a bed which had probably been erected there for me. I startled Trevor as I asked in a weak whisper, "How did I get here?"

CHAPTER NINE

Elizabeth

I had just finished taking a rare shower. My first in nearly two weeks. Piper's guard, Inge, had watched me like a hawk as I showered, brushed out my long hair, and put on the clothes that Inge had scrounged up for me. I recognized the stuffy khakis, light blue button up blouse, and dress shoes from my last visit. They were mine. I struggled when I thought about always wearing sweat pants and T-shirts. How had I gone so far off the deep end. I wouldn't have dressed that way before. Piper had stripped me of my clothes and placed me into the sweats and T-shirt combo as a punishment before throwing me into the dungeon on my last visit. However, today she insisted that I be clean like a Keeper should look. Complete with neatly brushed hair, makeup, and my old clothes. She probably wanted to show off my Keeper side in an attempt to get rid of me.

The room was jabbering as I thought about watching Marvin disappear. It was so hard to watch him and my friends begin their travel home without me. As Marvin turned to walk away from me, my mind screamed for him not to go. It was all I could do to keep my feet planted firmly on the ground. He looked back one last time and I tried to give him a confident grin and wave. Then he walked away into the darkness.

For the last nine dweller days, or twenty-seven Keeper days, I had told myself that there had been no choice. I had to be the last person standing. The truth was, I did not regret being the last one standing here. If I had left any of them behind, they would have been sent through the Black Arch or tortured. The beating Collin gave Tilly was unbearable to think about. I couldn't let them continue to torture her or hurt anyone else.

I had counted the days, just like Dustin and I had planned. On Dweller day ten, Dustin would return for me. It had only taken the group four Dweller days to travel, with Dustin as their guide, from the Black Arch entrance to Venema House. Even though Dustin had some type of carriage, Rhett thought traveling back would be slower going with Tilly. The plan was to meet my grandfather, Mr. Solliday, at the Black Arch where he would allow them back into the world of the Keepers.

My gut had screamed for the last nine Dweller days that eventually Piper would insist on punishing me for my group's escape. I was one Dweller day short of Dustin rescuing me from whatever she had in store for me. I held onto the hope that they would never hurt me, because I was one of them. For better or worse, I was royalty in the dark world of the Dwellers.

Samuel was a cruel drunk, but had one redeeming quality. He wouldn't let Collin touch me. Samuel did feel strongly that I should be punished for letting them all escape. However, he also believed, since he was my guard, he was the only one who should be allowed to push me around. He would be my disciplinarian. He kept repeating to everyone that we needed to bond. Day after day, he would visit me in my dungeon cell. An awkward silence would loom between us as he drank, sat, and stared at me from the opposite side of the room. Once he had too many spirits, he would pass out in my floor.

Collin didn't buy into Samuel's ideology. He was intent on punishing me for Tilly's escape. Once Samuel was in his drunken slumber, Collin would stand and stare at me through the bars on my door. He was like a shark circling, waiting for an opportunity. Samuel was the only one standing between Collin and me. That veil of safety was fragile and I had been waiting for it to fall apart.

On one hand, I remembered wishing that I was in my dungeon cell where I was safe from my Venema family. Then on the other hand, I understood that ending up before Piper was my opportunity to finish what my father had started.

The painful memory of watching my father leave and come back had haunted me the last nine days. As a child, I didn't know where he took his trips too. I only understood how distraught my mother was in his absence. Her demeanor became increasingly nervous as the days went on. She would stop eating and sleeping. Dad would return and a moment of happiness about being reunited would be followed by a deep sadness when she would always ask if he would be making another trip.

It wasn't until the darkness consumed both my parents that I learned my father was making trips into the world of the Dwellers. His mission for my grandfather, Albert Solliday, was to find their weapon. On my previous visit, I believed the Dwellers did have a weapon that allowed them to capture Keepers. If they had such a weapon, wouldn't my father have known about it? He was a Dweller and should have known their secrets. Maybe he knew that no such weapon existed. I questioned my own suspicions concerning it.

Back to reality, standing before my grandmother Piper, I took a deep breath. "You don't have a weapon like they think?" I questioned staring my family in the eye.

When no one paid me any attention, I screamed at the room, "You don't have a weapon like they think, do you?"

Piper appeared instantly angry at my interruption of their discussion as to what to do with me. She asked, "What are you blabbing about?"

"The event," I replied.

A calculating smile crossed her face as she replied, "You are your father's daughter." She sat down on her chair as she added, "Finishing his task, are we?"

"How did you manage to capture the Keepers you now hold captive as slaves?" I questioned.

"Well, they were a select few," began Piper. "Like Grace, your grandmother. I hand-picked her!"

"She was a lot of fun to play with," Collin said in my head as Tina laughed at his remark.

"Tell me," Deward began. "Did your escaped friend named Tilly hold onto her memory after using your locket?"

Piper instantly appeared angered at the thought of Tilly. I answered, "Her memory was fine." I thought for a moment about his strange question and then replied, "You captured them using their lockets?"

"Not their lockets," Geren coldly stated. "Once they were rounded up, they were outfitted with Dweller lockets."

"What's the difference?" I questioned.

"My dear sister, you know the difference," taunted Tina as she began to pace around me. "You spent months trying to figure out who you were and unfortunately, still have no memory of our sad life." As she shook her head in show she continued, "Our parents were tragic. I wish you could share in my suffering by remembering them."

Mom and Dad... Memories flashed into my mind like I was watching clips of a television show. I did remember them. I remembered being deeply loved by them.

I also remembered the night a stranger came into my bedroom. He stood over me and reached down, touching one of my arms. Then I had a swirling feeling and then felt a thud as I fell to the floor of this very room. That was my first visit to Venema House. It was Dad who grabbed me and placed me squarely behind him. I clung to his leg, shaking and not sure what had happened. My little sister stepped out from behind him as she peered around in pure wonder. Standing in front of Dad was a burly man who Dad seemed to know by the name, Xavier.

I don't remember all that was said that night. I just remember hearing in my head the pure evil of Piper saying to my father, "You are to be sent through the Black Arch."

Dad kept his hand on me as he begged for his existence. It was Geren who pulled me from my Dad's grip. I kicked him as hard as I could, causing him to release me. I ran for the corner in horror as I watched them push my father through their Black Arch. I remembered watching Tina through my tears. She stood in the center of the room bidding Dad goodbye. She appeared to enjoy the excitement of the event.

After Xavier was banished, Geren approached me, used his locket to return me to the world of the Keepers, and disappeared. They left us to take the blame for Dad's disappearance. Why hadn't Tina accepted their love? What made her hate them so much?

I always wanted my memory back. However, the memories seemed raw and overwhelming. The grief felt fresh. The weight of the world felt as if it were on my shoulders.

Tina staring at me taunted, "Our parents deserved what they got!"

"Don't talk about our parents!" I screamed at Tina, catching her off guard. Collin, being Tina's guard, was quick to restrict my arms behind my back to ensure I wouldn't attack her. I screamed in agony. The pain felt like my arms were being torn from my body. "Christina!" I added.

"Collin," reprimanded Geren telepathically.

He relaxed his grip and I began to think about the lockets. I knew Grace claimed to have no memory beyond waking up here. A Keeper who uses a Dweller locket to come here has their memory erased just like a... Then it dawned on me. I angrily asked, "I lost my memory going back to the dome because I am a Dweller using a Keeper locket?"

"Well, we do have a bright one before us, don't we?" Questioned Piper as she exchanged a glance with Tina.

"May I?" Tina asked Piper.

I watched in horror as Piper handed Tina a locket which I recognized to be my own.

"You see," Tina taunted. "We have decided to bestow a second gift upon you today. Your locket. Using it will take you back to the dome, but it will erase your memory. Imagine not remembering that excuse for a friend." Tina let out a catty cackle. Reading my dejected face, she stood beside me and grabbed my hand. With dark eyes that sent shivers through me she added, "Imagine not remembering that boy who proposed to you."

"Almost erase," corrected Samuel. "Won't she remember one detail?"

"What would she pick?" Tina asked with a calculated grin. "The secret weapon which alluded Daddy, her beau, and maybe her second boyfriend."

"Stuff it," I heard Collin say in his head.

"I agree she is to be punished for letting our slaves get away," Samuel stated gaining my attention and taking Collin's place.

"Punished?" I questioned as I looked at Deward. Using all the strength in my body, I tried to pull away from Samuel. He was too strong with his iron clad grasp on my arms.

"Unless you want to assume your natural place at our side?" Deward stated. The silence fell upon the room with every eye turned on me, waiting for my answer. "Just as I thought. You have never wanted to be one of our family,"

Deward stated to me. "Samuel may punish you for as long as he sees fit."

"But I am royalty," I objected.

Samuel's laugh was dark, pure evil. "Weak!" He whispered into my ear, "He will never forgive you for Dustin."

"I don't know why my boy, Dustin, seems to love you so much," Geren stated.

"Your boy?" I questioned as a smile crept across Geren's face. "He doesn't know."

"Yes he does," Piper disagreed. "He learned it when his mother, Mary Farris, came from your side."

I took a deep breath in and could feel Samuel's annoyance with my shock as I asked, "That is why she can talk to you."

"She knows how to make her mouth move," Samuel replied in utter annoyance.

"You mean telepathically?" Tina questioned as her eyes shot to Piper.

"You are more Dweller than you let yourself believe," Deward hummed in surprise as he peered at me.

"Did you hear me?" Samuel questioned. I shook my head no.

"Not fully," Piper stated to Deward.

I had missed something that Samuel had stated.

Samuel whispered in my ear, "Dustin intends to keep you here for himself."

If that were true, I didn't understand it. I could remember the journal, the love between us. Not only because I read it. I lived it. Long ago, we had been a couple. However, it was a different life. Dustin had accepted my decision about us before he left. "Why did Dustin go to Marvin to try to come here to rescue me?" I asked.

"He wanted to send Marvin through the Black Arch," stated Deward.

"Eliminating the competition," Collin mocked.

"You must be wrong," I disagreed. "He left with Marvin."

"Keeping up appearances," stated Geren.

"My dear sister," Tina began. "Dustin will come here for you only to find you have been sent through the Black Arch. The grief the Keeper boy will have, when he learns of the devastating news."

"Why?" I questioned knowing I only had tonight to do the unthinkable.

"We already told you sister. Dustin is ga-ga over you."

"He would have lived with you there," Geren said. "But you broke his heart when you chose the Keeper boy and left him for us to bring back."

"Sister, the hurt overtook his desire to simply be with you," Tina stated. To protect you."

"He now wants you all to his self," Collin said.

"His loyalty now lies where it belongs," stated Piper.

"With us," Geren stated. "Dustin will rejoin our ranks."

I had been a fool and tomorrow was the day Dustin was to come back.

Samuel placed the locket over my head and latched it into place around my neck. I knew the consequence of using it. He had called me weak. None of them thought I would be willing to use the locket knowing that upon its use, I would basically forget everything about myself. As I pulled my long hair out from under it I whispered to Samuel, "Thank you for keeping me safe from Collin."

"What?" Samuel asked from behind me.

"You heard me," I retorted back.

It was all going to change. The locket would safely take me home with the memory of what I was thinking about when I left. I now understood why I was so drawn to Lakeland. How clever to figure I would find Emma and eventually find myself. The question now was, what did I want to remember.

I could not help turning my engagement ring around my finger. My first instinct was Marvin. I wanted to have the perfect forever with Marvin. The love of my life. My mind wondered to the thought about what I would be giving up when I returned to home, my memories. I knew I would be forever tied to Marvin and in my heart his memories could never be taken from me. Or could they? I had once felt this way about Dustin. I forgot him!

This decision would forever affect Tilly as well. I could have never asked for a stranger, but truer friend. I knew she would continue to seek my protection, just as I had done my best for her. The thought of not remembering my best friend weighed on my mind. However, I decided she was strong enough to move on, without me if she chose too. My mind knew if she did choose to move on, I would not be affected by the loss because I would not remember.

However, today was the day. I couldn't wait anymore because I couldn't trust Dustin.

I could live a lifetime without ever thinking about this dark place again. It was selfish, but the truth. I had asked Marvin not to ever tell me about this place. All I wanted to do was forget about my Venema families' existence. He would keep me safe and I hoped he would keep his promise.

I placed my hand on my locket. I was ready to let go of my memories and let go of who I was. I had to trust that Marvin would keep me safe. I was ready. I would focus on Marvin in hopes I could remember him at the loss of everything else. I rubbed the locket and whispered, "Home," *while hearing my sister hum, "Trevor," in my head.*

Elizabeth

I opened my eyes slowly to find I was seated in a massive hospital waiting room. Everything was sterile white and I could not fight the feeling of not being safe. I ran my hands all over my arms and legs. Was I ill or hurt? Is that what landed me here?

Startled, a young man stepped through the swinging door that loomed next to the Nurse's station. My gut screamed that this was a repeat of a scene which had played out in my life before. Déjà vu overwhelmed me. The young man looked at me and smiled. He then turned to the nurses saying, "She is here!" The staff obviously was expecting me. Actually, it was more like I had been lost due to wandering away. I told myself I must be a patient.

As suddenly as he appeared, the young man crossed the space between us with a broad smile. He sat down in the chair next to me and appeared to be eagerly awaiting some response from me.

"Yes?" I questioned to his anxious stare. As an awkward silence grew between us, his demeanor changed. As his smile disappeared I asked, "Do you know why I'm in this hospital. I mean, am I a patient?"

"You don't remember me?" He asked with a hint of sadness behind those eyes.

"I'm sorry," I replied. "I don't know you.'

"I'm Marvin," he stated.

I held out my hand to shake his as I said, "Very nice to meet you. I'm…" Who was I? What was my name?

As he took my hand inside his warm hand, he asked in return, "Do you know who you are?"

This question left me baffled. Actually, no. Who was I? I had no idea who I was.

I was so deep in my thoughts, I did not notice the circle of people who had surrounded me. Standing in front of me was a girl about my age who looked dreadful. She was covered from head to toe with cuts and dark bruises. As eager as she seemed for me to recognize her, I didn't. She had to be a fellow patient. A tall orderly was holding her by the shoulders. The anticipation seemed to be killing her as she loudly popped her gum. "Can you tell me who you are?" I questioned in confusion wondering why they all were taking such an interest in me.

"Tilly," she responded. "I am Tilly!"

"Huh," was all I could respond. I just couldn't place her.

"I'm your best friend," Tilly stated as she leaned over to hug me causing me to tense up. As she pulled back, I could see the sadness at my lack of response to her. She peered directly into my face adding, "There will be plenty of time for me to tell you about our many adventures."

"Um…" I hesitated peering at her barely able to stand. "Have we possibly survived a car wreck?"

The orderlies eyes were about to bug out of their heads as Tilly's eyes flickered to Marvin's. She then answered, "Yeah, something like that."

They left me with the idea there was a major story behind her appearance.

The group surrounding us was growing and my head suddenly began to hurt with the realization that I didn't remember any of the remaining faces. I turned to Marvin and questioned, "Do I have amnesia?"

The orderly spoke up saying, "Only a memory fog."

"I'm sorry," I stated. "I don't know any of you."

Marvin attempted to grab my hand, as I pulled it away. Instantly, he held up his hand saying, "Sorry."

I peered at Tilly and she reassured me, "It's okay."

"This is all okay," I repeated to all the faces staring at me as I fidgeted in my chair.

Marvin called to me, "Elizabeth, let me…"

"My name is Elizabeth?" I asked in return to Marvin's nod.

"Let me introduce everyone to you," Marvin stated as he pointed around the group.

"And I should know all of you?" I asked.

"Yes you should," a gentleman stated to the side of Tilly.

"You can try to remember everyone later," Marvin piped up in a reassuring tone. He then pointed to the gentleman stating, "This is my Uncle Rhett. And…"

"Dustin Farris," the young man with spiked hair beside Marvin introduced himself as he extended his hand to me.

He was pale with dark eyes and rock hard hands. As we exchanged a handshake, I asked, "How are you related to the group?"

"Dustin is my best friend," added Marvin. "I would trust him with my life."

"And the best man at your upcoming wedding," Dustin added as he placed his hand on Marvin's shoulder. The two of them exchanged a long, odd glance at each other and both began to smile. It was like they had exchanged an inside joke.

"Who are you marrying?" I asked Marvin.

Looks exchanged between everyone in the group with the exception of Marvin. His stare seemed to be locked onto me. The more he peered, the more nervous I seemed to feel. "What?" Then I questioned him.

"Elizabeth, we are getting married," Marvin responded.

"Were getting married?" I questioned with a nervous giggle. Suddenly, the ring on my finger seemed to be a shining beckon announcing itself to me. "Oh."

He sat very quite to let me take it all in   I simply stared at him. Marry him? Other than this brief encounter with him, I had no idea who he was. The longer we sat, the colder I felt.

When I began to shiver, Marvin quietly asked, "Will you let me take you home?"

"What if I don't want to go with you?" I pointedly asked Marvin. As I looked around at the sad and shocked faces, I added, "I simply don't know any of you." I simply protested, "You are asking me to go with complete strangers."

The orderly asked, "If you don't let us help you, where will you go?"

I began, "I'm sorry."

"This is Trevor," Tilly interrupted me.

Trevor? Hmm... I peered at him. He seemed like someone that you were safe around. It was like I had known him for a long time.

"Sorry," Marvin quickly added. "I didn't exactly introduce him."

"I have something to ask you," Tilly stated between chomping her gum. "Do you even know where you live?"

"Well no," I admitted.

"I can tell you," Tilly stated. "You're my room mate. We live in Keeper House. You are in training to become a Keeper."

"A Keeper?" I asked.

She held up her hand to stop me. "You like pony tales, sweats, gingerbread cookies." She smiled as she said under her breath, "Especially the ones from the midget."

"Midget?" I again repeated.

"And you are indeed engaged to Marvin," Tilly seriously stated. "Don't you remember you're in love with him?"

"Actually..." I started to reply, but thought better when I saw him peering at me through the corner of my eye. The truth was, I didn't know the young man seated to my side.

"I can fill it all in for you," Tilly stated and then blew a big bubble as she stood. "What do you have to lose?" With her hands on her hips, she looked unsteady on her feet. Then she added, "I can see you shivering. I'm cold too. Let's at least continue this in the comfort of our room."

"Come on," the Uncle stated from beside Marvin. He seemed to be impatient. "We can't sit here all night."

I remained planted in my seat until Trevor stated, "Do you have a better offer?"

Well, no I didn't. Since Trevor was still holding Tilly up, he had to be a warm person. My gut said I could trust him.

CHAPTER TEN

Marvin

I leaned, patiently waiting, against the wall outside Professor Presnell's office. The door was ajar and voices from inside drifted out. From the tone of their voices, I could tell there was a very unhappy group crowded in the office. Professor Zirak, Mr. Solliday, Mr. Bradford, and a man which I was sure was Trevor's Father, Mr. Stillholm, was among those attending.

"Mr. Solliday," Professor Presnell coldly stated. "I will have you know, those three are done."

"Allene, I won't let you kick them out," Professor Zirak stated defiantly.

"You had better shut your trap on this one!" Professor Presnell growled. "They have been gone nearly a month! We have had every available guard looking for them!"

"The girls were in an accident," Mr. Solliday calmly stated. "They have an excuse."

"Where?" Professor Presnell challenged. "I demand to know where they have been!"

"What I would like to know is why we, the families, weren't notified of their absence," Mr. Stillholm sternly stated.

"Don't blame me for your lack of communication with your child," Professor Presnell returned.

"I hadn't seen Trevor in awhile," Mr. Stillholm stated sounding defensive. "With it being the last few weeks before graduation, I remembered how busy he would be."

"Your family has communication issues," Professor Presnell stated, dismissing his thoughts. "The other Stillholm boy didn't say anything to you? I'm sure he knew his cousin was missing."

"Do you know how many job interviews Eddie had over the last month?" Mr. Stillholm threw out. "None of this changes the facts. Trevor's Mother and I depend on you to communicate with us if there is a problem. We place our children in your care."

"They are really not children anymore," Mr. Bradford interjected.

"Again," Professor Presnell began. "Where have they been?"

"Does it matter?" Mr. Solliday returned.

"This is a school Albert," Professor Presnell stated. "So yes, it does matter. If they aren't here, they can't finish their studies. They have both fallen behind." She added with a huff, "Graduation is set for next week!"

"I will catch up Miss Bradford and Mr. Stillholm," Professor Zirak interjected.

"It isn't as simple as catching them up," Professor Presnell retorted at Professor Zirak's offer. "Even if a miracle occurred and they passed their final tests, they haven't been hired by anyone as a Keeper." She slammed something on her desk. "They didn't go on any job interviews!"

"They are both more than capable of passing the test," Professor Zirak shot back to Professor Presnell's rant.

"Yes, Miss Bradford is indeed brazen," Professor Presnell huffed. "Mr. Stillholm is too smart for his own good!"

"Today, I would agree with you on that point," Mr. Stillholm agreed. "I don't know how he could do something so childish as to skip a month of school, much less expect to get away with it."

"Trevor is a respectable young man," Mr. Bradford chimed in. "I am sure he had his reasons."

"I'm surprised to hear you, of all people, standing up for Trevor," Mr. Stillholm stated with shock in his voice. "I've never had any communication with you that wasn't your holding my son by his collar, as you returned him home in the middle of the night."

"He's growing on me," Mr. Bradford hummed.

"And why are all of you only concerned with part of the problem?" Professor Presnell questioned. "Does Miss Cantrell not concern you?" After an awkward long silence Professor Presnell demanded, "Well?"

"Miss Cantrell has amnesia," Mr. Solliday threw out. "From the accident."

"She remembers nothing?" Mr. Stillholm questioned.

Professor Presnell asked, "What about Mr. Lagedge?"

"What about him?" Professor Zirak retorted.

"Today, they were together outside," Professor Presnell stated. "Why do you insist on letting this girl pull the wool over your eyes."

"I believe she has no memory," Professor Zirak stated folding his arms in defiance to annoy Professor Presnell.

"You would," Professor Presnell growled with her face flushed from anger.

"Miss Cantrell will not continue training," Mr. Solliday stated.

"You can't just waltz in here and take her out," Professor Presnell huffed. "She needs to pay for her disregard of our school and Keeper House rules."

"First you don't want the three," Professor Zirak stated. "Now you tell him that he can't take one of them out?"

"To begin with, Miss Cantrell has no family to speak of," Professor Presnell spewed. "Where will she go?"

"I will ensure that Miss Cantrell is taken care of," Mr. Solliday stated.

"Why?" Professor Presnell questioned.

"Enough," Mr. Solliday stated. "Miss Cantrell will be moving into Dogwood House until her memory recovers. Unlike Mr. Stillholm and Miss Bradford, she will need to start training all over. I don't see the need to waste anyone's energy."

"You are making a mistake," Professor Presnell said under her breath totally annoyed with the adults present.

"Miss Bradford and Mr. Stillholm are your concern," Mr. Solliday continued. "Professor Zirak will see that they finish any remaining work and pass their tests."

"And a job?" Professor Presnell questioned.

"I will take care of that," Mr. Solliday stated.

"What makes them worthy of your help?" Professor Presnell retorted.

"I don't answer to you," Mr. Solliday stated.

"You do answer to the Council," Professor Presnell snapped back. "Did you clear this with them?"

That is when someone closed the office door. I moved towards the staircase wondering about the confrontational conversation still taking place. It was sure to be an explosive one due to the closing of the door.

As I climbed the stairs, I couldn't help but notice Tiffany standing at the top waiting for me. Just great.

"Look who it is?" Tiffany loudly cackled from her place for all to hear. "The girlfriend beater!"

I picked up my steps, spanning two at a time. "What are you talking about?"

"All those bruises," Tiffany stated with an innocent look for the crowd.

"I have never laid a hand on her," I adamantly stated for all the ears listening.

She leaned much to close as she whispered, "She seems to have no memory. Won't it be tragic, when I explain to her how dangerous you are." She placed her hand over her heart, playing innocent and said, "I couldn't live with myself, if I stood by and let you continue to beat the poor thing."

I could feel my hands clench into fists at my side. The thought of her publicly spreading such lies made me see red. I fought to control myself. If she dared to confuse Elizabeth...

"Whoa buddy," Rodger stated as he stepped up. "This isn't your girlfriend."

"No she isn't," I agreed as I stepped around the two of them. "I would never date such a witch!"

I left Rodger standing in shock. After a moment he yelled after me, "Hey! Hey! You can't say that to her!"

I briskly continued to the Keeper House door. Tiffany seeking revenge was really due to the feud she had with Tilly. A turn of events had left me with the feeling I couldn't trust Tilly, the wild card. I wasn't sure what she would or wouldn't do or tell Elizabeth. She lived to rebel and wasn't happy about the housing decision Mr. Solliday and I made for Elizabeth. She thought Elizabeth should continue to be her roommate at Keeper House. The truth was, Elizabeth wasn't completely safe with Tilly. I couldn't trust that Tilly wouldn't take her out on an adventure. Not to mention, as long as Elizabeth was with Tilly, she was in Tiffany's cross hairs.

With my adrenaline flowing, I pounded on the door.

The door opened quickly. Destiny appeared, "Is there a fire?"

"Only flame throwing Tiffany," I huffed.

"I'll get Elizabeth," Destiny hummed as she gave me an understanding glance.

"Actually," I stated catching her attention. "I'm here to carry her boxes."

"Moving huh?" Destiny questioned as she stepped aside letting me climb the stairs.

She was always meddling. As I stepped off onto the girl's floor, I received lots of stares. None of their stares had ever bothered me before. However, today I couldn't help but wonder if the stares were all caused by Tiffany's new line of bull.

I knocked on Elizabeth's door and it was Tilly who yelled, "Come in! Unless you are Destiny!"

I opened the door, passed through, and pushed it shut. There she stood. Elizabeth was as stunning as she had always been. "Good Afternoon," I stated.

"Hey," Elizabeth responded as if I were a stranger. She then brushed past me to round the end of her bed.

I peered at Tilly who handed me a stick of gum saying, "This day isn't going so well."

I mouthed, "Why?"

Tilly pointed to a single, empty box which was perched in the middle of Elizabeth's bed.

"Why haven't you packed?" I asked as she sat on the end of her bed.

"What would I take?" Elizabeth returned in a disgruntled voice.

"Your clothes," I replied as I pointed to the T-shirts and sweats hanging.

She got up and ran her hand down them. When she stopped to look back at me she questioned, "These?" Pointing down the line she added, "They are dreadful."

"I wouldn't say dreadful," I disagreed.

"I've asked Tilly why you all allowed me to wear all of those?" Elizabeth replied as she glanced at Tilly. "Really," she huffed. "I wore these out in front of people?"

Tilly gave me a look replying, "Don't even go there."

"You want new clothes?" I asked.

"I would love to go shopping," Elizabeth replied. "I could use some slacks, khakis… maybe some new jeans with beaded designs!" She stepped a couple steps down with a dreamy look upon her face. "Knee pants. Oh, colorful shirts with fancy buttons. Maybe a few dresses. Even shoes! What girl only has tennis shoes and flip flops." She pointed over at Tilly's shoe collection, stating in rambling chatter, "Tilly has a great shoe collection. The heels are a little high for me though."

I couldn't help but chuckle a bit out loud remembering the one night Elizabeth had tried to borrow Tilly's shoes. She could barely walk in them.

Having interrupted her shopping thoughts, she asked, "What are you chuckling about?"

"Nothing," I replied.

"Just look!" Elizabeth demanded. "Can you see one piece of clothing in my closet that is quality?" I shook my head as she continued, "I'm not taking any of this!" She once again strolled her fingers down her rack of clothes continuing, "Tilly has informed me, we aren't able to just go shopping."

"If it will make you happy, I'll take you shopping," I added.

She stopped dead in her tracks, frowned, and retorted, "Shopping with a guy trailing along. You must be joking?" She mumbled something inaudible under her breath. Then, "Like you would enjoy the makeup counters."

Tilly shook her head no and held up her hand signaling for me not to reply. The new Elizabeth sometimes lacked the quiet, timid, mildness that I had fell in love with.

A knock came at the window. Instantly, Elizabeth smiled as Tilly opened the window for Trevor.

"What are you doing?" I questioned Trevor as he crawled through.

"Don't start being a square now," Tilly hummed as she plopped down in one of the chairs.

"It doesn't matter," Trevor answered me as he sat down next to Tilly. "They are downstairs deciding our fate. In my mind we're getting kicked out." He shrugged adding, "Makes no difference."

"This is it," I questioned as I pulled the almost empty box to the side of the bed to pick it up.

"Yup," Elizabeth replied.

I looked around at the remnants of the life which Elizabeth once led, all the things a person picks up one day at a time. As I stared down into the box, I could see the choir robe I gave her neatly folded and tucked inside. It made me smile.

"You aren't taking the rest of your stuff?" Trevor questioned as he pointed to the closet.

I began to explain for Elizabeth, "She…"

"Those aren't anything I intend to wear," Elizabeth interrupted me as she stared at Trevor.

"You need to go shopping then," Trevor stated.

"Yes I do," Elizabeth smiled. "With someone who has some fashion sense."

"Isn't that what I just offered," I said under my breath.

Tilly's eyes flashed to me.

CHAPTER ELEVEN

Tilly

I couldn't get a vibe off the room as they prepared me a place setting at the table next to Trevor. They were simply the Stillholms, a loving family who cared deeply for each other. Trevor's sister was eating with one hand while baby Henry rested on her shoulder asleep. Her husband sat next to her cutting her pork chop as well as his, as she needed it. I don't even think he thought about it. Next to him sat Eddie with Kim perched at his side. His eating habits never changed. He ate the majority of his food with his hands. Eddie could be a caveman, not that Kim seemed to notice. Spread around the remainder of the table were Mr. and Mrs. Stillholm, aunts, uncles, and cousins.

I simply followed the path to Trevor's house, just like I had done a million times before, when things fell apart at mine. It felt natural.

Trevor wasn't exactly happy to see me. I knew his mother and sister seemed to share his demeanor. I wondered if they knew the sorted details of our disappearance or maybe our outing earlier in the day. Trevor was still hyper from the shopping trip. Elizabeth asked Trevor to tag along. I assumed it was to keep Marvin busy. When I stepped off the lift with Anthony, Trevor instantly seethed with anger. I could read it in his face.

My day of shopping and bonding with Elizabeth had just about been ruined by the senseless arguing between Trevor and Anthony. I now got the point that neither could stand the other. Everyone standing within a hundred feet of our group were aware of that fact. Trevor blamed my trips to see Anthony as the reason I was captured. Due to Trevor's unwarranted aggression towards him, Anthony disliked Trevor. They both held their own strong opinion, when it came to me.

Marvin had stuck to us like unwanted glue. He followed us from rack to rack, huffing when I suggested he sit on the man chair provided while we tried on clothes. He opted to stand outside the dressing room door in an annoying manner. At his crazed pace, he was going to drive Elizabeth nuts. The controlling square deemed she shouldn't be left alone for a moment. Normally, I would not have appreciated a third wheel? Despite both Trevor and Anthony waiting along the street side for us, I appreciated Marvin's insistence to keep Elizabeth safe from the darkness.

The only happy member of our shopping party was Elizabeth. Never did I dream the day would come when she liked to shop. With Marvin as her pack mule, she indulged the day away. Surprisingly, she squealed in delight over the color selections of button up, collared blouses. This led to new pants and shoes to match every color of blouse. Even I began to tune her out when we reached the makeup counter.

As I glanced around the table, I saw that everyone in the room was focused on Eddie. He had a new job as a Keeper and the room was buzzing about it. They were equally ignoring Trevor and I. The elephant in the room was the same disgust I encountered in my own home. We weren't graduating, we didn't have jobs, and it appeared we were in trouble for skipping a month of school.

"I guess you wouldn't be in the same boat if you had brought Ruthanne home," I smugly stated to Trevor.

"Ruthanne isn't walking at graduation either?" Kim asked.

Trevor coughed beside me trying to avoid the discussion. I answered Kim, "No, Ruthanne isn't walking."

"He knows how to pick them," Trevor's uncle stated under his breath rolling his eyes referring to me.

"For different reasons though," Eddie piped up. "Ruthanne didn't skip school."

Trevor glared at Eddie and his skin began to flush.

Turning to me Trevor blurted out, "Maybe they should ask you about your newest fling? Dating a Humling?"

Trevor's Aunt gasped in shock as someone from the other end coughed from choking at the news. Trevor's father loudly scooted his chair back giving the appearance he knew about Anthony. He held his palm up to the crowd around the table as though he would have preferred that my dating Anthony hadn't been announced.

"I'm always telling Trevor he has chick problems," Eddie hummed from his place.

As Mr. Stillholm stared at the two of us, he put his fork on his plate. "Tilly... let's step outside and talk."

"Good luck," Trevor stated to his father. He tossed his own fork on his plate and added, "She has a screw loose that just makes her have to see him!"

"Don't break my plate," Trevor's mother growled at the rough tossing down of the fork.

"I'm not simply talking to Tilly," Mr. Stillholm returned pointing to Trevor and then the door.

Trevor jumped up, making his own chair loudly scoot across the floor. "Oh no! I've had my lectures for today." He shook his head stating, "It is useless Dad! I've already tried everything to convince her that Anthony is wrong for her."

"Trevor," Mr. Stillholm called. "Outside!"

With a toss of his napkin to his plate Trevor continued, "The last thing she wants to do is admit that she is seeing him for the thrill of it. It is just another way on her part to rebel."

"Trevor," Mr. Stillholm called giving him a serious don't mess with me look.

Trevor ignored his father as he shook his head looking at me. "I have always dreamed…"

"Trevor Stillholm," Mr. Stillholm roughly demanded snagging his attention. "I won't put up with you disrespecting Tilly! A Stillholm man stands by and takes care of the woman in his life!"

For a moment, I could see pain flash across Trevor's face as he reached up and gently rubbed the left side of my face which was still discolored from bruising. "Mathilda Bradford, I can't watch you destroy yourself."

Trevor then pushed his chair further back from the table and stormed off. It was Mr. Stillholm who broke the silence as he moved to stand behind my chair, "Come on Tilly."

I stood as everyone stared. It had been a huge mistake coming here. For the first time in my life, it dawned on me that I really did, but didn't belong in the Stillholm house.

"I thought Ruthanne dumped Trevor?" I heard Kim say under her breath to Eddie.

Eddie's eyes flashed to mine.

"It's for the best," Trevor's sister hummed as her eyes flashed to her husbands'.

Instantly, I understood two things. It was true, Ruthanne had walked and Trevor preferred that I not be told.

To add to what I wasn't supposed to hear, Trevor's Aunt made a comment about my covered up appearance to the person next to her. In my desperate attempt to cover all my bruises and healing cuts, I wore a long sleeve shirt with a high neck. I wanted to forget, not relive the ordeal in the eyes of those who looked at me.

"Mrs. Stillholm, thank you for setting a place for me," I said as I neared her chair.

"You're welcome Tilly," Mrs. Stillholm answered giving me a warm motherly smile.

I walked out the front of the Stillholm's Victorian home. Stepping down a few stairs, I plopped down. Over the years, I had many private talks with Mr. Stillholm on the same front stoop. He was the Dad I had always wanted.

"What brought you here tonight?" Mr. Stillholm asked as he took his spot next to me.

"I couldn't stand the heat in my houses' kitchen," I stated.

"This time, I think you both deserve what you have coming to you," Mr. Stillholm stated giving me a knowing look.

"I know," I agreed.

Mr. Stillholm wasn't the only person to take my mother's side today. I recalled sitting with Anthony earlier outside one of the many shops we visited.

"What's wrong?" Anthony asked as I sat down on the bench next to him.

"You know I'm not graduating," I began.

"It's not your fault," Anthony answered as his hand reached for mine.

"Do you see that woman across the street?" I asked pointing to my mother.

"Which one," Anthony replied as he peered across the street. Several women were walking down the sidewalk, carrying bags filled with their shopping goods.

"It really doesn't matter, does it?" I huffed. "My mother saw me and yet she has turned in an effort to ignore me!"

"She won't be mad at you forever," Anthony tried to assure me.

He didn't know my mother very well. I had expected my mother to be upset as we ate together earlier. I wanted her to scream at me, or give me a lecture about not graduating. She once again proved what I already knew. She didn't really care. My bruises and welfare were of no interest to her. My not graduating, the bruises, and the gossip were apparently the last straw for her, or the fuel she needed to abandon me.

"I'm the one thing in her life which embarrasses her," I said under my breath.

A moment of shock flittered across Anthony's face as he looked across the street at a cold woman ignoring us. "Give her time."

"I am just stating the truth," I replied.

My mother ignored me at dinner. My mother's behavior did not come as a surprise, except to Anthony. He didn't know or understand my families' history like Trevor.

I suppose that is why I mindlessly wandered here tonight. Trevor understood me and always had been there for me when I needed a shoulder to cry on.

"What happened at your house?" Mr. Stillholm interrupted.

"My mother pretended I didn't exist," I answered. "I was a speck on the wall paper and nothing more!"

"Give her some time," Mr. Stillholm counseled me. "Your fooling around with a Humling, wandering off and getting into an accident, skipping school, and not graduating has given your mother a good reason to be angry with you."

"You would never ignore Trevor," I countered.

"No, I wouldn't," Mr. Stillholm conceded. "He got the brunt of my anger, a separate lecture from every adult family member, and a good dose of a reality check! I have laid out what the expectations are from this point on. He's a man who must step up to his adult responsibility!"

Poor Trevor. I hadn't considered how my folly would affect his life. If only his father understood that he was a good man who had placed himself second, and honored me first. Trevor would never be able to tell his family that he was now marked by my captor and tormenter, the Dweller Collin. Guilt overtook me. Why hadn't I saw Trevor's view point or considered the consequences he would pay. He had more to lose than me. He had a family.

"Tilly," Mr. Stillholm stated. "I consider you one of my kids and I'm honest with my children. I must tell you that I too am disappointed in you. You are basically an adult. It is time to stop the childish drama and behavior. You are at a point in which you must settle in to adult life."

"I know," I replied.

"In spite of everything, I believe in you," Mr. Stillholm stated. "I always have." He peered up at the sky.

He was laying it on thick, maybe his plan was to give me a guilt trip.

"Trevor blames me for the whole thing," I blurted out under my breath.

Mr. Stillholm let out a sigh, "You need to give Trevor some time."

"I don't think he wanted me here tonight," I replied suddenly feeling vulnerable and unwanted.

"He has a lot on his mind," Mr. Stillholm countered. "Not only is he worried about digging himself out of the hole he has put himself into, he has you to worry about."

"I can worry about myself," I disagreed.

"Tilly, you are to be a Stillholm," Mr. Stillholm began. "As far as I see it, taking care of you is Trevor's responsibility. The two of you chose this path when you went to the Earth Plane. You can't turn back time."

Even though Mr. Stillholm didn't see it, Trevor had taken care of me. He never left my side, even though being in the same room with Anthony tormented him. Trevor's hands were sadly tied when it came to me. I didn't think he would ever explain what really happened to his father. Mr. Stillholm would never fully see the man that Trevor had become.

"You are always welcome in our home," Mr. Stillholm continued. Again he stared off at the night sky. "Trevor will come around."

In his mind, time could heal all wounds. I was serious about Anthony and time could not fix Trevor and I. I peered over at Mr. Stillholm. He was so knowledgeable and patient. The thought of giving up Mr. Stillholm as my substitute father and the dream of finally having a family, made my chest physically hurt. They accepted me. Life with Anthony and his family was the unknown.

Trevor

"Get lost," Anthony spewed as he stepped out his door. "How dare you come here!"

"I need to talk to you," I tried to calmly tell him as I threw up my hands.

He aggressively pushed towards me as he demanded, "Get off my porch."

"Hear me out," I said as I stumbled backwards down the steps.

"Are you delusional?" Anthony spewed at me as I kept backing towards the gate. "I have no desire to hear anything you have to say." In one fit of anger he shoved me through the gate spewing, "You are a burr in my saddle. Why don't you just disappear?"

"What if I wanted too?" I threw back at him, as I waved my hands in air in exasperation. I couldn't believe I came here to hand Tilly to him and he wouldn't hear me out.

"You have one minute," Anthony stated as he crossed his arms across his chest.

"I have realized that I can't protect her," I stated to his fuming demeanor.

"Just realized you're not man enough huh?" Anthony spewed at me.

I took a deep breath knowing that I would tuck my tail between my legs if it allowed me to ensure Tilly was safe. "I don't want her to face the Dweller, Collin again," I threw out. "She has nightmares. I would do anything…"

"How do you know she has nightmares?" Anthony growled with a look of shock plastered across his face.

"If she goes with you to the Earth Plane, Collin won't be able to find her," I stated. "Then when the two of you return home from the Earth Plane, she will have a new identity."

"The only way she could go to the Earth Plane with me is to marry me," Anthony stated.

"It's the only plan I could come up with," I unhappily stated. "How else can I keep her safe?"

"I guess you don't love her as much as she thinks," Anthony hummed hitting my last nerve.

His comment left me speechless as I stared at him.

CHAPTER TWELVE

Tilly

My time with Anthony was fleeting and soon ending. His appointed time to leave and go to the Earth Plane had been reset by the Council. Unlike Trevor, he was in the hot seat for appearing to have run away from his responsibilities for nearly a month. Anthony wasn't his usual self around me tonight. He was antsy and nervous, matching the way I felt. I couldn't stand the thought of watching him drift away from me, but he was. What could I expect? The only thing certain about dating a Humling was that one day he would leave for the Earth Plane.

My mind drifted back to yesterday, which apparently was our last carefree day together. He wanted to fish and swim off a small paddle boat which he kept stored alongside their house. I never told Anthony about my one life on the Earth Plane and how the Dweller I married there tried to drown me in dark water. Rowing around the lake wasn't my idea of a great outing. However, I understood Anthony's need to escape Emma and spend the day with me. I went along with his whim and spent hours in the sun watching him fish and swim. I remained in my seat in the paddle boat.

He had just resurfaced after diving when he said to me, "You need to get in and cool off. You look really hot."

"I guess I can take that as a compliment," I spouted back trying to deflect any suggestion of my getting into the dark water.

"Tilly, you are beat red!" Anthony seriously retuned as he began to tread water.

"I'm fine," I replied waving my hand at him.

"Just take a quick dip," Anthony countered.

"I don't want to get my hair wet," I retorted as an excuse.

"Tilly," Anthony said in a stern voice as his hands found their way to the side of the boat.

"I'm not getting into that water!" I loudly stated with a note of finality.

"I can't have you dropping dead due to heat stroke," Anthony said.

"We're already dead," I snapped back. "You don't have to worry."

Anthony peered at me over the boat edge before asking, "Are you afraid of water?" As if a light bulb went off in his head he assumed, "You can't swim."

"Of course I can swim," I retorted.

"Then I don't understand," Anthony stated.

I was no longer the beauty Anthony once dated. I had scars and bruises that wouldn't go away. However, I didn't want to explain my fear of water. The details of my Earth Plane life were secret, locked away deep within, and mine to keep. I stood, took a deep breath, and jumped over the side of the boat ignoring the overwhelming panic welling up in my body. After my forced leap of faith, it irked me that he was acting so strange.

After our day of boating and swimming was through, I made my way back to Keeper House to attempt to make myself beautiful for our date at the dirt track races. However, Anthony couldn't wait to escape from his seat beside me on the metal bleachers for some reason. Tonight, watching Wyatt race didn't seem to keep his attention. The confident man I fell in love with had been reduced to a nervous Nellie every time he looked at me. His looking past the outward and inward scars was easy to do when no one was around. However, with his friends around, he appeared to be biding his time to get away from me. We were at the age, that everyone says, we should be enjoying ourselves. If this was the best time of our lives, it sure didn't feel like it. Anthony leaving was bound to happen and I needed to prepare to let him go. My soul mate and I were drifting apart and over. I had simply hoped we would hold each other until the end. He was creating reasons to escape me. If he were simply getting me a drink, why had he been gone so long?

Elizabeth had insisted that Anthony and I sit between her and Marvin. She didn't remember Marvin or how much they were in love. Her indifference to him was cruel. To her, Marvin was a stranger invading her space that she desired to keep at arm's length. No matter how much she attempted to push him away, he loved her in spite of herself. It might simplify things to tell her of the danger of her Venema family. Marvin had promised he wouldn't tell her. We were forbidden by him to do so as well. It was no wonder she didn't understand his smothering need to keep her safe. He had to seem a little demanding and overbearing to her. Thus, I was seated between them.

Elizabeth's lack of time was limited to Marvin. She hadn't given me much of her time, either. As I peered over at Elizabeth, it was Gary who caught my attention. He was staring at me. I thought about putting my fingers in my ear and waving them at him. He was driving me crazy as well as being rude with his staring. What was his problem?

I stood, unable to sit any longer. Then I began to step down the bleacher as Marvin called, "Tilly, where are you going?"

"Home," I said under my breath continuing to hop down the bleachers.

As I finished my descent, I made a dash behind the fence which led to the exit of the race park. Suddenly, I felt a strong set of hands grab my arm while saying, "Wait!"

I jerked my arm away from Marvin's unnatural touch. "What are you doing?" I spouted. It was an instinct reaction. In horror, I had a flash back to Collin's strong grip.

"Shouldn't I ask you the same thing?" Marvin pointedly returned. "I'm worried about you."

"Go worry about your fiancé," I curtly answered.

Marvin didn't turn his stare away from me as he countered, "You are not running off by yourself."

"I'm leaving," I stated.

"Why?" Marvin questioned. "Are you not enjoying the race?"

"Not really," I honestly answered.

"Why?" Marvin again questioned.

"Anthony can't stand to be near me!" I shot off. "I'm... I'm ugly now!"

"What are you talking about?" Marvin answered with a tone of concern.

"Haven't you noticed Anthony's friends staring at me?" I retorted. "They can't stop gawking and Anthony won't hardly look at me! Trevor can't even look at me."

"Trevor?" Marvin repeated shaking his head.

I turned to race away from him, but heard him matching my footsteps.

Out of annoyance, I turned and spouted, "Get lost Marvin!"

"No," Marvin answered. "You are wrong! Trevor..."

"Forget that I said anything about Trevor," I cut Marvin off.

Marvin stared at me before beginning, "Maybe Anthony is nervous to be seen with you!"

I turned to glare at him. What did the square just have the nerve to say to me? I was irate.

"Come on," Marvin said in an exasperated tone sticking his hands in his pockets. "My words came out wrong. That isn't what I meant."

"Right," I huffed.

"Think about it from his perspective," Marvin stated.

"Isn't that exactly what I am doing?" I spouted back.

"Have you stopped to consider how much trouble he got into for missing his appointment to plan his Earth Plane life?" Marvin asked.

"We all got into trouble," I reasoned. "It's my face that's the problem!"

"Get real," Marvin retorted. "You only dealt with the Professors. Right before coming here, he was summoned to the Council."

"How do you know that?" I asked. "What did you do? Have a little guy talk?"

Marvin had an expression which said it wasn't exactly what he meant.

"What are you and Anthony, new best friends?" I retorted.

"Did you consider that maybe he was warned not to miss anymore appointments," Marvin shot back. "He isn't supposed to break anymore rules."

"What does that have to do with me?" I questioned not getting his point.

"Are you kidding me?" Marvin retorted with an annoyed look on his face. "He is dating the one girl who could get him into the most trouble and sent through the Black Arch."

"How dare you," I spewed back at him.

"Are Keepers and Humlings allowed to date?" Marvin returned.

"You know the answer to that," I huffed.

"Humor me," Marvin said.

"No," I sarcastically said.

"That is why you could get him into serious trouble," Marvin reasoned.

"Trouble?" Anthony questioned as he walked up carrying my drink. "What is my beautiful girl doing down here?" When I didn't return his smile he asked, "Is something wrong?"

"Only how boring the intercession is," Elizabeth said as she rounded the fence separating us from the bleachers looking bored.

Gary was on her heels rolling his eyes.

"I'm ready to go," Elizabeth told Marvin.

"Good," Gary answered with wide eyes.

"I guess we will call it an early night," I added glancing at Anthony.

"Tilly," Anthony called as he suddenly set our drinks on the ground. I watched all the color drain from his face and for the first time, he actually appeared sick.

"You're dumping me," I said under my breath.

Elizabeth gasped.

"I knew you weren't acting right tonight," I whispered.

"No," Anthony said as he took my hands in his and peered into my eyes. "Don't ever think that!"

"Then you're leaving early for the Earth Plane," I retorted.

"Man, we'll miss the derby's while your gone," said Marvin.

Suddenly my self- centered mood shifted. Peering at him I knew, "I don't want you to go."

"Tilly, it's not that he wants to leave," Marvin reminded me. "He is a Humling! It's his duty."

Anthony inhaled a deep breath, dropping one of my hands. "I didn't want to do this here."

"No victory lap!" Gary chuckled from behind me.

Anthony shoved his hand in his pocket and looked undecided. Then taking a deep breath, he peered into my eyes. "Marry me, Mathilda Bradford. Marry me, and go with me to the Earth Plane."

I stammered back, "I can't. I'm a Keeper."

"Shh," came from Marvin as he looked around to see if anyone had heard me.

"Do you love me enough to give it all up," Anthony dared.

The tears began to roll down my face. His distance wasn't due to his changing his mind, it was his decision to commit to me. To make me his forever.

CHAPTER THIRTEEN

Trevor

I left early enough from Keeper House to avoid riding my skateboard with Eddie. I was tired of his rambling on and on about his new job, Kim, and just how well his life was going. I knew I shouldn't be anything less than happy for him. However, compared to Eddie's life, mine was in the gutter.

My family had given Eddie the task of keeping track of me. How ironic is that? I had always taken care of him, not the other way around. Now, his insistence to hang out was hindering my ability to complete my tasks for the Underground. Marvin had tricked Mr. Bradford into agreeing that we should be a part of the round the clock guard for Elizabeth. That is why I would be missing tonight. Marvin would relieve me, once he came back from the city on some errand he was running for Mr. Solliday.

As I knocked on the massive door to Dogwood House, Elizabeth opened the door. Standing before me wasn't the same girl who liked baggy T-shirts, sweats, and flip flops. She had replaced them with a constant look of button up blouses, khakis, and mini heels.

As she flashed me a warm smile she asked, "What are you doing here?"

"Just thought I'd stop by," I answered.

She simply stood peering at me.

"May I come in?" I asked.

"Why would you want too?" Elizabeth returned in a huff as she glanced over her shoulder.

"Something wrong?" I inquired as I tried to peer over her shoulder.

"Nothing other than all the prying eyes." Elizabeth leaned forward to whisper, "I feel like I'm a dog on a short leash."

"Oh," I stated.

"You try moving around this house," Elizabeth continued now loud enough for anyone behind her to hear. "Someone is always in my space!" With a sigh she continued, "I can't get a moment to myself."

"You are Mr. Solliday's granddaughter," I reasoned.

"And?" Elizabeth retorted.

She clearly wasn't enjoying her surroundings and lifestyle. Watching the look of contempt on her face, I asked in return, "How about we take a walk around the grounds and garden?"

"You think they'll let us do that, do you?" Elizabeth sarcastically asked.

"Come on," I said as I pulled her out the door. Once down the massive steps, I leaned over and whispered, "How fast can you run?"

"Run?" Elizabeth questioned as she peered down at her shoes.

"Yeah," I replied as her eyes flashed back to mine.

With a devious smile, she nodded yes whispering, "On the count of three." She removed her heels, holding them in one hand by their sling backs.

We once again began to walk down the sidewalk with our backs to the two royal guards who were now watching us from the porch.

I began, "One…"

"Two…," Elizabeth stated from beside me with big eyes.

I peered over my shoulder at the guards. Elizabeth and I weren't heading in the direction of the garden. With each step towards the paved path leading away from Dogwood House, the royal guard's were moving more rapidly following us. Although I understood their job, Elizabeth needed some space.

"Three," I yelled and taking her hand, we both took off sprinting like two road runners.

Once on the paved road beyond the grounds, we could hear the royal guards yelling, "Stop!"

"They're coming!" Elizabeth squealed in delight as we ran.

Once out of hearing distance, I once again peered over my shoulder. I could see in the distance the royal guards who had filed out into the paved path leading from Dogwood House. They just stood watching the two of us. I had met the majority of them and they understood I was on their side. However, I had assumed they would chase us, not just stand and watch as we ran away.

"Don't stop!" I yelled to her. Even though I had her hand, she was lagging back being slower than me. My legs were longer.

For the first time since her return, she had a broad smile on her face. With every moving step, I could tell she was running away from her new unwanted life. If she understood the magnitude of the situation and danger she was in, I felt sure we would be doing this in reverse. She would be running to protection, instead of away from it. While Marvin felt it was her wish not to know, his insistence to keep the danger from her was foolish.

Once we came into view of the Administration Complex, our frantic run slowed to a walk and I released her hand. She stopped briefly and rubbed the bottoms of her feet.

"I can't believe we broke out!" Elizabeth squealed as she breathed deeply trying to catch her breath and slip her heels on.

"That we did," I agreed laughing in response to her contagious mood.

As she lifted her arm to push her long hair back to allow her skin to drink in the sunlight, I couldn't help but notice a long, red, horrible scratch that ran down her arm. It led me to ask, "What happened to your arm?"

She glanced down rubbing the red line with her finger answering, "The cat got me."

"Dogwood House has a cat?" I questioned surprised.

"The thing hates me," Elizabeth replied while shaking her head yes. "I could live in a world without cats."

"Don't say that," I retorted. "Cats often befriend and help children on the Earth Plane."

"I doubt this hissing, territorial cat ever helped anyone," Elizabeth huffed. "They told me it came to Dogwood House from the Ghost Complex, a stow away in one of the portals." With a few more huffs she added, "Whatever that means."

"It does make sense," I agreed.

"It does?" Elizabeth questioned.

"Yeah," I answered. "Ghosts don't like cats. On the Earth Plane, cats can see them."

"Cats can see ghosts?" Elizabeth repeated. "None of this makes any sense to me."

Of course it didn't. One might think not remembering was blissful. However, I wouldn't want to be in Elizabeth's shoes and not remember simple things. I couldn't imagine living in a world in which I didn't understand. Elizabeth had gone back to pushing her long hair over her shoulder appearing deep in thought. Since her return, I hadn't seen a pony tail either.

As she glanced at me she sheepishly began to explain, "You know I have a memory fog."

"Memory fogs generally aren't permanent," I replied knowing Elizabeth's lack of memory really wasn't due to a memory fog.

"Tilly kinda said the same thing," Elizabeth said as we entered the garden outside the Administration Complex.

"Tilly?" I repeated.

"You haven't heard?" Elizabeth seriously asked.

"Heard what?" I asked.

"Oh," Elizabeth stated as she focused on her feet clearly wishing she hadn't said anything to me.

"What is it?" I asked.

"You better ask her," Elizabeth hem hawed. "I don't want to be the one to tell you. I've seen you argue about Anthony."

"Anthony," I huffed, pointing to a bench. "What has he done now?"

"Sit with me," Elizabeth said as she scooted over to allow me to sit next to her. As I sat down, she again said, "You really should let Tilly tell you."

"Just spit it out," I said looking directly into her eyes.

"Anthony asked Tilly to marry him last night," Elizabeth answered.

"Oh don't worry," I said dismissing the concern behind her eyes. "She's a Keeper, she can't marry a Humling."

"Why not?" Elizabeth asked looking confused.

"Tilly may be impulsive, but she wouldn t want to give up her place as a Keeper," I answered.

"So, if Tilly were to say yes…" Elizabeth hem hawed. "She no longer could be a Keeper."

"That is right!" I replied. "Besides, she is promised to someone else."

"Then you probably need to remind her,' Elizabeth said under her breath.

Elizabeth was peering at me and what she didn't say, she said. Tilly had said yes. How could she do that? Feeling my blood beginning to boil, I complained, "You don't commit to marriage on a whim." As I stood feeling my fists clench, I reasoned with myself, "This is Tilly we are talking about! Of course she would say yes, anything to get attention." How could she have agreed to this?

Mark

Something was off key in Lakeland. The whole marriage proposal thing between Anthony and Tilly stunk to high heaven. When I arrived home with Daniel in the afternoon, I found Emma crying. She can't stomach the thought of Tilly joining the Tabures family. She considers Tilly not worthy of her brother and feels completely helpless to stop Anthony. Although I disagree to hold him in such high esteem, I would forgive her since he was her brother. The story she told me through sobs proved something wasn't right.

The night before the engagement, Emma heard a strong knock at the front door in the wee morning hours. By the time she made it to the door, Anthony had already answered it. She peered out into the darkness expecting to see Tilly. Instead, she discovered Anthony was aggressively stepping towards Trevor, pushing him beyond the gate to their yard. Since it was the middle of the night and I wasn't home, Emma assumed Trevor intended to once again confront Anthony.

Quietly, Emma had slid past the front door and tip toed to the swing. As she watched from the porch, she waited for Trevor to show signs that he had enough of Anthony's badgering. The longer she sat upon the swing, the more she became aware that Trevor didn't appear to be hostile towards Anthony. He wasn't making any attempt to defend himself. Once Anthony had pushed Trevor to the opposite side of the path and almost to the water's edge, Trevor began wildly waving his hands. He seemed to be spewing something she couldn't hear.

Whatever the words were, they held a long discussion. Finally they stood staring at each other in silence. For Emma, it seemed like an eternity. It was Anthony who cut the tension as he offered Trevor his hand to shake. She watched in awe as Trevor shook Anthony's hand. Then, as fast as they shook hands, Trevor disappeared down the path into the darkness.

Emma asked Anthony what it was all about. He wasn't in a talking mood. However, if it weren't for Emma being so upset, I might think she had made the whole thing up.

Returning to reality and peering out my bedroom window to see what the ruckus was about, there stood Trevor. He appeared angrier than I have ever seen him and was in the middle of a hot confrontation. The cease fire had ended.

As I stepped out of my bedroom door, I almost ran over Emma.

"Mark, I think they may fight," Emma stated in an urgent voice.

I stepped around her and dashed down the hall, past the kitchen and living room, and out the front door. I could feel Emma hot on my heels as I jumped off the front porch and ran to the side of the house.

"Don't get wrapped up in all the hype!" Trevor yelled at Tilly. He was clearly exasperated.

"The hype?" Tilly retorted.

"Come on," Trevor stated as he reached out for her arm to leave.

"Back off," Anthony growled as he moved towards Trevor.

"Anthony isn't a passing phase," Tilly shot back as she stepped backwards avoiding Trevor's reach and placing her hand out across Anthony's chest.

"Get out of here," Anthony spewed.

Tilly stepped directly in front of him to hold him back.

"You've always wanted to rebel," Trevor stated with a hint of hurt as he looked at her. "You are taking it a little too far this time, don't you think?"

"Come on," I stated as I stepped up beside Trevor.

"Trevor," Tilly called as she moved to gently touch his arm. "This isn't about rebelling."

"Sell that to someone who will buy it!" Trevor sputtered in an angry voice.

I stood at Trevor's side demanding, "Let's go."

"I know you better than anyone!" Trevor yelled at Tilly. "I know you are enjoying the thrill's shock value of this stunt."

"This isn't a stunt! We are in love and getting married," Anthony growled pushing past Tilly. As I stepped between them, he continued, "Why is that so hard for you to believe?" Trevor's hands clenched into fists as Anthony said, "You're just a dumb ass who needs to get a life. Tilly isn't interested in you!"

"She isn't in love with you dude," Trevor spouted. Then as if it was funny, he smiled, "I'm not the one that's delusional."

Tilly and Emma both grabbed Anthony's arms. His nostrils were flaring with anger. I started pushing Trevor back saying, "That's enough." After stepping back a few steps I asked him, "What are you doing?"

"I came to rescue Tilly," Trevor answered. "Now, I know where she's getting this nonsense from. She's believing the load of crap he's selling! He really believes a Keeper can marry a Humling!"

"You!" Anthony growled as he lunged at Trevor hitting me in the back.

"Bring it," Trevor said as he pushed against me.

"Stop!" Daniel screamed at everyone from his place on the edge of the porch.

His small voice left everyone silent and standing still. Damn! We were all in trouble if he repeated this episode to anyone. This wasn't something he should have seen. I was on top of the hit list. Instead of standing between Anthony and Trevor, I should have whisked Daniel off to safety.

CHAPTER FOURTEEN

Tilly

With darkness all around, I stood on the manicured grass peering at the patrons of the country club through the big plate glass windows. While they ate, drank, and socialized, they had no idea of my watching them. I suppose I was not unlike the Dwellers who had been patiently stalking all of us. Not unlike the people inside, my friends and I had been living fake lives. We had walked around pretending to not have a care in the world while hiding deep secrets. We too had put on false faces to put on a show for those watching us. We weren't so different. Our façade was thin and the dwellers could see though it.

I would have never dreamed that I would be frozen here, eyeing and thinking of how I would miss my childhood eatery and the people within. Since my mother never cooked, I spent nearly every night of my childhood in the chef's kitchen inside. My kitchen family would whisk me off the moment we stepped in the door and always fed me well.

As I heard the cackling of my mother's laugh, I knew her and my father were arriving for dinner. Not wanting another confrontation with them, I made my way to the back of the building. The commercial door leading to the kitchen was cracked open as usual. A huge can of veggies was jammed between the door and the door frame. As if I were suddenly ten, my heart leapt as the familiar tunes floated on the cool night air from within.

I opened the door and stepped inside. "Tilly," Nathaniel greeted as he looked up from rolling out pie dough. "How has my girl been?"

"Yes, how has our own superstar been?" Rick piped up from over at the commercial stove.

"Great," I answered as I retrieved a hair net and pulled it over my hair, tucking my fly away pieces under.

"Great?" Lisa repeated as she moved towards me. "You look...." She paused as her smile wavered, turning into a slight frown. She had spotted the scar which appeared without my hair covering it. "What happened?"

My hand made my way to the scar as I turned away, "I had an accident."

"An accident?" Dalton repeated as he too moved towards me with a serious look on his face which I had seen before. He was the hard headed chef who was set in his ways, making few friends. As he looked up and down me for other apparent wounds or scars, he stopped dead in his tracks as his eyes focused on my hand. My engagement ring was the beaconing light he couldn't miss. His eyes flashed to mine as he said, "Mathilda Bradford, my sweet brown eyes. You came to surprise us."

I tentatively smiled at him as I help my hand up to show off my glistening ring to the room. Instantly, my scar was temporarily forgotten as both Lisa and Jill squealed in excitement. Lisa instantly flung her arms around me. Now, the whole room moved to take turns hugging me and ogling at my ring.

"So..., Mr. Stillholm finally asked?" Rick questioned from behind the sea of hugging arms.

"I am so happy for you," Jill mumbled into my ear.

"They're a great family," Nathaniel agreed to Rick's thoughts about Trevor and his family.

"None of you have heard the best part," Rowan stated as she stood in the far corner of the kitchen with her hands on her hips. As everyone turned to glare at her, she gave me a cocky grin. "Am I right?"

Their eyes immediately turned back to me.

Lisa broke the silence, "Pay no attention to her." Then she glared at Rowan, "She is a party killer."

"Really," Rowan sarcastically retorted. "Tilly is not engaged to Trevor Stillholm." With that she flashed me a cocky grin.

Everyone had an inquisitive look as they stared and waited for my response. Indeed, I wasn't marrying Trevor. He hadn't spoken to me since the day he found out Anthony and I were engaged. It had been nearly a month.

"Well?" Dalton prodded.

I began, "His name is Anthony. He is…"

"A Humling," Rowan interrupted me.

"Mathilda," Rick said in shock.

"Can you do that?" Jill asked the room. "Can a Keeper marry a Humling?"

"According to the Queen," Rowan interjected. "No!"

"Why don't you shut up," Lisa protectively retorted before I could reply.

"Lisa, you couldn't have said it better," Rowan continued in a smirk. "That is exactly what poor Mrs. Stillholm wanted the Queen to do. To shut up!"

Knowing I had purposely avoided the Stillholm family, I leaned back against the edge of the stainless steel prepping table. My mother dropping the news on Mrs. Stillholm wasn't how she should have learned about my intentions. They had always been so good to me and treated me as their own.

"Give it a rest," Dalton told the gloating Rowan. "Get back to work."

"I didn't ask to work on family night," Rowan sarcastically replied. "It's bad enough to have the Queen in the dining room. Who needs a princess in the kitchen!"

The gloom loomed over the room as the short haired blond hostess named Karen came through the swinging door almost hitting Rowan. She instantly smiled at me and greeted, "Tilly right?" I gave her a small wave as she too focused on my ring. "Is that what I think it is?"

"Yup," Jill stated.

She peered around in wonder saying, "Then why all the gloom. I thought all of you would throw a party when you found out!"

"They're upset that I'm marrying a Humling," I repeated for her.

"Yeah," Karen agreed like she had known it all along. "Last week during the Ladies Neighborhood Luncheon, Mrs. Bradford, told Mrs. Raderton all about it in front of Mrs. Stillholm. You should have seen their faces. Their faces read scandal."

I sighed.

"You knew?" Jill stated, clearly offended that Karen hadn't shared the news.

Dalton peered around the room and shook his head adding, "All of you get back to work too."

"Mrs. Stillholm seemed, extremely upset," Karen hummed as she picked up a rag and disappeared back through the swinging door.

"Tilly," Rick called, apparently unable to go back to work. Rick had always been concerned about any guy he knew I was dating. He had always been the father figure I didn't have. "Do you realize what will happen to you if you wed a Humling?"

"They will force you to become a Humling," Dalton answered clearly as concerned as Rick.

"Come on guys," I replied as I shuffled my feet. "You don't need to worry."

"We are serious," Rick stated. "Before the dome, when Keepers intermarried with Humlings, they lost their status as Keepers and became Humlings."

"Okay, got it!" I replied as I pulled off my hair net.

"Have you settled this with the Council?" Dalton asked.

I threw my hands up. I didn't come here to be put on the spot.

"Now don't be that way," Dalton retorted recognizing my sudden foul attitude. "I've always said you were an old soul. Only you know if he is worth the price."

"He is," I replied.

"Okay then," Dalton agreed forcing a smile onto his face.

Turning, I decided it was time to exit before I said something I shouldn't.

Nathaniel was once again working on his pies as I neared the back door. He peered at me, "Don't let them chase you off. If this fellow makes you happy, then I'm happy for you."

"Thanks Nathaniel," I replied.

"Do you have anyone in mind to make you cake?" Nathaniel asked as he began to hum.

"I actually came here to ask a favor," I replied knowing Nathaniel was a fabulous pastry chef. "I wanted to see if all of you would be interested in catering the reception. Also, I would be honored if you would bake me one of your beautiful cakes."

"Anything for my girl," Nathaniel happily replied. "Put a menu together and bring it back to me. I'll make you a cake no one will forget!"

I waved goodbye to all the unhappy faces. Clearly they were worried about my decision. Nathaniel once again began to sing with his familiar tenor voice. I hurried out the door into the cool night air. I had been listening to their songs since I was a child. I would miss all of them forever.

CHAPTER FIFTEEN

Trevor

The whole marriage fiasco between Anthony and Tilly was slow and painful. I felt I was left with no choice but to seemingly cut Tilly off. The decision had been hers. As much as I didn't understand the decision she made, I couldn't change it. I had been waiting for her to decide to go before the Council.

Today, when she didn't bother to complete our assignment for Professor Zirak, I heard over my radio receiver what I had been waiting for. She had taken the first step to abandon her life as a Keeper. It grieved me. That first step was her first true step away from me.

"Miss Bradford, I would think you had learned by osmosis what happens when someone doesn't complete one of my assignments," Professor Zirak stated.

"I'm not going to be a Keeper," Tilly defiantly stated. "So what difference does it make?"

"You're not married to the Humling yet," Professor Zirak countered with a tone of annoyance.

"Oh, I'm just temporarily lost," Tilly stated with a slight laugh. "That's your angle."

"No," Professor Zirak disagreed. "I don't have an angle."

"Good, because I'm not doing any of the make-up assignments," Tilly defiantly stated.

I could hear tapping on his desk. I assumed he was tapping a pen or pencil before he began, "You will make up the assignments and let me remind you why." Again the back to silence except for tapping. I could envision the power struggle between them. "If I am not mistaken, you are to marry Mr. Stillholm," Professor Zirak threw out. "Am I incorrect?"

The silence was eerie. I waited to hear Tilly's response. To hear her say we weren't meant to be together.

"What if the Council rules differently?" Tilly threw back.

"You are going before the Council?" Professor Zirak asked with a shock in his voice.

"I'm on the docket," Tilly answered.

Our path was now set. She no longer saw a world which included me. As much as we had denied the fact we were to be together, I never really put much stock in it. My heart had always raced for her.

"Until the Council informs you differently… I wouldn't hold your breath," Professor Zirak began. "You will be graduating and becoming a Keeper." I could hear him shift in his squeaky chair as he added, "Honestly, your antics!"

With that, I turned off the receiver. From there I found myself standing in the Underground before Mr. Bradford's office door. The time had come to ask for the help I needed.

I knocked on the door and heard Mr. Bradford mumble, "Come in." As I pushed the door open, he saw it was me. He greeted, "Trevor, it's not your night to come in. Is something wrong?"

"No and yes," I replied. "Sir, I have come tonight to talk with you about Tilly."

He leaned back in his chair grinning ear to ear saying, "Her latest stunt is fabulous, isn't it?"

"I don't think it's a stunt," I disagreed as I plopped down in the chair across from him.

"Come on," Mr. Bradford said in a dismissive tone. "You know she can't declare a Humling as her soul mate and marry him." Before I could answer, he waved his hand in the air while saying, "After all, the two of you are supposed to do this. Remember the Council?"

"You aren't going to help her, are you?" I questioned.

"Why would I?" Mr. Bradford asked with his mood turning serious. "She provides cover for me and always has."

"You're more concerned about this spy network?" I questioned.

"You're a rising star in the Underground," Mr. Bradford stated. "Tilly will provide cover for you too."

"You don't think you owe her something? Anything?" I asked to his serious but confused look. "You are supposed to be her father."

"I am not totally without heart," Mr. Bradford chuckled. "Tilly bonded with Mrs. Summors. I allowed it. Let me tell you I have paid dearly for that one. My wife hated dear Mrs. Summors because of who she was."

"Who she was?" I asked caught off guard.

"Tilly's great-grandmother," Mr. Bradford answered with a mischievous look upon his face. "You never suspected?"

"No," I honestly answered. "Mrs. Bradford hates her own grandmother that much?"

Mr. Bradford was lost in laughter as he stated, "No, she hates Rhett's grandmother that much."

"Wow," was all I could say.

"Then there was Bruce," Mr. Bradford threw out.

"Who?" I questioned.

"One of the cooks at the Country Club," Mr. Bradford answered. "He was planted to keep my evenings peaceful. A good baby sitter."

"Watch it!" I warned him.

Shortly after, I left with an understanding that Mr. Bradford wouldn't give me the help I needed. I then moved to someone I didn't know well, but had an interest in how things turned out with Tilly.

Standing before Rhett's door, I took a deep breath before knocking.

When the door opened, it was Marvin standing on the other side greeting me, "Hey man."

"Hey," I said as Marvin moved to let me in.

"What's going on?" Marvin asked.

"I need to speak with Rhett," I answered.

That is when I heard Rhett say, "Well come on in and have a seat."

I followed the voice down a dark hallway which led to the living room. From where I stood, I could see that Rhett lived an awesome bachelor life style. Big comfy couches and mismatched chairs loomed before a massive television. Before my last visit to Rhett's, I hadn't seen a television since the Earth Plane.

"Mr. Stillholm," Rhett called from his place on the couch.

"I still can't believe you have a television." I stated in awe.

"Some have wives, I have a television," Rhett answered with a chuckle. "What can I help you with this evening?"

"I need to talk to you about Tilly," I answered as I refocused on the task at hand. As Marvin sat down in one of the chairs I added, "Alone."

Marvin stood and left giving me a serious stare.

Once he was out of ear shot, Rhett asked, "What do you need tonight?"

"Your help," I answered as I sat down in an overstuffed chair.

"My help," Rhett repeated.

"Yeah," I answered. "I need you to help me go before the Council and ask them to reconsider their verdict that Tilly and I must marry."

"Whoa," Rhett hummed. "Shouldn't you be talking to your father about this, or Mr. Bradford?"

"I did try to talk to Mr. Bradford about this," I replied. "Only he didn't help me. The problem with him is that he doesn't act like Tilly's father." I looked Rhett eye to eye asking, "And why should he keep up the charade that he is her father?"

"How long have you known?" Rhett shot back.

"Since the start of our training," I replied.

"So you know the secret," Rhett stated. "Why haven't you told her?"

"And watch her world crash around her?" I shot back. "I don't think so. I chose instead to blackmail Mrs. Bradford. For a couple months, I was able to make her treat Tilly like a daughter."

"Until she realized you wouldn't tell Tilly anyway," Rhett surmised. "You're a good man Trevor Stillholm." He stared at me for the first time with a look of respect.

"Why do you want to go before the Council?" Rhett seriously asked.

"Anthony makes her happy," I replied.

"How do you know he makes her happy?" Rhett asked.

"Do you know about her life on the Earth Plane?" I asked in return.

"Belle told me a little of what she had planned before she went to the Earth Plane," Rhett answered.

"Did Belle tell you the Dweller she was married to tried to drown her?" I asked. "Tilly has a terrible fear of water because of that experience."

"I don't understand," Rhett said.

"She went boating with Anthony," I threw out.

"Boating?" Rhett repeated. "Wait a minute. You're basing your decision on her going boating?"

"She won't go out onto the water with me," I answered. "However, she trusts Anthony to take her boating. In her mind, he is the one that makes her world right, not me. She went swimming with him!"

Rhett looked dejected. "Honestly, the two of you have always confused me," he admitted. "Let me ask you one thing. How do you feel when you are near her?"

"Come on," I said shaking my head. It was obvious that Rhett wasn't kidding but serious and waiting on my reply. "When I'm near her …" How could I even begin to answer that? "I can hear her heart beat… her breath from across the room." Somehow the chair beneath me seemed to be the most uncomfortable chair I had ever sat in. "Her touch is electrical. It is like we become one. One current. One being." The truth couldn't be ignored. "Rhett she is my soul mate."

"How long have you known?" Rhett asked with a serious tone.

"From the first time I saw her as child," I said thinking of that fateful day. "My parents had just hung a new tire swing in the tree in the front yard. The problem was that Eddie and I couldn't reach it. So, we were digging holes in the yard and dumping the dirt under the swing. Out of nowhere a small, spit fire, toe head blond girl informed us while shaking her head that we were never going to reach the tire swing, not even if we dug to China." I shook my head when I noticed Rhett soaking up my memories of his daughter. "She pointed out we should just stand on our red wagon."

"She has always been strong willed," Rhett stated more than asked.

"I remember being mesmerized by her," I said remembering how I couldn't believe she was bossing us around. In the same thought, I didn't mind. "I have lived every day to be near her. She is the single most fascinating being in my life. I tried to move past her with Ruthanne. I couldn't."

"I could consider this a public statement," Rhett retorted.

"You would be a little late," I mumbled in response. "I all but did that in my life plan." I arose and paced a few times in front of the television. "Rhett… Don't you see it doesn't matter what I think, feel, or don't feel? What matters is that she is happy. That is all that has ever mattered to me!" I took another deep breath. "She is happy and has accepted Anthony's offer of marriage. I can't make her decisions for her."

"You shouldn't give up so easy," Rhett stated.

"It's done," I said under my breath. "I gave her the choice and she has chosen her path!"

"You gave her the choice?" Rhett questioned.

I paced back and forth before noticing him awaiting an answer.

"One thing I am is a planner," I began. "My plan was flawless and she took the bait." I took a deep breath.

"Took the bait?" Rhett repeated.

My thoughts went back to the dark night at Lakeland when I set my plan in action.

"Get lost," Anthony spewed as he stepped out his door. "How dare you come here!"

"I need to talk to you," I tried to calmly tell him as I threw up my hands.

He aggressively pushed me as he demanded, "Get off my porch."

"Hear me out," I said as I stumbled backwards down the steps.

"Are you delusional?" Anthony spewed at me as I kept backing towards the gate. "I have no desire to hear anything you have to say." In one fit of anger he shoved me through the gate spewing, "You are a burr in my saddle. Why don't you just disappear?"

"What if I wanted too?" I threw back at him as I waved my hands in air in exasperation. I couldn't believe I came here to hand Tilly to him and he wouldn't hear me out.

"You have one minute," Anthony stated as he crossed his arms across his chest.

"I have realized that I can't protect her," I stated to his fuming demeanor.

"Just realized you're not man enough huh?" Anthony spewed at me.

I took a deep breath knowing that I would tuck the tail between my legs, if it allowed me to ensure Tilly was safe. "I don't want her to face the Dweller, Collin again," I threw out. "She has nightmares. I would do anything…"

"How do you know she has nightmares?" Anthony growled with a look of shock plastered across his face.

"If she goes with you to the Earth Plane, Collin won't be able to find her," I stated. "Then when the two of you return home from the Earth Plane she will have a new identity."

"The only way she could go to the Earth Plane with me is to marry me," Anthony stated.

"It's the only plan I could come up with," I unhappily stated. "How else can I keep her safe?"

"I guess you don't love her as much as she thinks," Anthony hummed hitting my last nerve.

His comment left me speechless as I stared at him.

Breaking my thoughts and bringing me back to the present, "The bait?" Rhett repeated.

"It is probably fair that I give you the whole picture," I answered. "Tilly has changed. The time she spent in captivity in Venema House…"

"Broke her," Rhett finished my thought.

"She will never admit her feelings about being beaten so badly," I added. "Anyone watching her can see the outward changes. Trying to cover the scars with the full length shirts, long skirts, pants…" Again I paced a couple times. As I peered at Rhett he was patiently waiting for me to continue. "What you can't see is what is on the inside. I know she is terrified of that Dweller."

"That is exactly why she needs you," Rhett answered my rambling.

"She needs to be safe," I contradicted peering directly into Rhett's face. "I can't guarantee that she will remain safe as a Keeper. One thing I can guarantee, the Dweller will come back sooner or later for Tilly."

"You think they won't find her in Lakeland?" Rhett questioned like I was crazy.

"When she marries Anthony, she will go to the Earth Plane," I stated.

"For a time span she would be gone," Rhett agreed.

"By the time she gets back, they assume a new secret life somewhere beyond the dome," I added.

"How did you convince him to ask her?" Rhett questioned.

"Anthony and I had a heart to heart," I answered. "It really wasn't all that hard on his part."

"You're a good man Trevor Stillholm," Rhett said catching me off guard. "What do your parents think?"

"I'm going home to talk to Dad today," I answered. "I think I will need his help too."

On my way out of Rhett's, Marvin stopped me in the hall asking me, "What are you doing?"

"Letting Tilly go," I replied as I moved past him.

"I understand you must be doing what you think is right," Marvin reasoned as he moved with me.

"But?" I stopped to question. In my gut I felt he had more to say.

"Take it from me," Marvin began. "I tried to walk away. You can't walk away from someone you love."

"Then you tell me?" I demanded. "What am I supposed to do?" When he didn't answer I growled, "Tilly accepted Anthony's proposal. She is in love with him. Besides, our relationship has never been normal."

"You're cursing yourself," Marvin warned as I stepped out the door.

As I walked to my childhood home, Marvin's last words rang in my ears. They were true. However, I had to let her go. She made her own decision and so had I. This was all I could do to keep her safe. I loved her enough to put her needs first, even if in the process it meant letting her go.

Now, standing and looking up at my childhood home, I felt a deep sadness. For years, I had taken my entire family on this ride with Tilly and I. They had accepted her as one of their misfit children. Breaking my change of heart to them wasn't going to be easy. Their disappointment in me was adding up.

I was surprised when my Dad opened the door, stepping out. He simply peered at me stating, "Your Mom said you've been standing out here awhile." He stepped down a couple steps and took his place on the stoop. "I think I know why."

"Dad," I began as I moved to sit next to him. "I do have something to talk to you about." He sat quietly waiting for me to spill my guts. "I don't want to marry Tilly."

"Trevor," Dad began. "You aren't fooling me. You have always been smitten with her."

"Anthony asked Tilly to marry him and she has said yes," I admitted to him.

"I know," Dad stated. As I peered at him he explained, "Your Mom went to the ladies luncheon at the country club earlier this week. Mrs. Bradford told her."

"She was upset, wasn't she?" I asked.

"Yes," Dad answered. "Your Mom wasn't upset that she wanted to marry the Humling. She was upset about how it would affect you."

"I have to go on," I replied.

"What about the Council?" Dad asked.

"Tilly has a plan," I answered.

"She always does," Dad replied shaking his head.

"She is going before the Council to ask for a different decision concerning us," I said. "I'm not letting her go through with it though."

With a huff Dad warned me, "Don't go getting into trouble."

"That's why I came to talk to you," I answered. "I too am going to the Council. I already have my docket number."

"Trevor," Dad spit out shaking his head. "No!"

"It's important to me that you understand," I retorted. "It's time to let go."

Tilly

On the bench beside me, Elizabeth impatiently waited for the Council to call my docket number. Her mind seemed to be a million miles away. I understood the gum she was toting had given her for me by Marvin. He must have. The new Elizabeth hadn't taken the time to get to know me. I was edgy. Whoever was currently before the Council had been in there for hours. I fully expected someone to bring them lunch before long.

Noticeably missing were my parents. As always, they didn't offer me any support for my Council appearance. I hadn't really expected them to show up. They joked over dinner last night that I would never be able to convince the Council to dismiss their judgment that Trevor and I would marry. In anger, I made a comment about them accepting Anthony. They laughed it off, as well as told me that I could have their blessing to marry Anthony if I could convince the Council.

The one person who had always been there for me was Trevor. Although he had been notified of the hearing, today he was missing too. He had been distant and I guess my antics had finally ran him away. This was the last nail in the coffin between us. There was a hole in my life where Trevor should be. I did not like the feeling the hole evoked.

Catching me off guard was Rhett who seemed to appear out of nowhere calling, "Tilly."

"Hey," I replied. "What are you doing here?"

"May I have a moment?" Rhett seriously questioned.

"Um… Sure," I replied as I stood and began to walk down the lonely hall with him.

"Tell me what you are thinking?" Rhett pointedly asked me. "Are you seriously going to marry a Humling?"

"What business is it of yours?" I threw back at him.

Rhett sighed before beginning, "It's my business because I care. Hell, we've all been through a lot together lately."

"I have no doubt that Anthony is the one for me," I threw out.

"Where does that leave Trevor?" Rhett pointedly asked.

"You're concerned about Trevor?" I huffed. Rhett wasn't here for me either. "I see, guys sticking together."

"No," Rhett disagreed as he shook his head no. "It's just my understanding the two of you have always been thick as thieves."

"That isn't your concern," I stated as I turned to go back to my bench.

"Then why did you guys go to the Earth Plane together," Rhett seriously questioned from behind me.

I swirled around to meet his stare. "It was a foolish teenage prank." I took a deep breath and pointedly asked, "Anything else you would like to know?"

Rhett slightly shook his head as and raised his hands.

I turned on a dime and began to march back to my bench which was even lonelier than before. Elizabeth had disappeared. Now, I would feel the wrath of Marvin for not keeping an eye on her. I plopped down and all that was left to do was to ignore Rhett who was hanging around and now leaning against the wall.

I lived by the motto, throw caution to the wind. However, today I should have thought out a plan as to how to handle the Council. Trevor had always been the planner. Even though I might not have admitted it, I relied on him to do the heavy thinking. He would have already played out every possible outcome in his head. As for me with no plan, I could only hope they could find some compassion in their cold hearts.

When the door opened, I waited for the Council clerk to appear and call my docket number. From out the door came a stream of familiar faces; my mother, father, and Marvin. What were they all doing? Having a party in the Council room?

"Well, I never liked him anyway," my mother angrily huffed to my father.

"What is going on?" I asked the only friendly person around, Marvin.

"Trevor took care of it," Marvin told me.

"Took care of what? What did he do?" I asked the crowd.

"Said he didn't want to marry you," my father harshly stated with anger behind his voice.

"What?" I questioned noticing Rhett had stepped up to the circle. "Trevor is in there?"

Marvin shook his head yes.

Before I could muscle my way to the door, my mother continued her rant, "Good riddance! You know they are like rats. The Stillholms just multiply and burrow together. They are always creeping around. Opportunists!"

"Stop," I demanded feeling annoyed with my mother.

The Council clerk stepped out stating, "Please remain quiet in the hall."

Everyone was standing their ground with their arms crossed across their chest. I plopped back down on my bench. Did it matter that Trevor had fixed half of my problem? We had long ago decided we weren't going to marry each other. However, I had never imagined a life without Trevor. The rejection hurt. Not having a time machine, I couldn't change anything now or let what Trevor was doing bother me.

The door once again opened with the council clerk escorting Trevor's father out. Funny how all these people in my life came to hear what Trevor was doing.

Peering at Mr. Stillholm, he was very unhappy.

"Tilly," Marvin whispered. "Where is Elizabeth?"

"I'm sorry," I replied. "I was talking with Rhett. When I turned back around she was gone."

Marvin looked down both sides of the long hall as he began to jingle the coins in his pocket. Elizabeth wasn't only treating me differently. Marvin was patient and loving, but Elizabeth was unreceptive. He was delusional believing all would fall into place over time. My hope for them was dwindling. He should face the facts as I had. Marvin and I both were strangers to Elizabeth. She didn't know him. His overbearing insistence that she never be left alone was further driving them apart.

The door once again opened. This time it was Trevor who stepped out. Upon seeing me, Trevor's eyes stared into mine. I never meant this for us. "Trevor…"

It was Trevor's father who stepped up placing his hand on Trevor's shoulder interrupting me, "Come on son, we better head home."

Trevor turned and walked out of my life.

"Well, now you can tell the Council that you no longer have a problem," my mother happily continued. "We can get on with life and you can find a descent husband. Frankly, this is a relief."

"Olivia," Rhett called. "Don't you have a heart?"

"Tilly was dumping that nasty boy anyway," my mother retorted. "Why don't you go stick your nose into someone else's business?"

Ignoring my mother, Rhett looked at me directly and stated, "You are free. What are you going to do with your freedom?"

I was exactly that. Free. I could ask the Council to marry Anthony.

CHAPTER SIXTEEN

Marvin

I strolled up Dogwood Trail towards the home I shared with Uncle Rhett thinking every day was the same. Elizabeth spent her mornings wandering around the house and outside gardens she shared with Mr. Solliday at Dogwood House. At noon I would meet her for lunch. After lunch, I would see what her plans were and I would ensure that someone went with her. Of course Dustin watched from the shadows. But I always felt relieved to know someone else was with her as well. However, a note had arrived and she was meeting me at my house. I didn't like the break in our normal routine.

Elizabeth had an extreme dislike for the whole never be alone thing. If only I could tell her the reason behind it. However, I promised not to tell her. An impossible promise that I never should have made.

I could see Dustin meandering around the front door as I walked up. "I guess she is inside?"

"Yes," Dustin agreed. "And you have your hands full today."

I started to ask what he meant, but Elizabeth opened the door, "You're late."

"I'm sorry," I muttered. Work today had been demanding and I was late. But she really looked unhappy at the sight of my briefcase.

"And you brought your brief case," Elizabeth added. "You planned on working a little at home, didn't you?"

"Only so I could be near you this afternoon," I added.

"No need, I have plans," she happily stated. I glanced at Dustin who smirked at me as he followed me through the door.

"Plans?" I questioned, following her into the kitchen.

"I'm going to see Trevor," she said as she smiled at me.

"Trevor?" I repeated.

"I thought I might drop in at his office," she stated. "He could use some cheering up."

"I'll walk you," I said as I grabbed an apple off the counter. My lunch was going to be a lot shorter than I had planned today.

"We've been through this a million times," she protested. "That's not necessary. I can walk myself." Her frustration seemed to be building. "You're obsessive about my not going anywhere alone."

"You're right," I cut her off agreeing. "But can't I take a nice stroll with you?"

"No," Elizabeth sternly stated. "You only want to tag along because you want to ensure someone is with me!"

"I disagree," I contested. "You know I come home every day for lunch to see you."

She threw her hands up in the air. "I'm going to catch real life after my visit."

I could see the void Elizabeth's memory loss had left in her life. She was restless. As hard as I tried to keep her busy I couldn't fill the absence. The only thing she really enjoyed was placing distance between her and all of those who really cared about her.

As much as I was about to pay for this, I asked, "Whose going to be your partner in crime today?"

"Trevor, of course," Elizabeth replied.

"You led me to believe he didn't know you were coming," I retorted.

"He doesn't," she answered. "Isn't he going to be surprised!"

A pang of jealousy hit me. Trevor and Elizabeth had formed a tight friendship which reminded me of the friendship Trevor and Tilly had. Elizabeth was the new Tilly in Trevor's life. Trevor was filling the same void which Elizabeth had. I couldn't help but wonder, was Elizabeth confiding in him her deep secrets. She used to confide in me and I wanted that deep trust between us. Now, I knew why Dustin said I would have my hands full.

Mark

This morning started out the same as it always did on a day when we were expecting Wyatt to visit from the city. Breakfast was quick, followed by Emma rapidly flittering around picking up the house. As the time for him to arrive drew near, she would lock herself in the bathroom for hours and emerge with a hint of makeup, slightly curled hair, and a perfectly matched outfit. The look was beautiful, but her natural beauty on any given day far exceeded the dolled up look.

Wyatt arrived and Emma's demeanor became nervous and giddy with all of her attention focusing on him. She hung on every word and every glance he gave her as she twirled her long hair around her finger. Today's visit was the same. Wyatt was smiling and leading her on with no apparent consideration for her feelings. I didn't get what she saw in him anyway. When Tilly arrived shortly after Wyatt, I settled into a recliner to attempt to read when Emma followed Wyatt, Anthony, and Tilly outside. I couldn't watch.

Deeply frustrating was the topic of the wedding. The whole thing stunk to high heaven. Anyone, who really took the time to look under the surface, had to see what Trevor was doing. I understood the game he was playing. By separating Tilly form the world of the Keepers, the Dweller, who would come to recapture her, wouldn't be able to find her. So, it sickened me to listen to Tilly drone on and on about the wedding. She had been unbearable to listen to for weeks now.

Trevor had broad shoulders. I couldn't imagine going before the Council as he did. He wouldn't speak of all the details, only that he asked to have the Council ruling that he must marry Tilly overturned. He based his request on Tilly's acceptance of Anthony's proposal. The Council granted his request. Right on his heels, Tilly asked the Council for permission to marry Anthony. The Council granted her permission to marry on one condition, give up her place as a Keeper and become a Humling. Once she agreed to be his wife at the wedding, she would be a Humling.

Only then did they both learn that the intertwining of their lives would never end. The Council sent each of them notices informing them that, upon Tilly becoming a Humling, she would follow the marriage tradition of the Humlings by completing a life on the Earth Plane. Trevor was to become Tilly's Keeper. Not just for this trip, but for all the trips to the Earth Plane Tilly would ever make.

Suddenly, my thoughts of disgust were interrupted as Emma stormed through the door and rushed down the hall to her room. She had expected Wyatt to ask her to be his date for Anthony's wedding. I guessed it hadn't gone her way. Race car guy was a player who constantly led her on.

I slammed my book shut. I had told myself for months to stay out of it. I couldn't get involved with a Humling. It wasn't my place to do what Anthony should. It wasn't my place!

Now she was upset and I was completely torn. I left my place at the table and watched Wyatt working on Anthony's buggy from the window. It appeared Anthony and Tilly were taking Wyatt's buggy for a ride. Shame on Anthony for not putting his friend in his place. His concern was obviously living his life with Tilly. No matter how much I told myself not to get involved, I couldn't let it go any longer. I stormed to the door and out onto the porch.

As I rounded the corner Wyatt caught a glimpse of me greeting, "Hey Mark."

I nodded and moved to lean against the buggy. "Wyatt, how long have you known Emma likes you?" I asked.

"Emma?" Wyatt asked and then shrugged. "She's just Anthony's kid sister. Hand me a wrench?"

I looked at the tool box and picked out the tool I thought was a wrench and handed it to him. He took it in his hand and started to use it realizing it wasn't a wrench. He smiled and shook his head, placed it back into his tool box, and retrieved his own wrench.

"What did you do that upset her?" I pointedly asked.

"Upset her?" Wyatt repeated with raised eyebrows.

"What were all of you talking about?" I asked.

"Tweedle dum was teasing me about Cassandra," Wyatt said waving the wrench towards the forest that Anthony and Tilly had disappeared into.

"Cassandra?" I repeated.

"She's hot!" Wyatt said with a dreamy look. I must have unknowingly made some type of noise. He looked directly at me, "Look, I'm not dumb. I'm fully aware Emma has a small crush on me." He tossed the wrench back into the tool box. "No, she didn't appreciate the topic of conversation. It was as if she thought I would ask her to go with me to the wedding instead of Cassandra."

"You don't care, do you?" I questioned in return.

"Come on," Wyatt said appearing irritated. "No way did she really think I would ask her. And of course I care, she's Anthony's sister. Practically my sister as well. You don't mess with your little sister."

"Then why do you lead her on?" I questioned.

"I'm friendly without crossing the line. Besides," Wyatt answered putting his nose back into the buggy engine. "I would never date a vegetarian!" He glanced at me again asking, "Haven't you ever heard about the way to a man's heart is through his stomach?" He visually shivered asking, "How are you surviving on what she cooks? It's awful!"

"That is your opinion," I defended. "I disagree."

"Whatever man." Wyatt then said under his breath, "Guess Anthony isn't sharing his food stash with you."

"If you don't intend to have any type of real relationship with Emma," I began. "Then don't openly flirt with her and lead her on."

"And who do you think you are to be telling me this?" Wyatt asked.

"Just lay off Emma," I repeated. "She is a young lady who simply doesn't deserve for you to play with her feelings."

"Dude, don't," Wyatt warned. "I've known her my entire life. You don't have a right." He stared me down, "You should stick to baby sitting."

Baby sitting? I took a deep breath knowing I was done. He might feel he could play with Emma, but I didn't have to take his crap. As I turned to walk back to the house, I saw the curtains in Emma's room waving in the window. Why had I not considered how close the buggy was to the house? I suppose she heard the exchange. Smooth. Real smooth. Why did I get involved?

CHAPTER SEVENTEEN

Trevor

All that was left to do was to get through the wedding tomorrow. The old us officially ended and the new us began a month ago in room E329. Tilly arrived to plan her earth life. I sat across from her and Anthony as her Keeper. I spent my day seething at having to watch their hand holding. It was hard enough to live with letting her go, worse to have them flaunt their relationship in my face.

The only highlight from that day was watching Tilly disagree with Counselor McKay. True to herself, she didn't compromise.

"I won't say it," Tilly mumbled.

"You don't want to say the wedding vows?" Counselor McKay seriously asked.

"Oh I don't mind the majority of the vows," Tilly replied as she popped a huge bubble.

Without her saying, I knew what part she had a problem with. Obey. She would never agree to obey anyone, especially a man. It wasn't her character.

"So, there is a part you wish to write yourselves?" Counselor McKay asked.

"More like a part I want to omit for myself," Tilly countered. "I won't promise to obey Anthony." With a hint of a smile she added, "Anthony will say it though."

"Oh please," Emma huffed from the other side of Anthony.

"Won't you?" Tilly asked Anthony as she batted her eyes at him and ran her finger down his chest.

"If that is what you want," Anthony replied.

Unbelievable. She was still the man eating Tilly from my childhood.

Anyone looking at Emma could see she was seething over the comment. In general, Emma seemed generally angered over the whole wedding thing. We were in the same boat. Tilly wasn't going to be an easy person for Emma to cozy up too.

"Back to reality," I muttered.

I purposely hadn't seen Tilly the whole month. It was hard to look at her and not regret my decision. She was the spider in my life and I had always been hopelessly caught in her web. Tonight, our paths had crossed by fate. However, I was reminded again why Anthony was right for Tilly. I couldn't keep it from replaying in my head.

"Tilly, what's wrong?" I asked as I found her standing in the shadows of her childhood home's entrance peering up at her house.

"My room," Tilly sobbed as her hands clutched the wrought iron fence.

I moved to rub her arms. Before I could dangerously pull her into my arms, Anthony appeared out of nowhere. Tilly instantly let go of the fencing, turned towards him, and buried her face in his chest.

He cradled her while asking, "What's wrong?"

"My home," Tilly managed to get out between sobs. "My room."

I knew what was wrong. Tilly's mother had dismantled her room and thrown everything away. She appeared to have given, throwing all of Tilly's memories away, no more thought than taking out the trash.

"Calm down," Anthony softly said while rubbing Tilly's back in a consoling manner.

"My mother removed everything!" Tilly sobbed again pointing towards the house.

"From your room?" Anthony asked.

Tilly looked up at him as he wiped away her tears with his hands. "My mother threw away everything from my room. She said I didn't have a room anymore, because I don't exist anymore. She blatantly told me that she wished to erase any memory of me as if I never existed."

The tears once again streamed down her face while Anthony said, "I'm so sorry."

"She threw me out screaming to never come back. This isn't my home anymore," Tilly sobbed.

Anthony pulled her close to him and wrapped his long arms completely around her.

I opened my mouth to tell Tilly I had retrieved almost all of her belongings from the trash. However, Anthony interrupted me as he whispered into her hair, "You do have a home, Tilly."

"You don't understand," Tilly protested. "My walls were covered in photos and snapshots. I don't have any of those. She took them all! She took all my memories!" Tilly leaned into Anthony's chest as she sobbed again.

Again, I opened my mouth but Anthony beat me again saying, "Tilly, look at me." Tilly followed his instructions as he rubbed away the tears from her cheeks. "We will make new memories in our life together. You can paste them on every surface, every wall. Hell, cover all the walls if you want."

His words put Tilly at ease. A fact that reinforced my decision. All I cared about was her happiness and she would be happy with Anthony. Tilly had let him into a locked up place which I didn't have the key. Tomorrow I wouldn't stop them or ruin her opportunity to be normal. However, tonight I was going to Rhett's to barge in on their guy's night. Sorrow needs company.

Mark

Tomorrow was the big day and I couldn't sleep. Why did I allow myself to get involved? As much as I asked myself that, I knew why. I couldn't tell Emma no.

In my mind, I knew I should have. However, my gut wouldn't let me.

Upon successfully rigging my own listening devices, I overheard Tilly discussing her concern about Emma being dateless for the wedding with Anthony. In return, Anthony was to find a friend to accompany her. Somewhat relieved about this solution, I tried to put it out of my mind. Emma was Anthony's to take care of, not mine. Then I overheard Anthony explain to Tilly that he had asked every one he knew. No one would agree to take Emma. This caused Tilly to go into overdrive. Rather than tell Emma they couldn't find her a date, Tilly had a raw determined to fix Emma. The problem was, it came off to Emma as Tilly picking on her. One thing Emma didn't need was to be fixed.

Emma had finished serving everyone dinner at the table. She hopped up to fetch butter for Daniel when Tilly tried to give her some unsolicited advice.

"Meat Emma," Tilly stated as she pushed the vegetables and noodles around on her plate. "Maybe you should consider the way to man's heart is through his stomach."

"This is my favorite dish Emma makes," I disagreed with Tilly. I peeked at Emma and could see her hiding a smile over my comment.

"Most men like meat," Tilly continued ignoring me. "Maybe it would help you get that date."

Emma walked the two steps to the table and slammed the tub of butter down.

"Just saying," Tilly hummed in clear annoyance with Emma's reaction to her helpful hint.

"I'm going with Mark," Emma spoke up as she sat down in her chair.

"Mark?" Anthony returned as he glared at me.

"Well," Emma hummed as she shyly peered at me while nervously twirling her hair around her finger. "That is…"

"As long as you don't mind," I said to Anthony. His daggers instantly were shooting at me with his eyes.

Anthony did mind, but I took the heat. Emma was so mild, meek, and timid. Someone had to get helpful Tilly to pull back. All month I scolded myself for getting involved and buffering Tilly, but it felt natural to make Emma smile. My mind drifted…

"Have you picked your dress?" Tilly pointedly asked Emma.

"No," Emma responded as she began to twirl her hair around her finger.

"Why not?" Tilly demanded with her hands on her hips. "The wedding is eight days away!"

"Because you haven't told her what color," I answered for Emma.

"You'll love your color," Tilly replied directly to Emma. "Carrot orange."

When Emma didn't happily respond, Tilly let out a huge sigh. Tilly's assertive personality made Emma horribly nervous. Tilly huffed impatiently, "We'll go shopping. I'll help you pick out…"

"There's no need," I interrupted. Emma instantly glanced at me wide eyed. "We are going together to ensure we match perfectly."

Tilly stared me down, "The guys are all wearing tux tops, jeans, and matching…"

"Matching colored shirt with black bow tie," I finished. "I know. I heard all the plans. I just thought Emma might like a new dress from the formal wear shop."

"Are you kidding," Anthony said. "Emma likes to re purpose clothes."

"Maybe so," I answered as I flashed Emma a smile. "It's all up to Emma, she can get what she wants. I'll take her though."

Emma beamed at me for getting her out of a painful day of shopping with the overly helpful Tilly.

Elizabeth

"Tilly, I am so happy for you," I said twirling my own engagement ring around my finger.

"But?" Tilly replied.

"I am going to miss you," I admitted. Tilly and I… Well, our new relationship started out a little rough. It wasn't until I started looking past her rough exterior that I began to see what a true person she was. Over her marriage planning process, we were beginning to form a new bond. I don't know how it compared to our friendship before my memory fog. However, I had to think she could feel us getting closer. Besides, "You know me better than I do."

"What's ten years?" Tilly murmured to herself.

I thought she suddenly looked unsure.

When Tilly looked up, she said, "I'll miss you too."

"Our last girls night in our room," I reminded her as she tossed stuff around. "What's wrong, are you having cold feet?"

"It's just the whole Earth Plane thing," Tilly replied. "I didn't want to go the first time."

"Are you really in love with him?" I questioned as she threw herself on her bed and nodded. "Then that is what should be important."

"Thanks," said Tilly with a look of determination as she started putting her shoes on. "I've got to see my parents."

"Now?" I questioned as I looked at the darkness outside the window.

"I need to make them understand," Tilly responded and blew a big pink bubble and popped it.

Earlier tonight, Tilly discovered that her mother had thrown everything away in her room. Tilly was then informed that she was disowned. Even though Tilly was desperate for her parents understanding, it wasn't likely to happen. Especially at this hour.

"In the end, I want them there," Tilly stated as she stood. "I must fight for them to see."

"Don't be disappointed if they won't listen," I responded.

"I have to try," Tilly said. "It's silly of them to look down on Anthony because he is Humling. I need them to accept this."

"I'll wait," I replied as Tilly went out the door.

I laid back on my old bed and instantly found myself thinking of Marvin. He had the same problem, his parents didn't accept me. That was another decision made by someone in my previous life. The existence I didn't remember. It was Trevor who told me that. Instantly, in the hospital, I felt a bond with Trevor. He was easy to talk too and my gut screamed deep down inside that I could trust him.

Several of our deepest conversations have been about Marvin. Again, I felt the ring on my finger. Whatever had been between Marvin and I didn't feel right to me now. My gut screamed I had a destiny which was bigger than the two of us and that the promise I made to him I would have to break. Something else was on my horizon. I was certain of it. I shared this with Trevor and he assured me I should live in the now and not worry about some unknown future.

A knock on the door interrupted my thoughts concerning Trevor and Marvin. As the door creaked open, I saw it was Destiny.

"Want to have a girl's night?" Destiny asked.

"I should wait for Tilly to come back," I answered as I peered around the empty room. Destiny had a way of giving me knowing stares.

"I'm going to meet Janelle," Destiny continued.

"Have fun," I replied, feeling a pang of regret. It would be great to have fun with Destiny and Janelle tonight instead of sitting and waiting on Tilly to return.

"Okay," Destiny hummed as she started to let the door shut. Suddenly she looked directly at me, "Be careful tonight."

"Okay," I sarcastically reassured her.

Sometimes Destiny could be a space cadet and say weird things. Other times, her advice seemed to be so credible. That is why, when Destiny gave me almost the same exact advice about Marvin as Trevor had, I felt I should take it.

I had complained repeatedly about Marvin to both of them before they each assured me that Marvin was the one for me. They both told me stories about how we were deeply in love. I couldn't deny that when I was physically near Marvin, it felt like we completed one electric current. I could hear his heartbeat and we were one being not two. Beyond this physical attraction, Marvin was a stranger. Both told me to give Marvin a chance and stop being so standoffish. They said I should simply have fun and see where it led. Finding no sympathy with my closest two friends, I made the decision to be open and give a relationship with Marvin an honest try. What did I have to lose?

Marvin was slowly growing on me. In simple moments, I could see why a girl would fall for him. However, the moments of tenderness would fall away as his switch flipped. His fault was his overbearing insistence that I never go anywhere alone. Just when we would start to cut loose and have fun, the night would end and he would get down to business about my escorts for the following day. It was like he had two personalities.

Trevor had long ago told me Marvin's parents had disowned him. Tonight was the first time I thought about Marvin and his relationship with his family. He needed the same acceptance. How could I be so cruel in my past, forgotten life not to care about Marvin's relationship with his family? I decided to make the trek to Rhett's and discuss it with Marvin. I could add this to the list of things I did or didn't do in my forgotten life.

From the moment I stepped outside of The Hall of Knowledge Complex, I had the strange feeling to go back. I ignored this gut feeling and continued, descending into the park.

"Bethany," I heard an eerie voice calling as I crossed the bridge.

I stopped and peered over the railing. I didn't see anyone on the shore.

"Bethany," again I heard the voice call sending shivers down my spine.

I turned to look beyond the bridge. All I could see was darkness.

"Bethany," a female voice hummed in a taunting way.

Then I turned and saw a young strange man with ratty hair. My gut screamed that I needed to move away from him. Beginning to briskly walk, I could swear he was following me. I picked up my pace and he did the same. I started to jog and now he was jogging too. I broke out in a run, while I tried to keep my head turned to look at him. This wasn't right. He was wearing a black derby hat.

Who took an evening run wearing a black derby hat?

"Hello Bethany," the ratty haired young man seemed to say telepathically to me.

I knew I must be in view of the house when I was startled by running into someone who seemed to catch me. When I peered at the hands' owner, there stood Dustin.

"I see," the strange young man seemed to hum in my head.

I turned to look one more time at my assailant as I mumbled between breaths, "Sorry." The ratty haired young man seemed to be jogging in the other direction. I did a double take when he seemed to raise one hand and give me a short wave goodbye.

"Until next time," I heard him mumble in my head.

"Elizabeth, you look frightened," Dustin said regaining my attention. I stood panting as he bent down to look me directly in the eye. As I tried to catch my breath, he put his arm around my shoulder and began to pull me down the path leading to Rhett's house.

As we reached the door, my gasping for air subsided a little. I seemed to be catching my breath, "Dustin, I'm sorry I worried you. I am fine." He let go of me and peered at me and I knew he saw through me.

In silence he held out his hand to proceed inside. When we stepped though the door, I could hear a lively crew inside.

"Ash," Trevor stated as he held onto the metal disk while peering into the thin air over his head.

"Wild fire," a voice carried from beyond my view.

Guy's night was in full swing. I held out my hand to stop Dustin before the men around the table noticed us. Marvin was seated closest to the kitchen entrance and I could see Rhett, then Trevor, sitting at Marvin's side.

"I'm out," a disgruntled voice said.

"You're callin' it quits?" a southern twang questioned.

"Do you know the name of any noteworthy forest fires?" The disgruntled voice retorted.

"White ash," Trevor threw out. "Boiling lake, explosions, and earthquake."

"Volcano," another voice came from deep within the kitchen.

"Mount Unzen," a voice rang out.

"Still out," the disgruntled voice again called.

"Ooo," Trevor slightly hummed. "The mountainside ripped open and a dense black cloud shot out horizontally. Swept down the mountain and blanketed the town in under a minute."

"Mount Tambora," anther voice yelled out.

"No," Rhett stated shaking his head. "That eruption went up, not out the side of the mountain."

"You've just been covered by a volcanic flow?" Another voice bellowed.

"Nah," Trevor stated. "I'm sitting on the deck of a boat."

"Okie dokie," the voice with a southern twang began. "Get ta findin' a way to be narrowin' it down a bit."

"Fire people," Trevor threw out.

"Santa Maria," a voice called out.

"Bald Mountain," Trevor stated shaking his head no.

"French," a voice rang out.

"Mount Pelee," another voice stated.

"You got it," Trevor stated as he closed his eyes and let go of the rapidly rotating disk.

"Hmm," Rhett hummed. "Someone is thinking about disasters."

"You knew this one?" Marvin interrupted Rhett.

"Yeah," Rhett stated. "I knew which volcano when the clue was fire people."

With that I scooted out from the darkness to the stares of the men around the table. When Marvin saw all the stares, he turned to see me. Instantly, his face showed signs of worry before he covered his thoughts with a smile. "Why are you alone? Where is Tilly?" Marvin questioned as he got up from his chair.

"She went to visit with her parents," I replied as I glanced around at those in the room. The voice with the twang had to belong to the man in the cowboy hat. Then there was a guy in overalls, a hippy looking young man, and Mark. When I glanced at the man who looked stiff and pressed, his returning stare made me uncomfortable.

I was caught off guard as I felt Marvin's hand rest on my back. I let him lead me away from the awkward group's stares back into the hallway. When we stopped, I noticed Dustin had followed us out.

Marvin could feel how I was damp with sweat. He quietly asked, "Why are you wet?"

"I found her out front running from something," Dustin added with Marvin and him exchanging a look.

"I wasn't running from anything," I said and instantly knew neither seemed to buy it. Marvin was already upset about my being out by myself, which I was sure I would hear about. I didn't want to tell him that I just had a psycho moment and imagined that a jogger was chasing me. "I was getting some exercise."

"What's going on?" Asked Rhett as he too crowded into the hall with us.

"Elizabeth was running from something," Dustin stated.

With a deep breath, Rhett's eyes flashed to Marvin's.

Dustin's face got very serious, "Elizabeth, are you hearing people in your head?"

Marvin stepped in-front of me and I noticed his fists were balled up. He growled at Dustin, "What did you just ask?"

He knew, but I would not admit it, "No, I don't hear others in my head. That would be crazy."

"We won't think you are crazy," Rhett seriously replied.

"That's enough!" Marvin yelled. I hadn't seen an outburst like this from him before. Maybe this was part of his overbearing side. Marvin grabbed my hand. Suddenly, he was pulling me through the door. I wondered if I should tell Marvin that I do hear others. At the same time, I was irritated. Rhett and Dustin didn't deserve Marvin's outburst. I didn't understand.

When I opened my mouth to stand up for Rhett and Dustin, Marvin interrupted me, "Elizabeth, we're leaving."

I didn't argue, but I instantly felt guilty. I hadn't meant to ruin guy's night. I just wanted to talk to Marvin. "Marvin," I called as we stopped on the porch. "I don't want to pull you away from guy's night."

"Don't be silly," Marvin said as he pushed my hair behind my shoulders. He looked directly at me, "There is nothing or anyone as important to me as you."

In that moment I knew he meant every word. That left me to feel more confused about what just happened.

"You're dripping with sweat," Marvin said as his hands moved to hold mine.

"That's just because I ran from the lift," I mindlessly answered as I felt the electricity between us as we stood so close.

"She ran because she was being chased," Dustin said as he stepped outside.

"How?" Rhett asked as he followed. "There is no more darkness."

Marvin began to pull me down the path to Dogwood Trail. Where ever the discussion was heading, he didn't want me to over hear it. "What are they talking about?"

"Who?" Marvin asked.

I gave him a look. Was he kidding?

"Why did Tilly go to visit her parents?" Marvin asked to change the subject.

"She was hoping they would reconsider," I answered.

"I doubt it," Marvin quickly replied.

"Tilly getting married should be a happy event," I began. "But no one seems to be all that happy."

"Tilly always finds a way to go against the grain," Marvin answered. "The problem is that she wishes to marry a Humling.

"So?" I questioned. "Why does marrying a Humling have to be so taboo?"

"I suppose it's because most Keepers wouldn't want to give up their status as a Keeper," Marvin stated. "We're wired different. We are not Humlings. A Keeper's life is about helping others through our work. A Humling's life is about perfecting their own soul by making multiple trips to the Earth Plane." He shrugged and added, "We are just different."

"The whole thing is seriously wrong," I said. "Tilly should be able to marry and remain a Keeper."

CHAPTER EIGHTEEN

Tilly

As I walked up to my parents' stately colonial home earlier, the dwelling eerily towered and appeared more cold and impersonal than ever before. The wrought iron fence surrounding the grounds was cold to the touch. It was the first warning about the type of person who resided within. I made my way through the gate, down the path, and upon the long porch. For the first time, I felt small standing under the six white pillars which stood watching over the bare rock yard. With no trees, bushes, or flowers, it was lifeless.

It was odd to knock on my own door. However, my mother had made it clear that I wasn't welcome here anymore. Walking though the door in the face of that fact wasn't the right approach. As my knuckles knocked on the massive wooden door, I could hear footsteps beyond it. To my surprise, Grandmother Bradford opened the door. She was the one person who disliked me more than my mother. Could it get any worse?

"What do you want?" She demanded with her hands on her hips.

"I am looking for my mother," I replied.

"I am so glad that they have decided to disown you," she spewed as she shut the door behind her. "You are trash! My son has been saddled with you his whole life."

"Saddled with his daughter," I sarcastically stated.

A satisfying smile crossed her face. "You might find it interesting to watch your mother's declaration."

"What are you alluding too?" I asked.

"A mother always knows," she spewed. "Get off my son's porch!"

"Is my mother home?" I asked ignoring her demand.

"You are no longer welcome here," she again stated. "Leave or I will call for the guards."

"You are truly an unhappy, hateful person," I threw back at her as she turned to walk back through the door.

"At least I know where I come from," she spewed as she disappeared.

Grandmother Bradford's delightful attitude didn't shock me any more. Her comments however, although not surprising, didn't make any sense to me. Without Trevor's shoulder to cry on, I rushed to the Ghost Complex to catch Aunt Belle. Luckily, she was working late, so that she could attend my wedding tomorrow.

I ran my finger down the wall as I walked down the row of office windows which ran along the wall of the Elephant Room. Coming to the last office, a single desk awaited me with the same prim and proper lady seated behind the desk. Maybe the woman seated at the desk would remember me.

As I breezed into the room, she looked up giving me a warm, friendly smile. "Belle's niece?" She asked. "Correct?" I shook my head yes as she continued, "May I help you?"

"Once again, I'm looking for Aunt Belle," I politely said returning her warm smile.

"Really?" She retorted. "Belle doesn't work this late."

"Actually, tomorrow I'm getting married," I began.

"Congratulations," she returned.

"Thank you," I returned to her warm smile. "Aunt Belle is taking the day off and it is my understanding she is working late tonight to make up for it."

"I see," she stated as she began to thumb through a huge stack of papers giving me a sense of déjà vu. "Is Rhett by any chance coming to your wedding?"

"Rhett?" I questioned.

"Yeah," she answered. "He was in today talking about a big wedding he was going to tomorrow." As her finger suddenly stopped going down the page she stated with a frown, "Here it is."

"Is something wrong?" I asked.

"She is in the sprayer locker again," the lady stated. Then she leaned forward like she was telling me some great secret. "Belle is great at what she does. I don't know why they waste her talents by putting her in the sprayer locker to be a equipment clerk." As she leaned back she mumbled, "Sorry. It's kind of my soap box."

Even though I was an opponent of woman's rights, I needed to tread lightly and not get caught up in her personal rant. Putting my acting skills to use, I shook my head in disgust.

Feeling I was her counterpart in thoughts, she happily asked, "Do you remember the way?"

"I do," I reassured her. "Thank you for your help."

As I turned to make my way back out the door, she bellowed, "You're welcome."

As I quickly made my way to the sprayer locker, I couldn't help but be thankful for Rhett. My parents had wanted no part in the wedding and Rhett had volunteered to walk me down the aisle. Knowing how happy he was about my wedding gave me an odd sense of warmth inside. Geez, I was turning into a sap! Once before the locker room doors, I opened the middle door and trotted in.

My Aunt was busily placing orange tags on the sprayers which were setting on the marble white tile. As she looked up she squealed, "Tilly!"

"Hey," I greeted.

"Ready for tomorrow?" She asked with a grin.

All I could do was sigh. Tomorrow was to be the happiest day in my life, but it had torn so many of those in my life away. I felt raw and vulnerable. I just needed someone I could unload on.

Instantly her mood changed as she peered at me asking, "Is something wrong?"

"Cold feet," I nervously hummed.

"Cold feet is normal," she responded as she intently watched me. "I thought you were hanging out with your friend for your last night of freedom."

"I was," I responded. "Then I got to thinking about Mom and Dad."

"Tilly," my Aunt called. "Your parents are…"

"They disowned me," I interrupted as I felt a tear well up.

"What?" She retorted.

"Mom threw everything in my room away," I responded. "My clothes, my furniture, my memories. Then she threw me away as she informed me I was dead to her."

I could see my aunt's skin flushing from anger.

"Tonight, I had to give it one more attempt," I stated as the tears began to fall down my cheek. "I just wanted them to understand."

"You can't make your parents accept this," Aunt Belle stated as she moved to rub my back. "Your mother wasn't receptive tonight?"

"I didn't get a chance to talk to her," I stated. "Grandmother Bradford wouldn't let me in."

"What did the old witch do?" Aunt Belle asked catching me off guard.

"You know her?" I asked in surprise.

"Along time ago, she didn't like me," Aunt belle responded.

"Join the crowd," I huffed. "She hates me. Tonight she claimed my father had been saddled with me." I wiped my face adding, "Saddled with your own child?"

My Aunt let out a huge breath as she moved to sit on the oversized couch leaned up against the wall. Her hand reached over and patted the spot next to her, inviting me to sit with her. She seemed to mumble her own thoughts, "A burden shared always lightens your load."

As I moved to sit beside her, I assumed, "It's bad isn't it?"

Aunt Belle shook her head yes. "I don't think I should be the one to tell you." As if she were talking to herself, she added, "I can't believe you still don't know."

"Spit it out," I unhappily stated. "Whatever it is, just tell me already!"

"I shouldn't be the one to tell you," Aunt Belle repeated as she looked away deciding what to do.

"Mother is not a big fan of either of us," I threw out.

"Do you know why your Mother and I haven't talked for all these years?" She returned.

"Some deep dark secret," I half-teased. When she remained serious my mind drifted to another time. "I didn't know you existed until the day you visited the Hall of Records and I witnessed you arguing with mother."

"I remember," she said. "We were fighting about you. It was the last straw."

"Me?" I returned remembering how heated their discussion was. I had never seen anyone stand up to my mother like that.

"Our discussion that day…" my aunt paused. "Your mother and I had a falling out during our training."

"I know that," I stated figuring now was my chance to finally learn what it was all about.

"I didn't and haven't agreed with some of her decisions she made back then," my aunt stated. "Are you aware that Rhett and your mother dated during their training?"

"Big deal," I responded feeling utterly shocked. This must be why Rhett seems to be able to crawl under my mother's skin. "Do you know how many guys I have dated?"

"No, you don't understand," Aunt Belle disagreed. "Rhett was extremely attractive and smart, but he tested Department of Ghosts. Your mother always swore he flunked the entrance exam on purpose. She claimed he wanted to work in the Department of Ghosts."

"And what's bad about that?" I questioned.

"Nothing," Aunt Belle sighed. "They were deeply in love, but your mother felt anyone working for the Department of Ghosts was beneath her." I opened my mouth as she held up her hand, "Towards the end of training, she dumped him shocking everyone. Your mother had always claimed Rhett was her soul mate."

"What?" I shot back.

"Much to everyone's surprise, your mother instantly started dating your father," my Aunt answered without answering. "Thomas Bradford could provide her the lifestyle she wanted."

"All because of her prejudices," I concluded.

"Rhett tried to win her back in every way possible," Aunt Belle continued. "But your mother wouldn't have him. She told me he claimed he needed to work for the Department of Ghosts and had no choice."

Okay, so my mother's aversion to Rhett all made sense now. The night before she disowned me, my mother had asked who would be walking me down the aisle. Then she proceeded to flip a lid when I replied Rhett. "Honestly though," I mumbled, "I've dated my share." As I peered up at my aunt who was still intently staring at me, I continued, "So she is upset that her ex-boyfriend is going to walk me down the aisle."

My Aunt looked away.

"There is more?" I questioned.

"Your mother and I didn't talk for years after training," Aunt Belle continued. "What she did concerning Rhett and Thomas was wrong." After taking a deep breath, a pained look crossed her face as she added, "Then I found out about you." My aunt got up to pace. "She hid you from us."

"Us?" I questioned.

"You have never seen my parents, your grandparents," my aunt stated as she paused to peer at me as she patted my leg. "They were crushed."

"So you approached my mother," I surmised.

Once again she plopped down beside me. I could tell there was more. "I was mad at the treatment of our parents, but that is not why the argument got so heated." She once again paused and took a deep breath. "Rhett had confided in the morning I approached your mother that he…" She took another deep breath. "Tilly, I don't fully understand how. Rhett believes he is your father."

"What?" I questioned.

"Your mother didn't deny it," Aunt Belle continued. "She disowned her family in fear that we would find out and tell you."

"Wait a minute?" I questioned. "How can that be? When you get married you make your declaration. They didn't get married."

My aunt shrugged as if she didn't understand how it had happened.

All I wanted was to be alone with someone who comforted me, but Aunt Belle only left me with more questions. I really tuned her out as I sat thinking. Suddenly, my world had fallen apart, but made right in an instant. My whole life made sense. I was a reminder to my parents of Rhett. My father had always been distant and never willing to spend time with me. I always had thought he just wasn't a kid type of man. My mother had always treated me as if I were the bad end of a memory she wished she didn't have to look at. Mother disliked me because Rhett was her soul mate and my Father. I was a constant reminder of Rhett. All of our lives might have been happier, if my parents had not been so superficial. Mother should have married Rhett if she loved him!

Flashes of my life flooded my mind; never having dinner with them and being dumped in the kitchen, never allowed to play with children from the Hall of Ghosts, never visiting the Hall of Ghosts while she openly dragged me along to everywhere else with her and then dumped me on some low employee, never being loved.

Learning that Rhett was possibly my father was shocking. If it were true... I understood Rhett's fascination with me. His insistence to work with me, stand up for me when other didn't, and stick his nose where it didn't belong.

"Tilly," my aunt called.

"Huh," I responded.

"Did you hear me?" She asked.

"Grandmother Bradford told me to review my mother's declaration." I blew a big bubble. "I thought she was just being her hateful self."

"I'm really sorry," my Aunt stated looking sincere.

I half-listened to my aunt's nervous chatter before dismissing myself. I had the feeling she would stick to me like glue, if she were off work. Luckily for me she wasn't. I didn't need her tagging along where I intended to go. In a haze, I made my way to the lift and then to the Hall of Records. Most people would go to their childhood home. In my case, this was my childhood home and the only place left tonight to comfort me. As I approached the empty declarations room, I would have given anything to have Mrs. Summors present. She was wise and instinctively knew exactly what to say to ease any of my heartbreaks.

Over the years, I had watched many happy couples come to the Hall of Records to make declarations. Mrs. Summors would lead them away from the front desk and into the declaration room. I had peeked inside several times, but never watched exactly what happened in there. The happy couples were always given instructions by Mrs. Summors. Then they were left to make their declarations. Children were gifts from God and only he could grant a couple children. As each couple emerged, they would know how many children they were granted, but not the time of their arrival.

Thus was the reason I visited the Hall of Records tonight. I also knew that all declarations were recorded and documented by name and date. I patiently waited for the evening lady to approach the desk.

"Is it possible for me to view my own declaration?" I asked seeming to catch her off guard.

"Tonight?" She returned. "This late?"

"Well," I hem-hawed. "I'm getting married tomorrow…"

"I know who you are Miss Bradford," she interrupted.

"Then you know tomorrow I won't be a Keeper any longer," I assumed. "I won't be able to view it after tonight."

"This is not normally something we do at this time of night," she continued. "They are restricted and normally your mother approves all requests to view them."

"Of course," I let slip out. How better to ensure I never see it.

She stared at me intently. "I guess your own mother wouldn't mind you viewing the declaration that gave her you."

"If it keeps you out of trouble," I said forcing a smile across my face. "I won't say anything to her about it."

With that she disappeared into the confines of the restricted section behind the desk. When she returned she handed me a disk saying, "Go into the room and place this in the player. It plays just like real life."

"Thank you so much," I stated with my whole body meaning it.

I stepped up and through the door to the Declaration Room and instantly the light turned on leading me to believe it was on some type of sensor. However, the light of this room was intensely bright. It seemed to bounce off the white walls, ceiling, and floor. I had never noticed how bright it was as a child. Next to the door was the player. I pushed the button and the plastic CD holder came out inviting me to place my CD inside of it. After I did, I moved to sit on one of the two white pillows on the floor. The wall before me seemed to come to life. Only it was life twenty eight years before tonight.

"Olivia, my love. What's wrong?" Rhett asked as he sat beside my mother on the opposite white pillow on the floor.

"I can't do it," my mother sobbed as she leaned into Rhett.

"Then don't," Rhett pointedly stated as he wrapped his arms around her. "I still love you."

"And you would take me back?" my mother whispered.

Rhett nodded and kissed the top of her head, "Of course. I know we are soul mates."

"I have always dreamed of our life together," my mother sobbed. "Of the children we would have. Places we would visit…"

"It's not too late," Rhett added as he pulled her head up to look at him. "We could have all of that. And most importantly, we would have love. Tonight, my love. Marry me tonight instead of him tomorrow."

"But you love that department more than me," my mother selfishly retorted.

"Olivia, you know that's not true," Rhett disagreed as his arms fell to his side.

"If it wasn't , you would ask Albert to place you into one of the other departments," my mother demanded.

Rhett had a torn look on his face.

My mother rubbed it in, "See, it is more important. That's the problem."

"Please listen to me," Rhett said in anguish. "I love you more than the air I breath, more than life itself. However, I have an obligation that I must fulfill in the Department of Ghosts."

"What obligation?" My mother demanded. Rhett sat quietly and looked away. My mother suddenly pulled back from him and stood. "No, I will marry Thomas Bradford." As if resigning herself to the facts she added, "I will be Mrs. Thomas Bradford."

"So this is what will keep us apart?" Rhett questioned. "You won't trust me when I tell you I have no choice in my employment?"

"Thomas and I aren't married yet," my mother smiled. "May I have one last moment with you?

My mother sat back down before Rhett and grabbed him by the hand. He seemed helpless under her touch. Clearly he was lost in their connection.

"Shall we look into the future as to what would have been?" My mother taunt-ed.

"We can't" Rhett protested. "What if there were to be a new soul?"

"It's just pretend, we aren't married!" My mother shouted at him.

She firmly led his hand and hers to hover about the white and gold gypsy ball.

Rhett softly protested, "Yes, but you put in for marriage." Then as if his breath were taken away he peered at her hand asking, "Do you feel that?"

My mother was overtaken with emotion as she began to quietly cry. She shook her head in agreement. Rhett was soon rendered speechless as well.

I thought I was going to fall off my chair when I saw it. A small flake of what appeared to be skin fell from both of their hands and settled about a half inch off the globe. Suddenly Rhett attempted to pull back his hand. He pulled back with all his might using the weight of his body. The reaction happening under their hand appeared to be unstoppable. The edges of the two separate pieces of skin began to burn and this burning seemed to fuse them together. The globe lit up and I could see the form of a baby beaming out from inside. Not just any baby, I was looking out. As suddenly as I appeared, I was gone. The globe went fuzzy reminding me of the old television fuzz that would show when the station was off the air. Rhett had ceased trying to pull his hand back. He sat totally pale.

"What happens next?" my mother asked him.

"I guess we wait to see if there is another," Rhett quietly answered.

With that, they both sat still until the globe went back to its white and gold milky form. Then the single piece of skin became a fire ball and disappeared.

"What have we done?" Rhett asked as he was finally free to pull his hand away from my mother's. For the first time ever, my mother appeared to be speechless. "Don't you see we are truly soul mates?" Rhett pointedly asked my mother.

"My soul mate is Thomas," my mother disagreed as she dried her tears on the back of her hand.

"You know that is not true," Rhett retorted as he tried to grab my mother's hands.

"It is," my mother whispered.

"God only gives soul mates a baby," Rhett stated.

"Only my marriage papers aren't with you," my mother stated.

"Thomas is not stupid," Rhett said as his skin was beginning to flush. "He will know the baby isn't his."

"We will already be married by the time he knows," my mother stated. "Unlike you, he puts me first. I doubt he will care."

Not unlike the young Rhett I was watching, I was shocked at my mother's calculating scheme. It was too much for Rhett. He left the room and the screen went blank. I could feel my own tears flow down my face. Maybe life with Rhett would have been easier than the life with my parents.

As I made my way out of the declaration room, I was faced with a sight which scared me. My mother stood with her arms crossed, intently staring at me.

"Guess Trevor couldn't keep his mouth shut after all," my mother stated catching me off guard.

"Trevor?" I questioned.

"Yeah!" She sighed. "The weasel! Backed out on our deal. I knew better!"

"A deal with you," I sneered.

"All the energy I put into it. You must be kidding me," she stated. "I have been at your beck and call for months. I should have known he would back out when you pursued your whim to marry this lowly Humling."

"Wait!" I demanded. "Am I hearing you right? You made a deal with Trevor that he wouldn't tell me. In return you would be nice to me. Have the last few months have all been a lie?"

"You didn't know," my mother stated with a satisfied look. "Good! Direct your anger at him. It wasn't my deal, it was his. Threatening me! All of this, so he wouldn't tell Thomas."

"It always boils down to your social status," I stated as I turned to walk away. For my own health, I had to let her and her status go.

Trevor knew me. I had spent a lifetime wishing my mother was a mom. He had tried to give me an incredible gift. I missed his true friendship. That is how I found myself standing and looking at the Stillholm's Victorian home. Swinging in the breeze was the old tire swing; the very swing which Trevor was sitting under when I first met him. He was directing the other boy and had a plan. I remember thinking a stupid plan, but a plan just the same. I knew way back then we would be great friends.

I stepped through the gate and was going to swing on the tire swing for old time sake when I heard, "Tilly, come on up."

I looked up and focused my vision on the stoop where Mr. Stillholm was sitting. I made my way up the steps. As I sat down, I inquired, "How long have you been watching me?"

"For as far as I could see you," Mr. Stillholm admitted. "Would you like to talk about what is bothering you?"

"It's nothing," I stated.

"I could see you crying," Mr. Stillholm gently said. "If you think you are making a mistake, it's not too late to change your mind."

"It's not about Anthony," I quickly corrected him.

"Hmm…" was all the response Mr. Stillholm gave. "Have your parents changed their mind about your wedding?"

"No," I said as I peered out to the street. "They're not going too. They don't like Anthony and they're not happy with me. It doesn't really matter though."

"Sure it does," Mr. Stillholm disagreed with me. "If it didn't, you probably wouldn't be upset tonight."

"You have it all wrong," I corrected him. "My mother has never wanted me and my father has never been a father!" I said under my breath, "No wonder why!" Looking into Mr. Stillholm's prying eyes, I began to spill my guts. "I found out tonight that my dad isn't my father." I threw up my hands, "I know. Sounds weird."

"I've known for awhile," Mr. Stillholm replied in a serious voice.

"Trevor told you," I assumed.

"Only because he wanted my advice," Mr. Stillholm stated.

"Was it your idea to blackmail my mother?" I asked.

"Blackmail?" Mr. Stillholm repeated with a shocked look on his face.

"Yeah," I replied. "Make my mother be nice to me in exchange for not informing my father."

"Not my advice," Mr. Stillholm stated clearly offended that I might consider this his idea. "I told Trevor to tell you. However, I left the decision up to him. I never would have agreed to let Trevor blackmail anyone."

"Don't be mad," I stated. "He knew how much I have always wanted my mother to be a mom."

"I'm sure Trevor only was concerned with your feelings," Mr. Stillholm stated. "Your happiness is all he has ever cared about."

CHAPTER NINETEEN

Elizabeth

Early in the morning, I drank in my last few moments of peace before going to the carnival show, or Tilly's wedding. I found serenity in the massive garden which surrounded Dogwood House. As usual, Tiffany and Mrs. Farris had joined me. They were an odd, quiet pair whom I enjoyed spending time with because they seemed to ruffle the feathers of the overprotective guards. Conversation was always second as they to seemed to enjoy the peace. I purposely spent as much time with them as possible.

This morning had been different. When I mentioned Dustin, Tiffany's eyes fiercely shot daggers at me and Mrs. Farris. The mere mention of his name appeared to almost push her over the edge. I played the conversation over in my mind.

"You know Tiffany once dated Dustin," Mrs. Farris looked at me and said.

"Really?" I asked.

"Yeah, I did," Tiffany agreed who was visibly trying to control herself.

"What happened?" I asked.

"He cheated on me," Tiffany said as her eyes flicked to Mrs. Farris. "With a boyfriend stealing tramp!"

The look they exchanged and their shared laugh made me nervous. All I could muster was, "Wow."

"Yes, Dustin is a conniving, backstabbing, and cheating character," Mrs. Farris stated.

"I wouldn't trust him," Tiffany stated. She glanced at her watch and stood, "Sorry I have got to go." She leaned over and kissed Mrs. Farris on the cheek. I felt her stare towards me was menacing.

"I have kept you for awhile," Mrs. Farris turned to say to me. "You better be on your way too! I hear today is the big event."

I excused myself and made my way back to Tilly's dorm room. It was empty as when I left it the night before. Now, awaiting the lift I couldn't stop thinking about and feeling sorry for poor Tiffany. No one liked cheating scum.

The lift dinged announcing it's arrival.

"Princess!" The little dwarf of a man greeted as I stepped into the lift.

I glanced over my shoulder to see if perhaps there was someone behind me.

With expectant eyes he continued, "I have really missed you!" Before I could inform him of my memory fog he held up a small brown paper bag for me.

"Do I know you?" I questioned.

As the smile faded away, his wimpy arms lowered the bag to his side. "Of course you know me, Princess," he returned. "I'm Leo." He stood silent as his beady, deep blue eyes peered at me for any hint of recognition.

"Lakeland," I stated.

The midget of a man grumbled, "Destination card."

I dug in the small, tacky purse that Tilly insisted all the bride's maids carry to the wedding. I was sure the card had to be in there.

The midget man interrupted my hunting saying, "Never mind Princess." I peered down into his searching face as he continued, "Lakeland." His long skinny finger reached out to push the number five button. "I guess you are going to the bubble gum giant's wedding."

His description of Tilly made me smile. He must have seen her in the unusual wedding dress. Watching him swing the bag in his hand, I asked, "What's in the bag?"

"Gingerbread cookies," Leo peered up at me with an odd look upon his face.

"Really?" I asked.

"Don't you remember?" He asked as he slid the card into the slot.

"Actually I don't remember anything," I conceded. "I just woke up one day in the hospital."

"Hospital…" Leo mumbled.

"Imagine," I continued. "Waking up one day to find you have a fiancé whom you don't really care for and a best friend who is ill mannered. When I'm not being embarrassed by her, I'm bored out of my mind. Everyone wants me locked away."

"That's why I haven't seen you," Leo stated like it all suddenly made sense to him. Suddenly, he pushed the emergency red stop button.

"What are you doing?" I questioned as the lift made a sudden jerking stop.

"They haven't told you, have they?" Leo questioned.

"They've told me lots of stuff," I retorted as I leaned back against the cold steel wall of the lift. "I'm just not sure how much of it I believe."

"Then, you know you are the princess?" Leo pointedly asked.

"I have no idea what you are alluding too," I answered to his stare.

Leo, clearly flabbergasted, leaned back against the lift wall opposite of me. His beady eyes peered at me. I could read the indecisiveness across his face. As if resigned to divulge some deep, dark secret, he whispered, "You are a Venema."

The little creature was strange and I was a little annoyed. "Turn the lift back on," I demanded.

"You don't get what I'm saying," he stated as he stepped towards me. "You are half-dweller, Elizabeth."

"Right," I sarcastically retorted. "I am Mr. Solliday's grand daughter."

"Yes," Leo agreed. "You are that too."

"How do you know this?" I questioned. "If this were true... Don't you think someone I was supposed to trust in my life would have told me? Marvin, Tilly, Trevor, my grandfather!"

"They all know," Leo countered appearing steadfast. "You'll have to ask them why they are keeping secrets from you."

"Turn back on the lift," I demanded.

"Of course," Leo conceded as he stepped backwards once again pushing the button.

"One more thing," I growled. "Don't call me princess!"

"Guess she's back," Leo said under his breath as the lift began to move.

CHAPTER TWENTY

Tilly

It was my wedding and I was about to take my first step down the aisle towards the altar. Rhett was smiling a fatherly grin that over took his whole face. He was a good choice to walk me down the aisle. My father had his rightful place and he was genuinely happy for me. I stepped up to take his arm. We took a few steps and he stopped, placing his hand on top mine. He turned towards me and looked me directly in the eye saying, "It's not too late. If you've changed your mind, we can run!"

I let a giggle slip and then told him, "Thanks! I needed that!"

"And?" Rhett questioned.

"I'm sure," I answered. A thought crossed my mind. What if I fell in front of all those people?

Rhett could see the look on my face, "On second thought?"

"No," I reassured him. "Just promise not to let me fall."

"I promise," came a voice from behind me that I did not expect to hear.

I turned and their stood my fake father, Thomas Bradford, looking a little disheveled. Odd for him, he was always so well put together. He had gotten ready fast.

Rhett lowered my arm and hesitantly asked, "Should I?"

"That's up to Mathilda," answered my fake father. I turned away and he continued, "Honey, listen to what I have to say." He put his hands on my shoulder and turned me around. "You look beautiful."

I was dressed in my dream dress with a straight white strapless neckline, natural waist, and a tiered bubble gum pink staggered skirt. It skimmed the floor with over the top Victorian romance. My veil was a perfect bubble gum pink and flowed to my waist. I topped off the look with bubble gum pink lace gloves.

"I have dreamed of this day since you were little," my fake father continued. "Of you falling in love and finding a soul mate. My having a son."

"But you haven't given him a chance," I said.

"You're right," fake father agreed. "He just won't provide the life that I have dreamed for you."

I started to speak but he held up his hand.

"Today is not about my dreams," my fake father continued. "It's about yours. He has to be special to capture your heart."

"He is," I choked out.

"I couldn't miss this!" Dad begun. "My place is with you today." He hesitated. "I would love to walk you down the aisle if you deem me as worthy. I know I haven't acted the best lately. I am sorry."

I had never had a moment like this with my fake father. He was softening. I looked at Rhett who had started to turn pale while starting to step back.

"Did Mom come," I questioned.

"No honey, she didn't," my fake father answered softly.

"Do you intend to see me after today?" I pointedly asked. I could see Rhett stop dead in his tracks.

"Well, we will have to see," my fake father hem-hawed.

"It's yes or no," I demanded. "You can't come today and walk me down the aisle and ignore me for an eternity afterwards."

"What do you want from me?" My fake father questioned. "I'm here because I really want to be! However, I can't guarantee the future. I have to deal with your mother who will be furious that I even came today. But yes, in some form I want to be apart of your life!"

"Some form?" I repeated.

"We will never be able to be a regular family," my fake father half-shouted. "Your going to live with the Humlings! And that boy will never..."

My fake father stopped but I could finish his sentence. Just like the years of forbidden ghosties. That boy will never be welcome at our home. I could see Rhett take a couple steps towards us, then stop. He had something to say but seemed unsure. Suddenly he rushed forward saying, "Excuse me, may I speak with you?"

My father exhaled loudly while I followed Rhett far enough away that we couldn't be overheard.

Rhett looked nervous as he began, "Tilly, I want you to know I couldn't think of a greater honor than walking you down the aisle. It means more to me than you could ever know."

"I asked you because, when I look around in my life, there aren't many in my life that are truly family." I hesitated, "I don't really... I do but I don't... have family other than the life I have made for myself. Family isn't always who we are born into. Sometimes there is a greater family we find with friends. You're family."

He looked me directly in the eye, "And this is why I am so honored. I whole-heartedly agree, we are family." He looked away and said, "Ask me the same question you asked your father about his intentions."

I hesitated, "Do you intend to continue our relationship after today?"

"Yes, I do!" Rhett said. "Listen, I was forced into a decision long ago that I have regretted my whole life. Hold on to this happiness. I don't care that you are marrying a Humling. You are always welcome in my home and I assume I will be welcome in yours."

He was giving me the acceptance of a loving parent. Tears welled up in my eyes as I choked out, "Absolutely."

"Today," Rhett hesitated. He looked torn. "You should share this moment with your father. This moment won't come again. I don't want to take the memory from you of your father walking you down the aisle. If you don't let him, you will be closing a door."

That door had been closed my whole life. My mother had made the decision long ago to shut Rhett out of our lives. My fake father had shut me out since I was the secret daughter of Rhett. Rhett had missed out on my whole life. Today was his day to take his place as my father. "I will have my father walk me down the aisle." I stated as Rhett took a deep breath, clearly missing my meaning. "Rhett, I know what happened at the night before my mother's wedding," I blurted out.

He stumbled back a few steps, "What?"

I grabbed his hand, "Please, don't leave me today."

"I'm not going anywhere," Rhett reassured me and squeezed my hand. "So, that is why you asked me?"

"No, I asked you before my mother flipped out about you walking me down the aisle," I disagreed. "I went to look for answers about what her problem was. I went to Aunt Belle and..."

"And she told you," Rhett replied. "I guess now you know why your parents haven't wanted you to have a relationship with your aunt."

"Or with you," I added.

"Tilly, the choice I made long ago," Rhett trailed off.

"I don't hold against you," I assured him. "And with all that has gone on with Elizabeth, I understand. Sometimes, you have to look below the surface to see the actual truth. Mother didn't even try or give you the chance to show her." I paused, " I want you to walk me down the aisle, as my father."

"And what about?" Rhett questioned as he pointed to ... Mr. Bradford.

"Take my hand and lead me past him," I stated.

"I will, unless you've decided you want to run?" Rhett questioned to lighten the mood.

"I can't run," I hummed in response. "Not today."

"Oh you can run if you want too," Rhett replied as we breezed past Mr. Bradford. "Why would you say you can't?"

As we stopped before the massive wooden doors to the sanctuary, I turned to look at Rhett explaining, "I've come too far to go back."

"Are you doubting your decision?" Rhett quietly asked.

All I could think of was the conversation with Mr. Stillholm last night. "I have to face the music," I answered. "I burnt my bridge with…" I shook my head not wanting to continue.

"With who?" Rhett questioned. "Look nothing should make you sad on your wedding day. It's your day."

"Trevor," I let slip out. All my grief always led back to him. He was the one who could make any day better. Only, I didn't realize it until it was too late.

"Oh," Rhett stated. "I assume whatever you think he is upset about, he probably isn't."

"And why would you assume that?" I retorted.

"He is seated inside," Rhett answered with a puzzled look on his face.

"He's here?" I questioned.

Rhett dropped my hand and looked as if he desperately wanted to say something.

"I didn't think he was coming," I answered Rhett's intense look.

The usher opened the massive door before us saying, "It's time."

"One more minute," Rhett said to the usher.

"They are starting the music," the usher protested.

"Really, just a few seconds," Rhett insisted as the usher closed the door to give us privacy. "Tilly I must tell you my thoughts," Rhett said as he peered at me. "Everything Trevor does and has done has been for you."

"Trevor did this," I stated. "Do you remember that he went before the Council?"

"He did that because he wanted you to be happy," Rhett seriously stated.

Again the massive door opened with the usher saying, "We need to get started."

Conflicted, since I wanted Rhett to tell me what he knew, I took his arm which he was offering. He leaned over to ask me, "Are you sure you don't want to run?"

As the second, internal massive wooden doors were opened by the usher I repeated for Rhett, "I can't."

For the first time, I clearly saw all those who were standing and staring at me with smiles and open gazes. I could feel Rhett begin to pull me through the doors as the usual bridal music began. I whispered, "Don't let me fall."

"Never," Rhett assured me, giving me a genuine supportive look.

We slowly walked down the bubble gum pink aisle runner which was framed by a rainbow of colored roses. I smiled and attempted not to make eye contact with those whose eyes were fixed on me. Some were friends and others were gawkers, just there for the show. Then my eyes drifted up to Anthony. He looked like the cat who had eaten the canary. I focused on breathing deeply, moving my feet, and keeping eye contact with my groom. Suddenly, when we stopped just before the altar, I realized my French nails had a death grip on Rhett's arm. As I relaxed them, Rhett patted my hand and gave me a warm smile.

"Who gives this woman for marriage," Counselor McKay asked.

Rhett leaned over and whispered in my ear, "Last chance." He squeezed my hand. I shook my head slightly no. After a fatherly kiss on the hand, he said, "I do." Then he moved to place my hand in Anthony's warm, sweaty hand, who was obviously nervous.

As I stepped up the two small steps, I felt as if I could puke. I thought you were supposed to look at the other person and the room would disappear on your wedding day. All I felt as I peered at Anthony was nerves. As my skin began to crawl, I looked out towards the crowd for anyone which I could temporarily focus on while I caught my breath.

It was Trevor who caught my attention. He gave me a weak grin. He was more dashing in his dress clothes than I could have ever imagined. Suddenly, I realized I had never given him credit for all he had done for me. So many times he had put up with my antics, usually being my counterpart. No matter how crazy my stunts were, he was there for me. He was my gum totter and sanity. I had always been able to depend upon him to listen to my madness, analyze it, and somehow lead me through feeling safe, loved, and secure.

"Repeat after me," Counselor McKay said to Anthony. "I Anthony Wayne Tabures."

"I Anthony Wayne Tabures," Anthony repeated.

I held up one single finger whispering to Anthony, "Hold on. I'll be right back."

"What?" Anthony whispered back.

If I stopped to explain, I might never work the courage up. I turned on a dime and walked straight back to Trevor who was seated with his father. I leaned over, "I need to ask you something."

"Now?" Trevor retorted.

In a huff, I stated clearly annoyed, "Yes, now!"

Trevor rose to his feet as he peered around at all the eyes staring at him. Then he seemed to stare up towards the alter at Anthony who was locked into a deep stare at him.

"Come on," I said as I tugged on his arm.

Trevor allowed me to pull him back down the aisle and behind the massive wooden entry door. As it shut he began, "Tilly, what are you doing?" Temporarily at a loss for words, Trevor did something I didn't expect. He pulled out a piece of gum and handed it to me. He rubbed my arms as he said, "You're shaking."

I hadn't noticed that I was, until he pointed it out.

"I never would have thought that you would fall apart on your wedding day," Trevor stated with a concerned look on his face. "Take a deep breath and calm down."

"You brought gum," I said off the top of my head.

He peered at me. "Have you been drinking?" When I didn't answer he let out a sigh, "Of course I brought gum. I thought you might need a piece. I am your Keeper."

"My Keeper," I repeated as a tear rolled down my face.

"Now that's it," Trevor stated stepping back from me. "What is wrong with you."

"You are," I huffed and flung my arms around him. "I can't get you out of my mind! And now, you have went and brought me gum!"

That is when I felt his breath on my hair as he reasoned, "Tilly, I have always had gum for you."

He had always been there for me. From the moment we met as children to today, my wedding day. As Trevor held my trembling body tightly, I felt as if I melted into him. Ever since our return from the Earth Plane, I hadn't allowed myself to get this close to him. As I chomped my gum, I could feel my body relaxing. I could feel Trevor's heartbeat speed up to keep pace with my own. They were beating the same beat. As I breathed deeply, I could feel the current running between us. Hmm, I never felt a current with Anthony. Oh… Why had I not seen it before now.

"Why did you so easily let me go," I asked as I let go of him. "Why did you go before the Council? I must know."

"You want to re-hash us?" Trevor questioned. "This is why you are making everyone wait? You want to talk about the mistake we made as kids. A mistake, I might add, that I got us out of."

"A mistake?" I repeated as another tear rolled down my face.

"Tilly don't do this," Trevor stated to me. "Take this chance! Marry Anthony and let him give you the peaceful life he will be able to provide for you, the life I could never give you."

"What are you talking about?" I questioned.

"I will never be able to protect you," Trevor hummed.

"I don't need you to protect me," I adamantly told him.

Trevor shook his head in disagreement before spouting, "Do you really want that Dweller to keep popping back up into your life?"

We stood in silence. Of course I didn't want to face Collin.

It was Mr. Stillholm who interrupted our silence as he pushed open the massive wooden door and peeked through asking, "Everything okay?"

"Fine," I stated as I started to push past him.

Trevor once again caught my arm, "Dad, give us one more minute."

Mr. Stillholm peered at us with big eyes before disappearing back inside the massive door.

Trevor grabbed both my hands and gave me an apologetic look for bringing up Collin. "Tilly," he called. "Anthony can give you a quiet life away from the Dweller madness." He squeezed my hands, "If you won't do this for yourself, do this for me. Go out there and marry Anthony. Live the life I wish I could give you!"

"You can give me a quiet life," I disagreed.

"No," Trevor disagreed adamantly shaking his head. "You trust him."

"Not as much as you," I stated not sure what Trevor was getting at.

"I saw you go swimming with Anthony." Trevor threw out.

"What?" I stammered caught off guard.

"I watched Anthony row you out to the middle of the lake," Trevor said as he pointed towards the lake behind her. "Pure panic ran through my veins as I viewed Anthony dive in and leave you sitting in the boat alone. It seemed like forever as I watched your hands cling to the edge of the boat waiting for Anthony to surface. Then I saw it."

"Saw what?" I asked knowing what he was going to say he saw.

"Your smile," Trevor answered as he ran my fingers across my cheek. "You were smiling at him as he came and rested his hand on the side of the boat." As Trevor's hand lowered he continued, "You handed him a life vest for him to float on. Then he backed away from the boat and held out his hand inviting you to join him. He reminded me of a father waiting for his child to jump in the water."

"I didn't want to jump," I countered. I only jumped in because I couldn't confide in Anthony. I didn't wanted to explain my Earth Plane life.

"But you did," Trevor answered. "I thought I was going to have a heart attack waiting for you to surface. When you did, Anthony grabbed your hands." Trevor shook his head. "What doesn't kill you, makes you stronger," Trevor said under my breath. As his arms crossed his chest he questioned, "Don't you see? You have never gone swimming with me because I don't make your world right. He does."

"You have never asked me to go swimming," I retorted.

"You're right, I haven't," Trevor stated with a shrug. "I know how much the water terrifies you and I would never ask you to get into it." As if a light went off he stated under his breath, "Guess that's the difference between us."

"Ask me?" I dared Trevor.

"Come on," Trevor said looking at me like I had lost my mind. "You're in your wedding dress." Clearly exasperated he threw his hands up. "You're marrying Anthony today. Stop this non-sense!"

"Stop!" I yelled back at him. "Did you tell me to stop?" I turned and peered at the lake which ran beside the church. Getting married in Lakeland hadn't been my idea, but now I was happy to be so close to the water. I turned back to peer at him and started to slowly step backwards. "Ask me?"

"Tilly," Trevor called as he stepped forward matching my steps backwards.

When I reached the edge of the water, I stepped backwards once more letting my bubble gum heel sink into the lake bottom.

"What are you doing?" Trevor asked as I again stepped back. Trevor's hand grabbed and caught me from falling in as my foot sunk into a knee deep hole. As he held my arm, the wet lace of the tail of my gown rubbed my leg as I stepped back one more time making Trevor now step into the water.

I demanded, "Ask me?"

"Stop," Trevor begged. "Please stop."

"Ask me?" I again demanded.

"Ask you what?" Trevor begged.

"To go swimming with you," I answered.

"You would have taken a swim, if I hadn't kept you from falling," Trevor argued as I tried to step forward.

"I have never trusted anyone like I trust you," I stated to Trevor who had a firm grip on my hand as he steadied me. "You can so easily let me go?"

"I thought Anthony made you happy and I didn't," Trevor answered as I stepped out bare foot. "I let you go before Anthony ever asked you to marry him."

"You orchestrated all this?" I questioned. "Damn you Trevor Stillholm!"

I pushed past Trevor and stormed back to the massive door. As I passed Mr. Stillholm in the doorway, he asked, "Why are you wet?" Then his voice trailed after me as he asked, "Where are your shoes?"

I ignored him and breezed past the crowd of seated wedding guests back to my place in front of all the gawkers. I held up my wet dress to keep it from clinging to me. If that's what Trevor wanted, it was exactly what he would get. I looked at Anthony who had a serious questioning look upon his face.

He leaned forward whispering, "Why are you wet?" As Anthony shook his head and rolled his eyes, he whispered asking, "Did he push you in?"

"Trevor wouldn't push her in," Elizabeth whispered from behind me. "This is typical Tilly."

The counselor asked, "Everything okay?"

"Let's get this show on the road," I stated as I grabbed Anthony's hand in my wet pink lace gloved hand ignoring all the questions.

Glancing back towards the door, Trevor was entering. The crowd all turned to peer at him. He was somewhat wet also. No one could miss Mr. Stillholm bending over to peer at Trevor's wet pants and shoes. Then you could see him do a double take when he noticed Trevor was carrying a pair of soaking wet, dirty bubble gum pink heels that he had rescued from the lake bottom.

"Once again, repeat after me," the Counselor requested. "I Anthony Wayne Tabures, take you Mathilda Ann Bradford."

It was Rhett who caught my attention as he walked up and stood between Elizabeth and myself. He was apparently concerned about my odd behavior and my being wet.

"I Anthony Wayne Tabures," Anthony stated as he squeezed my hand to regain my attention. I peered at him. He said looking at me, "Take you Mathilda Ann Bradford."

What was I doing? Did I really feel the same way about Anthony? I had wrongly assumed he was my soul mate. My mind flashed to watching Rhett and my mother. One thing I wasn't, was my mother. So, why was I content to repeat her mistake?

"To be my soul mate," the counselor stated.

Soul mate? If I hadn't been in Trevor's arms, I wouldn't have realized who my true soul mate was.

"To be my soul mate," Anthony repeated once again squeezing my hand.

I could have sworn that I heard Anthony's heartbeat matching mine. Had I just dreamed it?

"To have and to hold for all eternity," the counselor stated.

I had to know. I flung myself at Anthony, sinking my head into his chest while my wet wedding dress bottom dripped water all over Anthony's shoes and the altar rug.

He tried to push me back as I shook my head no. The crowd of guests once more gasped. I felt Rhett's hand on my back letting me know he was there for me, no matter what.

Anthony began, "What…"

"Shh," I interrupted him. I closed my eyes and breathed deeply. I could hear his heart rapidly beating and it did match mine. However, soul mates should feel as if they were one continuous electric circuit. I waited and breathed deeply, but I waited for something that didn't come. I pulled back and stared at his questioning face. Of course our hearts would beat the same. We were carbon copies of each other. That didn't mean we were soul mates.

"To have and hold for all eternity," Anthony stated directly to me.

How could Trevor do this? He knew we were soul mates. I glanced back at him one more time.

"To love and too cherish," Counselor McKay continued.

Once again, I glanced at Rhett and tried to convey I needed help.

"To love and too cherish," Anthony repeated.

"From this day forward for all eternity," the Counselor stated.

"From this day forward for all eternity," Anthony repeated.

"Miss Bradford," the counselor called as he gently touched my arm to get my attention which was not on the vows being said or Anthony.

"Huh," I replied.

"Repeat after me. I Mathilda Ann Bradford," the counselor said.

I glanced over my shoulder at Trevor. I had never really seen him. I wanted so badly to run to him. He stood and I knew he was leaving.

"Repeat after me," Counselor McKay called again. "I Mathilda Ann Bradford."

"I..," I hesitated once again peering at Rhett.

With one nod, he gave me all the permission I needed. I peered back into Anthony's worried face saying, "I can't." I whispered to him, "I am truly so sorry!"

Then I quickly turned and ran down my bubble gum pink aisle runner as fast as possible to catch Trevor, the one man who had always loved and been there for me, no matter what. That included letting me have a thrill seeking, buggy driving, idiot version of myself.

Trevor

All I could hear was Tilly screeching my name over and over, drowning out the sound of my skateboard wheels rolling away on the pavement. I skidded to a stop and peered back to see an amazing sight. Tilly had become a barefoot runaway bride who was making a mad dash. As shocked on-lookers poured out of the massive, wooden church doors, Tilly continued to run as fast as her legs would carry her. One of her hands was focused on holding up the wet, clinging, lace dress while the other waved wildly attempting to get my attention. I never dreamed she would chase me down when I got up to leave.

As she neared me, I began to hold out my hands warning, "Tilly, slow down. Stop!" With a thud, her body hit mine. The force was too much for me to steady myself. We toppled over into a bush beside the paved path. As her body rested on top of mine, I asked, "What are you doing?"

"Trevor Stillholm, we are soul mates," Tilly stated staring down into my face as she sat up, legs straddling me. "You knew it and were going to let me marry that oaf!"

Suddenly, the scene the gawkers were seeing, dawned on me. Tilly must have appeared to have attacked me. However, from where I was sitting, the view was perfection. Tilly was gorgeous. I marvelled at her flawless skin, her rosy lips perfect in shape, her hair flying out from the wedding up do, and her slightly tarnished and wet wedding gown clinging to her perfect figure. The woman I loved, and never thought would be this close again, was actually... sort of attacking me.

I grinned up into her face as she said with a hint of annoyance, "What is so funny? Did you not hear me?"

"I heard you," I answered. As a tear streamed down her face, I lifted my hand to wipe it away. "You know you shouldn't cry on your wedding day."

"You're impossible," Tilly huffed.

As I sat up her body slid to sit in my lap. Before I could say anything, Tilly's finger was perched on the end of my lips. Her other hand retrieved the gum from her mouth and she flung it into the Lakeland forest.

I leaned in and our lips met in a fiery explosion. Instantly, my skin felt hot and I knew I was lost in Tilly. As my lips moved down her face and onto her neck, I could smell the hint of perfume mixed with the smell and taste of bubble gum. Her hands wrapped themselves around the back of my neck as she gasped in delight and tugged at my hair. Our lips met again with a sloppy kiss as my hands found their way down her back, across her buttocks, and down her hips. She felt good under my hands. Then...

"The two of you stop that," my father's voice demanded, interrupting my bliss. "Get up!"

Somehow, we had once again laid down lost in each other. When I peered up at my father, I saw that he appeared to be totally embarrassed.

"I mean it!" My father growled. "If you want to act like you are kids, then I'm going to... To..."

Tilly hopped off of me as I interrupted my dad, "Okay."

"Okay," my dad repeated. "This is not okay."

As I peered around, I could see the crowd on the lawn outside the church intently watching. I also could see the shock of our close friends who were slowing moving closer. Mark and Marvin both had faces which screamed they thought the scene was awkward, and they wished they hadn't seen it.

"Actually," Tilly began. "Today is great!"

My dad let out a huge sigh and shook his head as he peered at us. You could see he was clearly flabbergasted and without words.

"I mean," Tilly continued. "How often do you finally realize who your soul mate is?"

"I will consider that a public statement," Rhett answered her as he walked up.

"Hang that up with these two," my father stated under his breath. When he noticed Rhett staring at him he added, "Come on, don't give me that look Rhett. They have went round and round, with every turn breaking a rule. You never know what to expect from them and I want off the merry-go-round."

"Dad," I called. "We are soul mates."

"See," Rhett happily stated at my announcing this.

"I'm not holding my breath until either Trevor or Tilly gets married," my dad stated. "Doing so might cause me brain damage."

"Well, are we going?" Tilly asked as she grabbed my hand inside hers.

"Going where?" Marvin asked as he joined the crowd with Mark and Emma.

Tilly gave a shrug like it was no big deal before saying, "The reception."

This is when my dad appeared as if he were going to lose it.

"Well why not," Tilly said in a frown to the sour faces. "We planned a great party tonight with great food and dancing. White Crew is going to make an appearance." With her free hand on her hip she continued, "As far as I'm concerned we should celebrate today. I found my true soul mate and…"

"I agree," Emma piped up happily beside Mark. Every eye turned to stare at her as she moved to almost hide behind Mark. With her fingers nervously twirling her hair she quietly said, "Today is a great day to celebrate. My brother is free! We should have a party."

As Tilly and Emma smiled at each other, I couldn't help but think that they had finally found common ground. They both saw today as a celebration. Tilly found herself and Emma got rid of her.

CHAPTER TWENTY-ONE

Tilly

"Breathe Tilly," I could hear Trevor telling me as I stood on at the edge of the portal which would take me to the Earth Plane. I felt like I had been sprayed with one of the sprayers from the ghosties. I was frozen numb.

I was gasping for air. Panic concerning Elizabeth disappearing had begun to sink in.

"Breathe," Trevor once again demanded softly while rubbing my back as I bent over about to collapse.

I grabbed onto his arm for support.

"Take deep breaths, Trevor commanded.

I began to feel faint as I realized how helpless my situation was.

"Breathe Tilly!" Trevor now demanded. "Breath in and out!"

I took a deep breath in as I felt a tear stream down my face. My world was coming apart at the seams.

I tried to concentrate on Trevor's voice as he patiently demanded over and over, "In. Out. In. Out."

I had a sense of déjà vu. Barrett had once helped me with a panic attack. This moment of stress was worse.

No matter how many deep breaths I took, I couldn't catch my breath. "How can I leave when Elizabeth is missing?" I managed to ask between breaths. I felt as though my legs were sticks breaking below me. Suddenly, I lost my balance and fell to the cold tile of the Hall of Records hallway. I sat in a collapsed condition.

Trevor bent down and gently turned my face up to meet his saying, "I promise we will find her."

"Don't make me promises you can't keep," I retorted weakly between breaths.

"Just breathe now," Trevor again stated. "In. Out. In. Out."

"Trevor," Marvin called from down the hall.

I waved Trevor on saying, "Go."

"Let me see what he wants," Trevor said as he produced a piece of gum from his pocket. "I won't leave though." He then placed his hands on the sides of my face, looked me directly in the eye, and then picked up one of my hands and kissed it.

I grabbed the gum from his other hand muttering between deep breaths, "Okay."

I closed my eyes and instantly my mind drifted to our reception. After Trevor and I gave our wedding guests a steamy show outside the church, we hadn't let go of each other. At the wedding we both thought we were letting each other go. Our draw to each other wouldn't let us be apart. Facing the truth which we had tried to bury away deep within us, we realized we were one. We were soul mates.

Not unusual, gossip about us spread like wild fire amongst the Keepers. My mind instantly replayed the events at my wedding reception. As I looked around the country club, I understood most of those in attendance had come to be a first hand witness to how my dumping of Anthony and embracing Trevor was going to unfold. When the tables filled with bodies, the dance floor filled up with those who couldn't find a seat. I didn't let the looky-loes faze me. I happily danced amongst them, totally wrapped up in Trevor and his arms. Who cared if those in attendance were only interested in gawking. There was standing room only along the walls. Those waiting to get in were compressed against the big glass windows watching. The final act of our sordid tale would come when I left to go the Earth Plane. I recalled feeling like we were guppies in a fish bowl. However, I could have cared less.

I should have seen trouble brewing when Trevor and I sat down at our table to have a drink and rest between songs. Marvin and Elizabeth were already seated at our table.

"Marvin, are you ready to dance?" Elizabeth impatiently asked.

"My feet are kind of sore," Marvin replied to the impatient Elizabeth.

With a huff she turned back to stare at the dance floor. Elizabeth had been in a foul mood all day and whatever was bothering her, she wasn't in the mood to talk about it. None of us could penetrate the wall she had up and most of our day had been spent dodging her snaps at us. On days like this, I missed the old Elizabeth.

From over at the next table I heard a male voice say, "My date had the same problem. She went home!"

I turned to see a guy, roughly my age, sitting at the next table. He was kind of gross with pale, blotchy, pitted skin and oily hair.

He stood and stepped over to our table saying, "Yeah, my date went home early with a phony foot ache." He then extended his hand to Marvin, "I'm Trey!"

Marvin stood to return his handshake saying, "Marvin."

Then the crude fellow held out his hand to Elizabeth's as he asked, "And you are?"

"Elizabeth," she answered as she smiled and placed her hand in his.

He bowed his head saying, "It is nice to meet you."

With his head bent down, I could see a tornado of dandruff waiting to escape the oil on his head.

As he dropped her hand Elizabeth questioned, "Your feet don't hurt?"

"No," Trey said smiling. "I'm used to dancing. I take lessons."

"Lessons?" Marvin questioned while rolling his eyes.

I glanced at Trevor and could read the look plastered on his face. I knew he was questioning, what kind of guy takes dance lessons?

"My name is Trey," he repeated as he turned to Trevor.

"Trevor," replied Trevor in return as they shook hands.

"I think you might have picked the wrong date," Elizabeth hummed before there was a chance to be introduced. As I frowned at her she gave me a slight shrug before continuing, "A dancer should be accompanied by another dancer."

"Thank you for pointing out the obvious," Trey sarcastically answered while returning Elizabeth's smile. "You wouldn't want to dance, would you?"

Elizabeth instantly hopped up smiling, but then turned to look at Marvin. I knew in that moment, she saw him as dead weight.

Trey followed her sight to Marvin before asking, "Of course, it is if you don't mind."

"His feet hurt," Elizabeth answered not giving Marvin a chance. "He doesn't mind as long as he doesn't have to move. Besides, I would love too!" As she looked over and huffed at Marvin, "Here's a partner whose feet don't hurt."

Marvin watched her make her way to the dance floor with Trey. He hopped up and yelled after them, "I'll be keeping an eye on my girl."

"Better wash your hands," I muttered to Trevor. Then I peered over at him. He had a broad smile leading me to ask, "What is so funny?"

"Nothing," Trevor stated. "Ready to dance?"

"No," I adamantly stated shaking my head. "I mean what I say. You should go wash your hands."

Trevor's eyes flashed towards Marvin who was rolling his eyes. They shared in their look of disbelief.

"What is it?" I questioned. "Some type of private joke?"

"Tilly," Marvin called. "Are you jealous?"

"Jealous?" I returned in a huff.

"You always get more than your share of attention," Trevor said under his breath as a chuckle escaped him.

"I am not jealous," I sputtered.

"Hmm...," Trevor hummed. "Let's go dance."

I let him pull me back out to the dance floor, knowing my gut screamed that Trey was trouble. It had been a long time since a boy turned me off so repulsively. Greasy haired Trey was a rarity.

Trevor and I had danced most the night away when I happened to see Elizabeth standing with her hands on her hips with Trey in flank position. Not knowing what she appeared so mad about, I pulled Trevor towards the table. When we were close enough, I heard Elizabeth spew, "My lack of singing ability and your knowledge of it... Just another secret you are keeping from me."

"Um," Marvin hummed clearly unsure what to say.

"Actually, your singing ability simply hasn't come up," Dustin defended them both.

"Sure it has," Elizabeth snapped. "When the two of you want a private joke."

The look on Elizabeth's dance partner was one of total shock. As if he wanted to cut the tension, he began to speak, "Should we..."

"Go back out and dance," Elizabeth finished his sentence. "Yes."

Elizabeth spun around and left all of us standing in place as she stormed away.

"What was that about?" I questioned.

"She's gone off the deep end tonight," Dustin hummed under his breath.

Watching Elizabeth shun the protection of all those who cared for her, I knew she was in trouble and this stranger was blindly leading her into it. Marvin should just tell her so we didn't have to attempt to baby sit her. In the moment, I wanted to pull her aside and tell her. Walking blindly through life is dangerous.

Now, I regretted that I didn't.

The sound of Destiny sobbing brought me back to reality as I sat on the floor of the Hall of Babies. The time for me to leave for the Earth Plane was nearing. I peered around, barely able to see Trevor and Marvin through the crowd of Tilly gawkers. Destiny had joined them and I could hear that she was clearly upset. Since she was the cause of Elizabeth's disappearance, she should be distraught. The power of her words had pushed Elizabeth over the edge. However, I didn't see what the nosy neighbor had to offer at this point?

Elizabeth had given us all the cold shoulder. She continuously snapped at all of us before her disappearance. The private joke between Marvin and Dustin had pushed her over the edge and intertwined her path with Destiny's. Earlier in the evening, I caught Destiny trying to spill the beans about Elizabeth's heritage. I was fuming. On one hand I fully believed we should tell her. On the other, I didn't want her to hear it from Destiny who wasn't in our circle of trust. Who did she think she was? The nosy neighbor had taken her intrusion into our lives too far. I could just see the conversation replaying in my head.

"Hell," Elizabeth spewed at me. "You guys never give up." She shook her head saying under her breath, "Eavesdropping."

"Elizabeth," I called.

"Don't," she huffed at me.

"I just wondered where you were," I stated defending myself. "You wandered off…" Alone, I thought.

"Taking a page from Marvin's playbook," Elizabeth returned. "You are just as bad as him." When I didn't know how to answer, Elizabeth continued, "Don't stop Destiny from telling me what you already know."

"You do not know whatever it is you think you know," I stated back.

Elizabeth began, "I know that…"

"You know nothing," I loudly stated feeling all my pent up anger, from her mistreatment of me over the last couple weeks, coming to the surface. Her treatment of those who truly cared for her, left something to be desired. "You know nothing of the sacrifices we have all made for you."

"Right," Elizabeth sarcastically replied.

"You didn't tell her about all that bruising?" Destiny inquired.

"So your accident was a tall tale too?" Elizabeth questioned.

My fear was realized, I was nothing more to her than a second rate friend. She couldn't fathom what we were all willing to do for her to ensure her well being. She couldn't remember the torture I suffered at Collin's hands.

"What should I expect?" Elizabeth continued her rant. "What a habitual liar you are Mathilda Bradford!"

As a tear escaped and rolled down my cheek, I began to feel my anger boil over. No one made me cry.

"Painted with the same brush..." Elizabeth paused her taunt peering at the ring on her finger. In an instant she pulled it off and tossed it at me. "Same brush as my ex-fiancé Marvin."

As I moved to pick the symbol of their love off the floor I shouted back, "You're are truly stupid!" Her worst treatment was reserved for Marvin. Whether she chose to believe it or not, "He really does love you and you are soul mates." I yelled and then tried to take a deep, calming breath. "Both of you have publicly declared each other as soul mate."

"What difference does that make?" Elizabeth retorted.

"I have tried to reassure her that they are soul mates," Destiny had the nerve to chime in. At the same time I pinched my nose. Her choice of bad perfumes hadn't improved.

"You?" I questioned.

"She comes over every afternoon," Elizabeth yelled back at me. "She is at least a truthful friend."

"Elizabeth," Destiny began. "Giving back the ring... Breaking off the engagement..." She seemed to wring her hands. "It feels wrong."

"Your feelings should control her actions?" I questioned.

"The two of you were deeply in love," Destiny continued as she ignored me.

Elizabeth's yelling was reserved only for me. She turned to Destiny and held out her hand and touched her arm countering, "That's right. At one point we probably were in love, only I don't remember."

To my total shock, Elizabeth seemed to digest Destiny's words. My best friend wasn't my best friend anymore. She no longer trusted me.

Flashing back to reality, I felt the tears streaming down my face. Soon I would be leaving for the Earth Plane and I wouldn't remember any of this. I leaned forward, placing my hands on the cold floor and then placing them on top of my head. In my own private huddle, I simply let the tears flow.

"Poor thing," I heard a passer by mutter.

"Do you think she is worried about leaving?" A bystander asked as they gawked at me.

Another person answered, "Her cold feet earlier at the wedding must be kicking in again!"

They shared a chuckle as another voice added, " What else could happen?"

Cold feet? Ha! I knew all, who were watching, simply thought I was freaked out about going to the Earth Plane. If only it were so simple. The cares of my youth had long ago given way to the worries of the adult life I was now embarking upon.

After the blow up earlier with Elizabeth, I had just enough time before my date with the Earth Plane to put one last Tilly plan in motion. The best thing I could do for Elizabeth was to prove to her that Marvin was her soul mate. Her safety would be in his hands, whether I liked it or not. I had found my soul mate and felt compelled to help my wayward friend once again find hers. However, I had been delusional to think that I had one last opportunity to make her trust him. My best effort had left me feeling helpless and empty.

Still sobbing in my silent place, I replayed the details of my flawed plan in my head. It had seemed so simple when we started. Upon arrival at the Hall of Records earlier with Marvin in tow, I tricked Carmen into the restricted section. Then I proceeded to lock her behind the glass door. With her out of the way, I was free to contend with Elizabeth when she arrived.

The lift opened as I heard Elizabeth say, "Thank you Leo!"

I could see the distant, but familiar, brown paper bag which I knew contained gingerbread cookies.

"You're welcome," the leprechaun of a man returned.

As Trevor and Elizabeth exited the lift, she was hanging on his arm. Instantly, I felt a twinge of jealousy. Rationally, I knew Trevor was mine, but why had I not let myself see how close they had become?

Elizabeth stopped dead in her tracks when she spotted me. As Marvin approached, her hands dropped from Trevor's arm. "You too," Elizabeth said in shock to Trevor.

Instantly, Trevor's hands were in front of him as he countered, "Elizabeth, you know me."

"Too well," I said under my breath.

"Elizabeth," Marvin called.

"How could you too be involved," Elizabeth said to Trevor while stepping backwards.

"Hear them out," Trevor pleaded matching her steps. "They have something to show you."

"Elizabeth," Marvin again called.

"I don't care what they have to say," Elizabeth screeched back, plainly ignoring Marvin.

"Well you should care," Marvin stated as he stopped jingling the contents of his pockets.

"I have nothing to say to you." Elizabeth then pointed to me, "Did she give you back the ring?"

The hurt was visible across Marvin's face for a split second.

"Just listen," I demanded. "What are you afraid of? What we might say?"

"Come on," Trevor continued. "Here them out, for me?"

"For you?" Elizabeth retorted as she stepped backing away from Trevor. "You lied to me too."

As he neared her, he grabbed her hand saying, "I've never been anything but a great friend to you."

At the sight Marvin began to pace behind me.

Elizabeth stood peering at Trevor with her hand still inside his. With a deep sigh she continued, "I have this overwhelming feeling that I should trust you."

"Then do," Trevor answered.

"Well spill it then," Elizabeth spewed as she turned to me. "I have plans tonight."

"It's less about what I have to say," I began. "And more about what I have to show you."

"Show her?" Marvin questioned.

With a smile, which I knew was devilish, I led my friends towards the empty Declarations Room.

As Marvin began to wonder if the Declaration Room was our destination he asked, "Where are we going?"

"To make a declaration," I answered.

"Tilly," Trevor called as he left his spot by Elizabeth and closed the gap between us. "You can't make a declaration." He grabbed my arm. "You didn't get married."

I stepped around Trevor and once at the door I answered, "I'm not making a declaration."

For a split second Trevor looked relieved. Then he turned to look at Marvin and Elizabeth.

The magnitude of what I was saying meant nothing to Elizabeth. However, Marvin fully understood.

"You can't be serious," Marvin stated. "Only happy people come here to make declarations."

"What is a declaration?" Elizabeth asked.

"This is foolish," Trevor retorted. "Whoever is working the front desk will never let any of us in there."

"Already taken care of," I said as he pointed towards the restricted section.

Everyone turned to see Carmen screaming from the glass door.

"How could you have done that to Carmen?" Elizabeth asked.

"You shouldn't have done that," Marvin, the square, reprimanded.

As I opened the declaration room door, I hummed, "I know."

"What is a declaration?" Elizabeth again asked as she stepped through the door, triggering the light to turn on.

"Proof," I answered Elizabeth.

"I've seen this light before," Elizabeth hummed as her eyes scanned the room.

"Where?" Marvin asked from behind me as he squinted at the intently bright room. Elizabeth shrugged as Marvin added, "This isn't going to work."

"What if I knew you only had to declare each other as soul mates?" I retorted blinking to get my eyes to adjust as the white light bounced off the white walls, ceiling, and floor.

"How would you…" Marvin began but stopped holding up his hands.

"What do you have to lose?" I whispered to him.

"Let's just get this over with," Marvin stated.

Trevor was clearly guarding the door while I watched Elizabeth wander the room before stopping back at the door to fiddle with the disk player.

"Don't play with that," I said as I held my hand out towards the two white pillows on the floor.

With a huff she went to plop down on the pillow. "I still don't understand what this is all about."

"Couples come here on their wedding day to make the declaration of soul mates," Marvin answered as he set on the pillow opposite Elizabeth's. "Children are gifts from God and only he can grant them. He only grants them to couples who are soul mates."

"Children?" Elizabeth repeated. "Who's talking about children?"

"As couples emerge from this room, they know how many children they are granted," Trevor piped up.

"So you are attempting to trick me into parenthood?" Elizabeth spouted.

"No," I disagreed.

"Tilly has a delusional plan that this will prove to you we are soul mates," Marvin threw out.

"Everyone says we are," Elizabeth stated. "However, if we were wouldn't I still feel it?"

"I feel it enough for both of us," Marvin said with conviction. I watched as he firmly held his hand over the white and gold gypsy ball.

Elizabeth was intently staring at Marvin. I could have fainted when she placed her hand on top of his. "Do you feel that?" Elizabeth asked with big eyes.

The gold began to swirl within the milky globe beneath their hands. Then, a small flake of skin began to bubble on their hands before falling and settling about a half inch off the globe.

Trevor moved to place his hands around my waist. With his head resting near the top of mine, we watched. It hadn't gone unnoticed that we had a front row seat to a very private moment between our two friends.

Marvin simply peered at Elizabeth while she seemed mesmerized watching the edges of the two separate pieces of skin began to burn. Once the pieces of skin were fused together, it split right down the middle. It was like invisible hands were tearing a piece of paper. One of the pieces of skin began to shine like a light bulb. The globe lit up and I could see the form of a baby beaming out from inside. Both Marvin and Elizabeth were intently watching the globe. It was Marvin who seemed mesmerized by the baby looking out. When the globe grew dark, the bright skin became a fire ball and disappeared before the globe returned to its original milky color.

The second piece of fused skin began to glow. It lit on fire reminded me of a match lighting. Then suddenly the fire was gone leaving some black and brown ashes hovering. A dimly lit globe showed the face of another baby staring out. As if the roles reversed, suddenly it was Elizabeth who intently peered at the globe. As suddenly as the face appeared, it was gone as well. The ashes then gave a final poof and disappeared.

When the globe returned to the milky white and color and the gold stopped swirling, slowly both hands pulled back.

"Don't you see?" Marvin softly questioned.

"Do you really think I'm falling for these parlor tricks," Elizabeth retorted. "Where are the cords?"

We all watched in horror as Elizabeth attempted to pick up the globe.

"There aren't any cords," Marvin answered as his skin drained of color. "You don't see it?" Marvin hopped up and shoved his hands in his pockets. He focused on Elizabeth. "Don't you see we are truly soul mates?" Marvin yelled.

"Give it a rest," Elizabeth shouted back as she got to her feet.

"God only gives soul mates a baby," Marvin retorted.

"I think it's babies," Trevor threw out. "There were two."

"Come on," Elizabeth stated as she pushed past all of us.

"What a great idea Tilly," Marvin sarcastically stated to me.

"I'm sorry," I replied. "I thought she would see."

Marvin stormed out of the Declaration Room and into the Hall of Records foyer. He stood with his arms crossed across his chest as he turned around looking for Elizabeth.

"Where did she go?" Trevor asked as he too seemed to be turning circles.

The lift dinged and we heard Dustin call, "Marvin!"

Marvin swung around answering, "Yeah."

"Where is Elizabeth?" Dustin asked sounding panicked.

"We don't know," I answered him.

"They are here!" He leaned in and whispered, "The place is crawling with Dwellers."

"Elizabeth!" Marvin frantically yelled into the building.

Dustin suddenly seemed to be staring off into space and listening intently to something none of us could hear. Then, he gasped and stumbled a few steps. I knew.

"They have her," Dustin mumbled.

Elizabeth was captured.

I felt someone brush up against me, bringing me back to reality. I quickly dried my tears, raised my head from its place upon my arms, and peered down the hall at the growing group standing around Marvin. Mark had joined the group. For the first time tonight Emma was missing from his side. If Mark wasn't careful about his innocent date with her, coupled with the obvious chemistry between them, he would land in the same place I was. He would win a free trip back to the Earth Plane.

This trip to the Earth Plane was going to render me useless to help find or recover Elizabeth. There was no choice in my going and no choice in the trust

I would have to place in my family of misfit friends. I wouldn't even be here to help with the babies as foretold in the Declaration Room.

The Earth Plane gate keeper was walking towards me. The moment I had dreaded was very near. I had rehearsed what I would say to Trevor a million times. Only that was when I was married in my head. Now, I wasn't married and he was my soul mate. I had no words. What could I possibly say to tell him goodbye? This wasn't going to be easy.

"Trevor," is all I could choke out.

When he turned around and saw the gate keeper, he instantly moved towards me. I flung myself into his arms and cried into his chest. I was secure in his arms and this is how it had always been between us. I knew those watching were here for the show and watching our loving embrace. I didn't care.

As I could hear his heart pounding he said into my hair, "I love you Mathilda Bradford!"

I would try again, "Trevor, I'm sorry."

He pulled back to look at me and leaned back against the brick wall and sighed, "Tilly, what do you have to be sorry about."

"Where do I begin," I muttered.

"Only about leading a guy on and then crushing his heart," Wyatt chimed in from behind me.

I turned to see Anthony abruptly staring at us, flanked by his own posse.

Anthony playing the tough guy answered everyone before Trevor could defend me saying, "I have always known that Tilly and I were never meant to be." As he looked straight at me he continued, "We are simply too much the same and would smother each other. Simply, self-destruct!" Then he gave Trevor a menacing stare adding, "I'd run now while you can still get away from the psycho jezebel."

"Watch it!" Trevor warned as he stepped towards me.

I placed my arms around him to hold him back as guards held onto Anthony's arms.

"You're one to talk," Marvin retorted with a hint of sarcasm in his voice causing a guard to peer at him.

The whole group stood in an eerie silence.

"No, it's okay," Anthony growled as he pulled his arms free from the guard's grips. "I can't wait to get away from her."

"It's going to be a long Earth Plane life," I heard his Keeper say under his breath.

I understood. Anthony and I had planned a life together on Earth Plane. Even though I had chosen not to marry him, it was too late to change the details of our charts.

I turned to Trevor quietly asking, "Trevor, promise me one thing!"

"Promise not to let me exit the Earth Plane with Anthony," I begged.

"I promise," Trevor answered.

"It's in my chart," I said off the top of my mind as I began to panic. "If I exit with him, the Council will make me marry him!"

Trevor chuckled a little. My hands flew to my hips as I stared him down.

"I don't think even the Council could make you do something you don't want too," Trevor half-joked while gazing at me.

"I'm serious," I growled back.

"Remember who I am?" Trevor questioned.

"The love of my life," I replied.

"And?" Trevor questioned.

"My Keeper," I answered.

"There is no way I will let you exit at the same time," Trevor seriously stated. "I have never broken a promise to you and I don't intend to start now."

"I love you Trevor Stillholm," I softly stated.

His hands cupped my face. He peered into my eyes, "And I love you."

CHAPTER TWENTY-TWO

Elizabeth

As I opened my eyes, I had a sense of dejà vu. I felt as if I had once been here in this dingy home library. I was tied to a chair and I couldn't believe how I had been so stupid. The first thing I thought about was the final conversation which led me here.

"Can you believe it?" Emma had mumbled to me as she wandered over to me at the reception hall.

No, I couldn't believe what had just happened. Trevor, Tilly, and Marvin had tricked me. Worst yet, Marvin angrily claimed we were soul mates. Like some gypsy tricks could prove it to me. What they dreamed up was far out.

"What's wrong?" Emma asked interrupting my thoughts as she nervously began twirling the end of her hair around her finger.

"They forced me into that Declaration Room to try to convince me that Marvin and I are soul mates," I answered her.

With another long twirl she added, "He no longer makes you happy, does he?"

"You knew me before my memory loss?" I asked.

Emma nodded and once again began to twirl her hair.

"Tell me honestly," I stated as I peered at her. "Were Marvin and I really in love?"

"Yes," Emma answered. "Head over heals in love."

"The others continue to search the Hall of Records," I heard a menacing voice in my head.

I peered around the room attempting to see where the voice had come from.

Emma followed my looking around. Turning pale she asked, "You hear them, don't you?"

I stepped backwards. She was keeping secrets from me too. "You know too?"

She matched my step saying, "It is important. Where are they?"

I shook my head as I again stepped back.

"Where's Mark?" Emma asked as she spun around looking for him. When he left a group of men he was speaking with, she stormed towards him looking really frightened.

Trey instantly stepped up behind me as Emma stormed off. I felt a tear roll down my face . I felt so betrayed.

"What is going on?" Trey questioned with a concerned look.

"They are all lying to me," I answered.

"Your friends?" Trey questioned.

I shook my head yes.

"Let's get some fresh air," Trey stated as he grabbed my hand and pulled me through the sea of people still partying.

I let him pull me outside and into the edge of the forest. I thought we were taking a romantic walk, only to find he had a more menacing plan. My body ached, reminding me of the several day hike we had embarked on. However, I didn't remember coming to a home. I didn't remember anything after the cuts and scrapes from the thorns and bushes, the blisters on my feet, and the sunburn on my skin took their toll. I could only assume Trey had carried me the remaining way here. Now, I sat tied to a familiar chair.

The frosted glass door opened with Trey sauntering through. "You're awake."

"Won't be long now. What a waste." Trey's mind stated.

"Do you know what Tina intends to do with you?" Trey asked. I ignored him and looked away. I didn't understand, who was Tina?

"Tina will owe me," I heard his mind state.

He ripped the tape from my mouth. He stuck the tape to the leg of the chair. Once I caught my breath from the pain of my lips, I stated, "It doesn't matter what they do with me as long as I am away from you."

"These won't be the last tears you shed today." I heard his mind state.

"You will be begging to stay with me," Trey smirked. "Tina is going to send you through the Black Arch. Piper, Deward, Tina. They all want you gone."

"What's in it for you?" I questioned.

"I've patiently waited," Trey stated. "To answer your question, my reward is you. I can do anything I want to do to you."

He leaned in for what I thought was an attempted kiss. I turned my head as far to one side as possible to deter his thoughts. This caused him to get down on his knees in-front of the chair. Now looking directly into my eyes, he leaned forward and in one swoop of his hand shredded the front of my shirt. "Stop," I begged.

"Oh yes, please beg." I heard his mind say.

He leaned in and tried to kiss me again. I sealed my lips. When he pulled back I spit in his face. His eyes turned black! Peering in them, I could see pure evil.

"You won't do that again," I heard his mind state.

"You catch more flies with sugar. Didn't anyone ever tell you that?" The tape was suddenly back across my mouth. "My second reward for capturing you. I get to send you through the Black Arch myself. I was considering a request to keep you, but not after that!" He grinned at me as he began to kiss my neck and moved to my collarbone. His hands wrapped around my waist under my shredded shirt. Touching my bare skin. I felt sick and helpless. His hands were becoming more aggressive and all over me. I closed my eyes and concentrated on steadying my breath. I would not make a sound to give him satisfaction.

I felt him suddenly stop, falling off me. I opened my eyes. An old man was standing behind Trey. He grabbed Trey by the shirt collar and shoved him backwards. Trey hit the floor hard. The old man then moved towards me, untied me, and tore the tape from my mouth. I rose and backed away from him.

He held up his hand, "I mean you no harm. You must go quickly." He paused for a moment staring at me. "Where is your locket?"

"My locket... He took it," I answered.

I watched as he rummaged through Trey's pockets, retrieving the locket. He then gave me a warning. "You must listen. I know this will come as a shock to you. If you should happen to see Mrs. Farris, run from her."

"Why?" I questioned.

"Take this book," the old man stated as he shoved a book with a black cover into my hands. "It will answer all your questions, including why he brought you here. Your friends should have told you everything." Then his hand outstretched offering me my locket. "Put this on. Do you still remember how travel by locket works?"

As the locket dropped into my hands I shook my head no answering, "Travel by locket?"

"Put it on," Mr. Farris demanded as Trey made a moaning sound. "Rub it and think of someplace safe. Where ever you are thinking, the locket will take you there."

As I struggled to fasten the locket with trembling hands I felt a tear stream down my face. The kind old man, who had saved me, had no idea that I had no one I could trust in my life. "There isn't anywhere safe," I blurted out.

With a confused look written all over his face he answered, "You need to go to the Lagedge boy."

"Marvin?" I let slip out. "Why does all roads lead back to him?"

As Trey was beginning to stir, the old man demanded, "Now!"

Elizabeth

"Elizabeth, oh, my love, are you okay?" Marvin gently asked as he pushed the blanket off the top of me, revealing my disheveled look. I had not given much thought about the scrapes, cuts, dried blood, and bruises all over my arms and body until I noticed him hesitate to touch me. His eyes quickly settled on my torn shirt. He held up his hand to someone behind him who grabbed a shirt from a hanger above me. He then pulled it over my head while I pushed my arms through the sleeves. I cringed knowing how much my body hurt. Marvin saw me grimace. Then, I was wrapped in his arms as he picked me up and swept me to the bed. I buried my head into his chest and cried, I suddenly felt safe and the relief was overwhelming.

I could feel his hand on my back and was aware someone else was in the room with us. I was too ashamed to turn to see who it was that was sharing this private moment with Marvin and myself.

"Why have you been keeping secrets from me," I choked out.

I was startled when the answer came from behind me and in my head, "Because he promised you."

I clawed Marvin's arm, digging my nails into them, while I tried to get him to release me. I panicked and screamed at Marvin, "Just when I thought I could trust you." I then began to hyperventilate, when I saw it was Dustin behind me. This knowledge did not calm me, "You are one of them!" Marvin could not hold me any longer. I backed into a corner as Rhett came through the door holding up his hands, "Elizabeth, calm down."

My mind was racing, was he in on it too? I could no longer breath and felt my knees buckling.

I woke from my fainted moment on Marvin's bed. He was holding my hand with one of his hands and his head in his other. Dustin was sitting on the other side of me with his head leaned back against the chair with his eyes closed. I raised my hand and noticed my arms seemed to have some type of sap rubbed on them. With my movement, Marvin raised his head and sat staring into my eyes. No matter what beef I had with Marvin, I knew he would not hurt me. It had to be Dustin who was deceiving us all, and possibly only a matter of time before he would hand me over. I would need to convey that in a rash manner to Marvin, "I'm sorry, I don't know what I was thinking."

"It's okay," Marvin said looking exhausted as he moved up and kissed my forehead. Then he sat back down and placed my hand in his.

"Marvin, you were right, I hear them," I whispered.

"I know," he replied in a calming voice. "And it's okay."

"No, it's not okay!" I said in a harsh voice. "What else have you conveniently forgot to tell me you know?"

"It all centers around the only thing I have kept from you," he replied as he looked away.

I was now aware Dustin was awake. Hurriedly, I scooted away from him and closer to Marvin. I could not control my shaking, something that neither of them could not help but notice. Having experiences Trey's abuse, I was now terrified of those I could hear in my head.

Dustin moved back from me as far as he could, "My thoughts in my head, I have learned not to project them, but it slipped, and I'm sorry I scared you."

"Elizabeth, I have been bound not to say anything, because of a promise I made to you. I promised because you didn't want to remember," Marvin said.

"None of us have told you because Marvin insisted we must honor his promise and your wishes," Dustin added.

"Whatever you are keeping from me has placed me in danger," I said as I stared up at the ceiling with my mind drifting to Trey and my body shuddering. "The horror couldn't be worse than my last few days."

I watched Marvin grimace.

"I want to know," I said directly to Marvin.

"You are like Dustin," Marvin answered my pleading.

"Like him how?" I questioned.

"You and I are part Dweller," Dustin started. "Only you are a Venema."

"Who?" I questioned.

"The royal family of the Dwellers," Rhett answered me from the doorway. As he walked to the foot of the bed, he questioned, "Marvin, what made you change your mind to tell her?"

"There really wasn't a choice," Marvin answered. "You saw how frightened she was when she heard Dustin in her head."

"When you wandered off from Emma and Mark, were you with someone that you heard?" Rhett asked.

"Yes," I replied to Rhett. I peered over at Dustin and asked, "The Dwellers are dark souls?"

Dustin nodded his head yes.

"Your father was a Dweller," Rhett stated from the foot of my bed.

While with Trey, they were coming for me. The Dwellers were coming from me. I trembled.

"Who is Tina?" I asked.

Dustin buried his head in his hands, as he mumbled, "Your evil sister."

I hesitated, "There were two other names."

"Deward and Piper," Dustin asked confirming in my mind that these people did exist. "They are your Dweller grandparents. They lead the Dwellers."

"He kept saying..." I stopped thinking about Trey spouting that he could do anything he wanted to me. "That my Dweller family wanted to see me sent through the Black Arch. What is the Black Arch?"

"They told you then," Dustin answered without answering.

"Yes," I answered. "What does it mean to be sent through the Black Arch?"

Marvin breathed deeply in causing me to look at him.

"You would no longer be able to return to us. You would live one Earth Plane life after another if they send you through the Dweller's Black Arch," Dustin answered.

"I would never come back here?" I questioned as Dustin shook his head no.

I turned to look at Marvin, "They are coming for me, aren't they?"

"They are," Marvin conceded. "However, we really believed, once their was no darkness, they wouldn't be able to come here and you would be safe. So, our promise."

I nodded, "Right, I didn't want to remember."

"No, they frightened you," Dustin assured me.

"They frighten me now," I muttered.

Rhett seemed to be deep in thought and the commented, "I don't understand how they are doing it."

I sat up as Marvin put his arm around me and knew I could answer Rhett, "I might know how they do it."

They all three seemed to look at me astonished. I continued, "Take Mrs. Farris..."

"You have seen Mary Farris?" Asked Rhett.

"Yes, she sits everyday in the garden across from my house about mid-morning," I said. I stopped for a moment noticing they all looked visibly upset. "Anyway, I always hear her thoughts but Tiffany..."

"Tiffany is visiting you with Mary Farris?" Dustin questioned. I could see his hands ball into fists.

"Oh yes, they are quite close," I said as Marvin gasped. "Tiffany let it slip this week that Mary Farris was once a Keeper. Is she now a Dweller?"

"Yes," Rhett replied. "Do you want to know why she is a Dweller?" I nodded and Rhett continued, "She tried to help them capture you."

"So, now I can hear her," I thought out loud. I had trusted the two women's friendship and they were waiting to stab me in the back. "You see, that is how they are doing it," I replied.

"You think they are using Keepers who were sent to the dark side to come back," Marvin asked.

"It makes since," Dustin said. "They would be like Elizabeth and myself, they could walk in the light."

They all three were deep in thought when I turned to Marvin, "We need to warm Emma and Mark."

"You think they are in danger?" Marvin asked.

"Yes," I replied. "Trey, I can hear him. I thought he was harmless."

"There is more isn't there?" Dustin asked.

"I really did think he was harmless Marvin, I'm sorry," I started as he took a deep breath. "Emma went to find Mark and I was angry with her because I discovered she too was keeping something from me. I let Trey pull me outside and into the forest of massive trees. I followed him away from the building."

Suddenly, Trey turned to face me and his thoughts..." Marvin pulled me closer to him and his arms comforted me. "Trey's thoughts weren't friendly anymore and his eyes turned black and cold. He grabbed my arm and I couldn't get away, or scream. I was suddenly paralyzed with fear and he jerked my locket off of my neck."

"I understand, Elizabeth," Marvin stated in unconditional love.

"Trey and I walked through thick forest for what seemed like forever," I said. I took a deep breath as Dustin sat on the edge of the bed. Marvin began to breath unsteadily. "Marvin, I just kept thinking about all the times you told me never to go anywhere alone and how I always gave you such a hard time. I was foolish."

He was shaking his head no, in disagreement, "You got all of the scrapes and cuts in the woods?"

"Most of them," I answered as I looked at my arms. The cuts and scrapes. Yes. The bruising from the ropes and rope burns. No. Marvin seemed to calm down and I wondered how else did he think I get all of the cuts and scrapes. My mind wandered to my first memory of Tilly and how ghastly she looked. "The first time I saw Tilly, she was covered in cuts and bruises. They did it to her, didn't they?"

"Yes," answered Rhett. "They captured Tilly to get to you and she suffered greatly."

"How did she make it back?" I questioned.

"You had strength that none of us had," Marvin replied. "When she didn't come home, you went to look for her and they captured you. From the world of the Dwellers, you protected Tilly. Then you stayed to ensure we could get her home.

"So, I chose to stay?" I reiterated.

"Yes," Dustin replied. "When you arrived at the hospital, we realized that you gave up your memories to save all of us."

Guilt over took me. I had not given anyone a fair chance, nor did I realize the sacrifice I had truly made for them. And Tilly... I had treated Tilly so badly. "Tilly has already left, hasn't she?" I questioned.

"Yes," Marvin answered.

"Where did Trey take you?" Rhett asked.

"We eventually ended up in a town called Stonehenge," I answered. "We entered a house that I strangely felt was familiar."

"Mary Farris's house is in Stonehenge," interjected Dustin.

"Trey tied me up," I trailed off remembering his thoughts, how sick I felt, and his actions. I hesitated, I didn't want to say this in-front of everyone in the room. My heart started beating fast and I felt I couldn't breath. Marvin could feel it as he held me tighter. Quickly, I just needed to go through it quickly. "I heard Trey saying they were coming. All of a sudden, and older gentleman knocked out Trey and untied me. He dug my locket out of Trey's pocket and told me to use it." I took a deep breath to calm myself, "He gave me a chilling warning about Mrs. Farris."

"What did he say?" Asked Dustin who seemed to be less interested in the answer than genuinely concerned about the obvious panic attack I had just experienced before their eyes.

"He told me if I saw Mary Farris to run," I replied.

"But you came here with your locket?" Marvin questioned.

I nodded and asked, "How many days have I been gone?"

"Three," Rhett said. "But we don't know how long you have been in the closet."

"Why were you in the closet?" Dustin asked curiously.

"I started out sitting on the bed. Then they were here looking for me. I could hear them in my head, so I crawled into the closet to hide."

"Didn't you hear any of us?" Rhett asked.

"I did hear movements within the house, but I was so scared of being found by them, I didn't even read the book the old man gave me. I was afraid someone would hear me turn the pages," I explained.

"What book?" Marvin questioned as he moved from holding me, to the closet to look.

"He said it would answer all my questions," I replied as Marvin continued to dig in the bottom of the closet. "I knew you would eventually come into this room and it would be safe to come out."

"It is a good thing I could hear them as well as you. I knew they had lost you," Dustin said as he began to point at Marvin who was once again standing next to me with the book in his hand. "Marvin wanted to go to the Dwellers to find you."

"No, promise you won't ever do that," I demanded in a new wave of panic.

"Oh no, I'm not making anymore promises. Especially that one," Marvin said as he moved to look me directly in the face. "If they had you, I would come get you."

"Where else do you hear them?" Asked Rhett who had taken to pacing at the end of the bed.

"Here and there. I hear Mary Farris on a regular basis, and others the night when I told you I was jogging," I answered ashamed.

"We all knew," Marvin answered.

"I heard them too that night," Dustin stated. "I was outside looking."

"You were mad because they asked me if I could hear them and you didn't want them to tell me," I stated now understanding Marvin's fit of anger.

"Keeping this secret from you is the single hardest and stupidest thing I have ever done." Marvin stated.

I heard a small whimper come from the hallway causing me to sit straight up. "What was that?"

Marvin's eyes flashed to Rhett's.

Then I heard the loud shrill of a baby.

CHAPTER TWENTY-THREE

Elizabeth

Totally unexpected, I was a mother to an infant named Sophie. The beautiful baby girl in my arms had arrived during my disappearance. She had pure, soft, silky skin with rosy cheeks. I hadn't put her down since discovering her. A steady stream of close friends had visited and they were all shocked to meet her. I guess Marvin and I visiting the Declaration Room, without being officially married, was somewhat taboo. Now, everyone whispered about Sophie as a situation.

The only friend's face which had been genuinely happy for me was Trevor. He awkwardly held her and nicknamed himself Uncle Trevor. Marvin and him had already started discussing what they would do when boys started coming around. While listening to them, my mind screamed over and over that she would never see a normal childhood. Their concerns and bantering about boys was silly. She would be plagued with bigger problems than simple childhood milestones.

"Dustin, I need to ask you to help me put an end to this," I stated. "I just can't do this to Sophie."

"At this point, what can we do?" Dustin asked.

"If you brought Sophie and myself to Venema House, would you be forgiven?" I asked.

"I would never take you, much less Sophie to them!" Dustin said. "Why would you want to go back?"

"Answer my question," I demanded.

"Yes," Dustin said. "I'm sure forgiven and rewarded."

"Yes," I responded. "I guess we are the number one target."

"You are the number one target," Dustin interrupted. "They don't know about Sophie. However, none of this matters. I would never betray you by turning you over."

"Don't you see this would not be a betrayal?" I questioned.

"I don't understand," Dustin answered shaking his head in dismay. "You're going to have to explain this to me."

"The Dwellers want to send me through the Black Arch, don't they?" I asked to remind him of the conversation. He nodded and I continued, "They don't know about my declaration or Sophie. They want to send me through the Black Arch and if they see me go through, they will not look for Sophie."

"Don't," begged Dustin. "I can't stand the thought."

"It is the only way," I disagreed. "You will need to be the one to do it. It will make it easier if you're the last face I see. Most importantly, Sophie will be left here to be taken care of. You would be there. If they ever found out, you could warn Marvin."

"I am your guard, not Sophie's. I could never push you through!" Dustin disagreed.

"Sophie is the most important part of me, my future. If you now guard any part of me, let it be my future. You would be guarding her. Guarding my most important secret," I disagreed.

He sat shaking his head. "Please do this for me," I begged. "Protect the only part of me that can go on."

"I can't," Dustin said.

"Don't you see they will never stop," I stated. "They won't stop until they have Sophie." I peered down at my precious, sleeping baby. "This is the only way to make it stop."

"How can you ask me to do this to you?" Dustin asked.

"It's not doing this to me, its doing this for me," I replied in a pleading voice.

"You can't believe Marvin will go along with this," Dustin stated as if grasping at straws.

"No, he won't," I agreed. "I have no intention of asking him."

"He would want to be involved in this decision," Dustin stated.

"After all the rotten things I have done and said to him," I began. "I can only hope he understands."

"You will spend the rest of time, living one life after another on the Earth Plane. Have you thought about that?" Dustin questioned.

"Yes," I stated. "Is it really so bad that my life would go on, only on the Earth Plane?"

"I'm not telling you yes," Dustin answered. "I need to think this through."

"I want to do it now," I stated as I struggled to get off the bed with Sophie in my arms.

"No," Dustin disagreed.

I ignored him as I went out the door of the bedroom and headed for the staircase.

"Elizabeth, no," Dustin called as he followed me.

I stopped and growled at him, "Now is perfect." I knew I couldn't let this sink in or I would never have the courage to do what I needed to do for Sophie. "Now is the time before Rhett and Marvin get back." Time and space would only make my decision harder and make it easier for Sophie to be discovered.

"No," Dustin stated adamantly shaking his head.

"Then don't go with me," I growled back at him. "It has to be now!"

"What is going on?" Mark called from the bottom of the staircase.

"Nothing," I quickly replied.

Mark stared me down as he wiped his perpetually runny nose.

"I want to get some items from my room at Dogwood House," I lied.

"Not by yourself," Mark cautioned.

"I'm going by myself, if Dustin won't accompany me," I answered as I carefully began to descend the staircase."

"I can take you," Mark said in a tone of finality.

As I stepped off the bottom step, I whispered, "I can't leave Sophie with him."

"I heard that," Dustin stated in his mind.

Mark gave me a knowing look as he held out his arms for Sophie. This was the first and last time I would leave her. *"Dustin, please take her. I can't."*

Dustin, caught up with me, leaned in, and gently removed Sophie from my arms and then placed her in Mark's waiting arms. Not unlike Trevor, Mark had an uneasy hold on her.

As my eyes teared up, Mark cautioned, "Elizabeth, I promise to take care of her while you are off getting your belongings." Then with a goofy, raised voice he said to Sophie, "Uncle Mark is here."

"Are you ready to go?" I heard Dustin question in my mind.

I stood looking at my daughter, as I tried to distance her in my mind. Wow. All that I would miss in her life seemed to be flashing like a photo album in my mind. I just knew she would be beautiful . My sacrifice would allow her to live a full, happy life, grow up and meet someone of her own. One day she would have her own Marvin. I couldn't second guess myself. This was right.

It was a blur. I scribbled a quick note for Marvin, before Dustin and I moved on in perfect silence. The park was empty with a warm breeze. Peaceful.

"Elizabeth, are you sure?" Dustin asked.

"I have said my goodbye," I responded. I took a huge, deep breath in, "I am giving them a life free of my troubles."

He leaned over and kissed my cheek, "I will do whatever I can to watch out for them."

"Thank you," I replied with my hand on his cheek. I knew he meant every word.

I put the locket that hung around my neck between my fingers and held out my empty hand for his. Once our fingers were interlocked, I closed my eyes. Venema House, and my fingers rubbed the locket.

It all happened quickly. We were standing in a room full of others. I looked up and could see the arch, the Black Arch. Dustin grabbed my arm and forcefully pushed me towards it before anyone else could react to the sight of the two of us. "You have caused me nothing but problems," Dustin began. "I have waited long enough to bring you back here. I am tired of your whining about the problems your Venema family bring you. You should be proud to be a Venema!"

"Proud!" I retorted. "I would rather exist eternally on the Earth Plane than to join this family. They are evil."

He placed both hands on my shoulders, looking me straight in the face. I could see the pain in his eyes, "I'm sorry to do this too you. You could have easily loved me, if it weren't for him."

I was caught off guard, "What?"

He held up his hand to the now visible Samuel standing behind him. "I will take her." Just as suddenly he jerked my locket from my neck.

"Take me where?" I questioned as my sight began to blur. He gave me no response. I suddenly recalled what they told me the last time I was here. Dustin wanted me all to himself. I didn't believe it then, but I saw it now. My own stupidity had allowed him to double cross me. I screamed at him, "You promised!"

"Of all the things I told you, why didn't you know that I would never send you through the Black Arch!" Dustin shouted back at me. I tried to jump towards the Black Arch. He grabbed me by the arm. His grip was strong and he pulled me quickly away from the others.

Once in the bottom depths of the building, he opened a door and tossed me into the dungeon. The door closed behind me. What was I to do now?

Marvin

"Hey Marvin," Mark yelled from the Living Room.

I passed down the dark hall finding Mark rocking Sophie in one of the recliners. "Is Elizabeth upstairs sleeping?"

"No man," Mark said. "She went to get some of her stuff from Dogwood House. I didn't think you would mind, since it was basically crossing the yard."

"Alone?" I questioned Mark.

"No, with Dustin," Emma replied.

"I wouldn't have let her go alone," Mark said. "She left a note on the table for you."

"Hello all!" Rhett said as he entered the door, dropping his bag on the table. "Where is my favorite niece?"

I watched as he kissed Sophie's sleeping head as she laid across Mark's lap. He brushed Mark and whispered, "Sorry."

"Uncle, she sleeps through anything," I reminded him. "There is no need to whisper."

"Elizabeth sleeping," Rhett questioned us.

"No, she is out with Dustin," Mark replied.

"She left this note for me," I told Uncle Rhett as I shoved it into my pocket. I took Sophie from Mark's arms and took her to the kitchen to lay her in the playpen. I then plopped down into a chair beside her to read the note.

Marvin,

I must start by telling you that you should never doubt our love. I know you love me which only makes this harder. Please try to do the following for me.

I have decided to protect both you and Sophie from the danger that I bring into our life. It all must end with me. You and I both know they will never stop until they have taken me.

Sophie will have no future in my arms. The Dwellers will target her too. The decision will be yours. I hope you will decide to never tell Sophie about her heritage. Marry someone and let me be replaced in her mind. I don't want her to grow up and wonder about me. She won't one day go looking to answer the questions in her mind only to discover the horror that is the truth of my past. Marry someone and build a future with memories with whomever she may be and Sophie. Build a life. Take them boating, on walks, and to the races. Do these things for her.

Don't ever let anyone give her a locket. Mine has caused me nothing but trouble.

I don't want you to be mad at Dustin. I had a hard time convincing him that this was the only way. You know he loves me too, and is the best Uncle Sophie could ever have. He is protecting the only part of me that will remain, my future. If they discover her, he will return to tell you.

Lastly, don't be foolish and follow me. I will already be gone by the time you read this. When I arrive at the Dwellers, I will quickly enter the Black Arch without haste.

We just didn't have enough time to say all of things that are now left unsaid. I will love you forever and a day. You know you really love someone when you can let them go, when letting them go is what is best for them.

Elizabeth

My words had come back to haunt me. I had told Elizabeth long ago, when I felt I could not protect her, my reasoning for letting her go. It was what was best for her. Now, I was on the receiving end of those words. I never fully believed in love at first sight. However, from the beginning her memory overtook all sensibility and replayed again and again in my head. If I only had known it would lead me here. I now wonder, would I have changed anything? As I looked across the room at my daughter, I knew I would never change anything that brought her into my life.

I could hear a knock at the door. "Jessie, it's been a long time," Rhett stated. "Come in."

"Is Marvin here?" Jessie questioned.

"I'm not sure this is such a great time," Rhett responded.

"It's important or I wouldn't be here," Jessie insisted. "May I sit and wait?"

"Be my guest," Rhett told him. In sorrow and shock, I could not move from my chair. I could hear the floor creak under Rhett's footsteps as he rounded the corner towards me.

"Marvin, you look as white as a ghost," Rhett stated as he stopped to take a good look at me. "What is it?"

I mustered all the strength I had, "She is gone."

"Gone where?" Rhett questioned me as I shoved the note in his hands. I pushed past him, faintly aware of the shock that was spreading across his face and the stares from Mark and Emma who had heard me. Once standing at the table, "Jessie, what do you want?"

Jessie started, "It's private, can we go outside..."

"Whatever it is," I demanded. "Spit it out."

I noticed he glanced at Mark, still conscious of saying anything in-front of him.

"Shall I leave," questioned Mark.

"No," I replied. "Jessie?"

"I saw Elizabeth today," Jessie said. "She was with Dustin."

"Yes, they are friends," I agreed. He had this irrational thought process when it came to them.

"No Marvin," Jessie disagreed. "She was holding his arm with her head leaned against it as they walked."

"Where did you see them," Rhett asked from behind me.

"They were in the park," Jessie answered. "Then they stopped and he cradled her in his arms. She was crying and looked absolutely distressed."

I pulled out a chair and sat. I placed my face in my hands. "Yes, she is gone."

"I know," Jessie agreed. "That's why I am here. I saw him take her. They simply disappeared using that locket."

"No, she left so they wouldn't come here and find Sophie." I retorted and then pushed the chair back and walked over to Sophie rubbing her small back. I picked her up and the smell of baby powder filled my nostrils. Everything would now be about her. My future..., my only future.

CHAPTER TWENTY-FOUR

Elizabeth

I stood in the middle of the small room, watching the back of Samuel's head. I knew who he was, my memory had once again returned. Then, I heard a commotion outside the door. Oh no, it was Collin. The door opened and Collin stepped through against Samuel's warning. Collin smiled, "Look at you." I backed as far back as possible with my body hugging the wall.

"Collin, out of there!" I heard Geren shout in my head.

"Another time then," Collin's mind returned.

The swinging door opened once again with Dustin stepping through. "Samuel, Deward wishes to see you. I will guard her."

"I don't think so," Samuel started. "You will let her go!"

Geren walked up behind Samuel, "He is not going to let her go. Deward wishes to see you. Go!"

"Why?" I asked Dustin.

"Because I am a selfish creature," Dustin retorted. "The light half side of me wants you to love me."

"Dustin, I don't love you," I began.

"No, you don't," Dustin agreed. "But you will learn to over time."

I glared at him, "What about…?"

"That is exactly why you will choose to love my son over time," Geren stated and began to grin.

Dustin looked resigned to this fact, "Marvin can have your love child. She was never a part of my plans. Your declaration was never part of my plans. Those events wouldn't have happened, if Trey hadn't got greedy."

"Trey?" I questioned.

"Yes, it was the perfect plan," Dustin said while smiling a devious smile. "Lure you away and bring you back."

"He told me they were going to send me through the Black Arch! That he could do anything he wanted to me!" I screamed at Geren.

"It didn't matter what he told you," Geren stated. "He has paid for being a little too adventurous though."

"It was true, they did want to send you through the Black Arch," Dustin confirmed. "My father worked it out so that I could keep you, if it were my desire."

"Why?" I questioned. "Why would you do this to me."

"Because I love you," Dustin stated. "You should have known I would never send you through the Black Arch myself. I need to be with you."

"Love, would never do this too me," I stated.

Our types of love are different," Dustin stated. "Your love is unconditional and pure. My love is selfish and unkind. With your supposed love of Marvin and…"

"I assume you will want them too be safe," taunted Geren. "You will stay with Dustin or I will lead them directly to your child. Then, I personally will see to it she goes through the Black Arch."

"You wouldn't!" I yelled.

"Is it a price you are willing to pay?" Geren questioned. "If so, disobey me and see."

"Why would you betray them by allowing this charade? This lie?" I asked as I looked at Geren.

"My son deserves happiness," Geren simply stated. "Unfortunately, you seem to be what he desires to be happy. I will allow this because he is my son. Don't forget what I will do, if you cross Dustin or myself." He then turned to Dustin, "As I told you, it is now up to you to convince her to take what we offer her and stay." He turned and walked out the dungeon door.

I threw myself on the dungeon bed and buried my face into the oily, dirty pillow. I could feel Dustin sit on the bed and begin to rub my back in a consoling manner. "If you give me a chance, I will make you happy." I knew that somewhere inside, he sincerely meant it. "Elizabeth, I will give you what you want in return for trying to love me. Safety for Sophie."

"They will find her anyway," I replied. "When they do, anything I promise you will have been for nothing."

"I will warn Marvin if they ever decide to go looking." Dustin replied. "Do you accept the offer to stay with me?"

"I trusted you to bring me here," I stated. "But you betrayed me. Betrayed my wishes. You told Geren the one secret I did not want anyone here to know. Why did you tell him?"

"I needed him to convince Deward and Piper to give you an opportunity to stay," Dustin replied. "He was the only one who could talk them into this."

"How can I trust Geren won't betray us?" I questioned in horror.

"He is my father," Dustin stated. "I trust him. He trained me, took me in as a child. If you trust me, then you can trust him."

"How can I trust that you will warn Marvin?" I asked.

"I don't want either one of them in my life!" Dustin growled. "I don't want either of them here. Looking at her would always remind me of Marvin and you." I turned to look at him. When our eyes met he said, "If Marvin had never entered your life, we would have been happy together."

I had always been drawn to Dustin in the early days. Maybe he was right, we could have been happy. But this was not a path destined in my life. I knew

Dustin was not the one for me. "My answer is No," I replied. "I don't belong with you."

He stood, "You have made your decision. If I don't want you they are going to send you through the Black Arch. Only, you wont' be alone. I won't be able to stop my father."

"Dustin, please," I begged.

"Sophie will be reunited with you by nightfall," Dustin stated.

He turned to walk away and I quickly sat up. The moment was now. I ran towards him and flung my arms around him from behind, holding him as tightly as possible. "Please. Dustin, please," I begged.

I could feel him sigh. He never turned around, but placed his hands on mine across his waist. "Do you accept the offer to stay with me?"

"Yes," I replied. "Anything you want."

He whispered in return, "Thank you. I will make you happy."

ALSO BY JJ HULL

The Keeper Saga

Letting Go (Book 7)

Order these titles from

www.paranormalcrossroads.com

VISIT THE SAGA

WWW.THEKEEPERSAGA.COM

www.ingramcontent.com/pod-product-compliance
Lightning Source LLC
Chambersburg PA
CBHW070854180626
46817CB00003B/775